Now I Lay Me Down to Sleep

BY LUDWIG BEMELMANS

The hero of Ludwig Bemelmans' first novel is one Leonidas Erosa, a South American general heavy with years and money, residing in Biarritz with his retinue. This includes a paragon of a cook (no Bemelmans book would be complete without fine food); an Indian to care for his dogs; a fabulous secretary; a mistress; and the faithful English governess, Miss Graves, who carries her coffin with her when they travel. This sportive party, at the approach of war, sets out for America. Their adventures in Casablanca, in New York, and finally on the old hacienda in Ecuador, are a saga of life, love, death, and birth. In it appear lovely ladies and graceful men, sad Indians and knowing servants, and incidental celebrities who might be straight from today's most fashionable gossip columns.

Bemelmans himself must tell—to each reader in his own way—the meaning of this tale. Its setting is the nostalgic world of night clubs and champagne and diamond clusters. Bemelmans has loved that world and made much of its naïve splendors, even when he suspected that it was falling into green decay. This is his gay and irreverent novel about it. Let the reader beware who expects a conventional novel. It's a book that tells a story about some people; but beyond that it's a great many other things, all of them entertaining. Call it a small lamp hung out in the darkness of our time, to cheer us on the way.

Now I Lay Me Down to Sleep

BY LUDWIG BEMELMANS

NEW YORK : THE VIKING PRESS : 1944

Copyright 1942, 1943 by Ludwig Bemelmans

Printed in U. S. A. by H. Wolff, New York, N. Y.

Published on the same day in the Dominion of Canada
by The Macmillan Company of Canada Limited

THIS EDITION IS PRODUCED IN FULL COMPLIANCE WITH
ALL WAR PRODUCTION BOARD CONSERVATION ORDERS.

The author's thanks are given to Harry Bull, editor of *Town and
Country,* in which portions of this story appeared serially, partly
under the present title and partly under the title *Man of the World.*

Contents

NOW I LAY ME DOWN TO SLEEP

IN THE days when the King of Spain's only concern was that no one should clip a second off his record run from San Sebastian to Biarritz. . . .

Amidst the boom-tara of unending fiestas, of gala dinners in blossom-lined ballrooms in which a thousand songbirds were released, half of them to be swept out the next day. . . .

In the good old days when the amateur mechanic, the Marqués Ricardo Soreano, amused himself by pushing a button under his table that ingeniously released a menagerie of tigers, lions, and crocodiles, which suddenly stared into the dining room through the large plate glass windows and frightened his guests to death. . . .

When the young and radiant Natasha Brailovski shot herself through the heart over her father's grave with a ridiculously small jeweled revolver that was practically made by Cartier . . .

. . . and the handsome, immaculately groomed Antonio de Portago, dream man of the American debutantes, married, had all his debts paid, and later died for Franco. . . .

When, at the height of its fashion, this affluent municipality was graced with the presence of both the Grand Dukes, Dmitri and Boris; and the unbelievably beautiful Bebecita de Gainza—who set the fashion in Biarritz with her chic mother, Selmira de Gainza—married Nicki de Sangro. . . . When Elsa Maxwell promoted the dressmaker Patou and introduced the O'Briens to society. . . .

At that time there lived in his villa in Biarritz, in seclusion and in comparative simplicity, the South American General, Leonidas Erosa.

3

The Villa Amelita stood in vast grounds along the road that leads from Biarritz to Saint Jean de Luz. The varied landscape composed itself of opposites, and achieved harmony out of princely households set against the bonhomie of sardine fishermen's houses and their craft, of the fragrance that the sun drew from the fallen needles of pine trees, and the mimosa that was tended with extreme care in the gardens of the Villa Amelita.

No one was anonymous here, or footsore. Nothing merited the attention of the tourist in this good corner of France. It was blessed by an absence of museums, venerable cathedrals, ancient monasteries, historic curios, or scenic wonders. It was doubly protected by the total absence of cheap lodgings.

Like most wealthy South Americans, Leonidas Erosa preferred to live in France rather than in his native land. He had been home to Ecuador on two occasions, but he had quarreled with his relatives and left after a few days. He had never been to the Argentine to visit the properties that were the source of his enormous wealth. Out of respect for the famous Erosa herds, the Argentine republic had made him an honorary general, and he used the title on every possible occasion.

On a day when von Uff, one-time President of the Dresdner Bank, an expert in disaster, who had amassed a fortune during the German inflation, told the American expatriates that it was high time to close the shutters of their villas, pack up and go home, Señor Alfonso Lopez appeared at the ornamental bronze gate of the Villa Amelita, in haste and in a frail conveyance.

He came in a very small car which was mounted on four bicycle wheels and painted red. The car was propelled by a man who sat beside Señor Lopez, as if they shared a little bathtub. The man propelled the car with his feet. He occasionally tooted a horn by squeezing a black rubber bulb. The sound of this horn was like the hysterical squeal of a dog.

It had been impossible, at the railroad station, to find a taxi. Don Alfonso was the size of a jockey; he was a desirable passenger. The man who had pedalled as far as the villa refused to go on— the rest of the way up to the Villa Amelita, he said, was too steep for him. He helped Don Alfonso open the heavy iron gate. The passenger paid, smiled, lifted a bowler not much larger than half a cocoanut, and entered the complicated landscape of pine trees, mimosa, and shrubs that led directly to the door of the villa. Halfway up the hill, he swung off into one of the walks that wound about like leftover pieces of spaghetti on a green plate. Along these paths were statues and shaded benches beside small waterfalls; and on one of the benches, facing a Grecian nude, Don Alfonso sat down, took his hat off, rested and drank in the odor of warm pine needles.

From this part of the park, high and far away, the marble and stucco villa was visible. The villa was as bizarre as the garden. The salmon-pink facade was broken by balconies, winding staircases and balustrades supported by the crouching figures of Atlases, lions, allegorical animals and stucco festoonery. It was choked with ornaments and figures, and a small child could have climbed the outside of the four-story building from the ground floor to the roof without any danger to himself.

As Don Alfonso got up to walk on, he saw his way blocked by two salt-and-pepper-colored Schnauzers, standing with one paw half raised and trembling with rage. This was part of the protective system devised by Leonidas Erosa. Three Great Danes lay in deep sleep most of the time up on the terrace of the villa. The vigilant Schnauzers began to bark, and this brought on the Great Danes.

The five dogs stood in a circle around Don Alfonso and kept him there until an Indian appeared. The Indian shouted a Spanish phrase of welcome over the barks of the dogs; he threw a handful of sand at the Schnauzers and chased them away, said his phrase of welcome once more, and informed Don Alfonso that General Erosa was in his lookout tower, eating.

Following after the Indian, Don Alfonso wondered, as always, at his presence. The sight of the giant gardener, his black-blue hair, his costume, was like receiving a picture postal card from home. Alfonso Lopez was a distant relative of the General, a banker who handled Erosa's affairs in Paris.

He found Leonidas Erosa at a large table in the tower of the villa looking out at the sea. In front of him was an assortment of silver dishes. A butler poured wine for him, Roederer 1928 brut, which the General drank like lemonade. He had finished a kidney stew and asked for more wine when the sand crunched under the small feet of his visitor.

Don Alfonso was excited and warm; he stuttered and fanned himself with his bowler. The purpose of his visit, he said, was to give the General a warning. He knew someone, he said, who had the confidence of Gamelin. He advised the General's immediate departure.

He said, "I believe that this time they will steal everything, the Mona Lisa, the wine, the silver."

The General asked where he should go.

"New York, of course," said Don Alfonso; "there is no other place left fit to live in. Good hotels, opera, night clubs, people, all the pleasures . . ."

"I am not an opera man," said the General. "I don't like to go out to eat. I would hate to leave all this now and then have the French cover themselves with glory and hang up victory emblems while I am in America. I love this place, I am happy here— I will stay here. And now I wish to pray."

Leonidas Erosa stopped at each of the fourteen stations of the cross which stood along a path that led from the tower to the villa. Don Alfonso, who was an opera man, walked about and hummed an aria, and when both were done, they went into the villa.

The General and Don Alfonso lunched together in the baroque dining room. After coffee and cigars, Don Leonidas advised his visitor to remain calm, and he said goodbye to him in front of a forty-thousand-dollar bouquet of roses painted by Renoir. As Don Alfonso left, he was again surprised to see the giant Indian gardener sitting silently behind a screen in the foyer.

In European cities, on the belfries of city halls and other venerable edifices, you sometimes see complicated musical clocks with figures which appear at the stroke of the hour, move slowly around the belfry, and then go in again. The General's lookout tower was like one of these antique clocks. At specified times of the day all the important members of his household came there. The first was usually Miss Graves, an English governess whom the General many years before had rescued from drowning in the Seine. He had no need for a governess, his only daughter being grown by the time Miss Graves joined the household. Miss Graves came alone to the tower at seven in the morning.

At ten the General's second breakfast took place there. At noon Mlle. Borotra, the General's housekeeper, opened the door of the tower and looked out to sea. She was much younger than either the General or Miss Graves, and had traces of Castilian beauty which she accented with pendulous amethyst earrings, a garnet cross on a gold chain, and an unwieldy tortoise-shell comb. She always sat in a niche of the tower where her somewhat faded beauty was safe from the sun.

The only irregular visitor to the tower was the Indian, Anselmo. He came when no one else was there, climbed down the stairs inside the tower, and lay on the rocks below, with his feet dangling in the water, for hours. He had been taken from his home in a mountain valley to the hacienda of the General, when the General's little girl needed someone to play with, and he was brought along to Paris as a living toy. If they had left Anselmo in his native land he could hardly have grown up wilder than he had in France. He knew a few words of the language; the pictures of the Eiffel Tower and the Jardin d'Acclimatation were in his mind, and he knew how to order vanilla ice cream and pay for it; but his idea of quantities more than ten was clouded and confused. Across his large handsome face wandered simple emotions, never more than one at a time, and the thoughts when they came were always sad and the same, like someone making music by knocking two sticks together. What affection he had he gave to the dogs. When he was alone with them he embraced them, put his cheek to theirs, and talked to them. His favorite was the biggest of the Great Danes—Attila. He fed the dogs, washed them, and took care of their wounds. When he squatted on the floor down in the basement, they sat around him as if they too were Indians. And at night as many as could get on it were allowed to sleep on his bed.

He walked loosely, with the elegance of an animal, and managed to give a suggestion of the exotic to the white linen suit he always wore by carrying a red blanket over his shoulder as if it were a poncho. He also wore a wide-brimmed gardener's hat of blue felt which cast deep shadows on his coffee-colored face.

He might have been sent back long ago to Ecuador, except for one thing: the General was subject to fits, and needed someone strong enough to control him during these fearful attacks. They came at intervals of two or three months, and there was always a definite warning—the General's left cheek started to twitch shortly before the seizure occurred. When the fit was over he slowly regained consciousness, and was surprised to find his clothing disarranged. For several days he looked exceptionally well. His cheeks were rosy, his eyes sparkled, and he was much more intelligent than usual. During the months when the General had no need of him, Anselmo was free to wander about under the warm-smelling pines and the mimosa that lined the roads of the villa. The other gardeners ignored him.

When Anselmo lay on the sunlit rocks beneath the tower there were two daydreams that he gave himself up to. The first was of his mountain home. In his mind's eye he saw a road winding up from a valley and a low house with a floor made of earth stamped down by bare feet. This hut was filled with smoke and had an opening for a door and no window. In the center, on a poncho, sat an Indian woman and two Indian children. The fields outside were warm and soft like the skin of a llama. All around stood mountains that were copper-colored in the sun and silver when the moon rose. High up near the mountain peaks condors were circling, and in the hills below Anselmo could hear drums and the mournful flutes of shepherds.

As this dream faded he crawled to the edge of the water, held his head out over it, and wept. In his sad hesitant soul, shaped by the ancient Spanish boot and spur, the whip, and the padre, Anselmo carried his homesickness with him wherever he went. It felt like a stone. He tried to throw it into the water at the foot of the tower but he always got up with the weight still inside him. And after that he gave himself up to the other dream, which was

so much simpler—to take General Leonidas Erosa by the throat
and choke him to death.

The interior of the Villa Amelita was an auctioneer's paradise
of flowered carpets, tassels, and draperies, Biedermeier, and Louis
Seize. Of the many rooms, General Erosa's bedroom was the most
museum-like. It was a shrine dedicated to the memory of his dead
wife. Three full-faced and two profile paintings of Donna Amelita
hung here, and with them a portrait of the General's daughter,
Beatriz Mercedes, who was now married to an Englishman and
living in London. Donna Beatriz resembled her Peruvian mother
closely.

The furniture in this room, as in all the others, was ornate.
On a rosewood table whose marble top was supported by the
golden legs of two cranes reposed the Erosa family album, bound
in velvet, embossed, and the size of a lexicon. In a large glass case
next to the rosewood table were preserved a number of relics of
the General's marriage: his wife's wedding dress, the small doll-
like madonna to which she had prayed, a sword and silver spurs,
two dried bouquets of flowers, and a row of the scented candles
which had burned at her bier. Four people could have slept in
the General's bed, which was heavily inlaid with mother-of-pearl.
Over it, on a branch, sat a stuffed condor which the General had
shot in South America. At the door of the bedroom, on a golden
bracket, swung a polished turtle shell containing holy water.

The General was awakened by the sun each morning when his
valet drew back the tasseled curtains. Although he was seventy,
he was still a man of tremendous strength. He had the torso of
a bull, and almost no neck whatever. People who saw him sitting
in bed thought a very tall man would get up, but his powerful
legs were extremely short. His arms and legs were covered with
black hair, and his chest looked like a sofa ripped open.

The General's day was as evenly divided as the face of a watch.
From the moment he woke he was passed from one pair of hands
to another, like someone in a flying trapeze act. The valet dressed
him, walked him to the private chapel of the villa, and pushed
him through a carved oaken door. On the other side the curé

would take him over, whisper a few devout sentiments in his ear, guide him to a pew, and begin to say the Mass. With the General knelt his entire household, except Miss Graves who belonged to the Church of England. Anselmo served as altar boy. He repeated the Latin service day after day without knowing the meaning of the words, and went through the ritual with automatic precision. He had learned it thoroughly as a child.

The curé stayed for breakfast, blessed the bread, and brought the gossip of Biarritz into the glass-enclosed verandah where he and the General ate. After breakfast the chef would appear, bringing with him Escoffier's *Guide Culinaire,* and a heavy scrapbook filled with recipes and menus. He and the General nearly always had a difficult time rowing through a sea of soups, sauces, ragouts, and all the ingredients that go into them. They disagreed about what birds to cook, what to garnish and stuff them with, and how to balance it all with the proper savory, the right wine, and the General's mood. This was the hour in which the General was most alert. He aroused the temper of his French chef, the table was struck, and voices were raised. It was fortunate that the curé was present to bring master and servant back into proper accord. As the chef left, Miss Graves entered.

The curé waited for that moment as a dog waits for a bone, because it was then that the General called for a silver casket in which he kept his cigars, and from it presented the man of God with a soft, round, perfectly balanced brunette cigar—a British cabinet selection. The two men always lit their cigars with separate matches.

After the curé left, Miss Graves read the mail, which consisted of daily appeals for help from charitable organizations, and occasionally a letter from the General's daughter. On those rare occasions when the General decided to answer a letter, he would inform Miss Graves of his sentiments and she would translate them into a polite and brief answer.

At ten the General proceeded to the lookout tower, followed by a butler who carried an elaborate assemblage of copper marmites. This equipment had been designed for an outing in the Pyrenees, but was used to transport the General's second breakfast, which consisted of meat puddings, small curries, sweetbreads, kidney stews, and coquilles of seafood.

At eleven Professor Hubert Roselius, a German refugee portraitist, waited for the General in a small garden house, where he was at work on one of a series of portraits of the general in a soldierly coat, holding a sword, and looking into the distance. Herr Professor Roselius was only a mediocre painter and had no talent for business, but even to his dull senses it was clear that a man who had three pictures and a statue of Napoleon in his library, who walked with his right hand stuck into his coat and insisted on being addressed as "General," might secretly fancy himself to resemble the Emperor. Herr Professor Roselius had remarked on this curious accident, after having several swallows of Napoleon brandy served in an inhaler with a large golden N engraved on its belly, and the result was his present commission and what seemed to be a life work ahead. The finished pictures, all of them more like Bonaparte than like Erosa, were stored one after another in an attic, like the scenery of plays that had ended their run, and immediately a new one was begun.

The General's lunch was served at one, in the lookout tower whenever the weather permitted. He usually ate in the company of his doctor or Miss Graves. After luncheon he went to sleep for an hour and was awakened by the masseur who appeared at three. At four, having passed through swells of soapsuds, sponging, slapping and rubbing, kneading, and the heat of the electric cabinet, he was taken to his swimming pool. He swam up and down three times, like a large turtle, and crawled out, to be dried and placed in the sun.

The Paris papers arrived then, and tea was served on the terrace of the pool. Miss Graves read to him the items that interested her, which were mostly about the Court and the Royal Family; she avoided the more disturbing news. She had to stop reading sometimes when military planes flew overhead, but the General did not regard them either with interest or with anxiety.

After tea, with Anselmo beside him, he made the stations of the cross once more. Then the valet took over, and helped him dress for dinner.

There were always guests. While the food was on the table, the General's appetite confined his thoughts and hands to his knife, fork, and spoon. He smoked one of his fine cigars after dinner, and for dessert slowly peeled himself a Calville apple. After he had finished, he always looked from face to face around the table, as if he were sorry for them all, got up abruptly and went to his bedroom. The valet undressed him, drew the curtains and left. For a moment the trapeze act seemed suspended. In sudden fright, because there were no outstretched hands to catch him, he yelled for the Indian. Anselmo came in then and stayed with the General until he fell asleep.

Shortly after the visit of Señor Lopez, the peace of the Villa Amelita was disturbed by two visits from the authorities. The first time it was the agents of the Deuxième Bureau. They hustled Herr Professor Roselius off but allowed the General's laundresses —two German women whom he called the Andirons because they looked exactly alike—to remain at the villa. They were even permitted to keep the little radio with which they listened, as they bent over their washtubs, to the broadcasts from Cologne.

A few weeks later the villa was visited by a French army surgeon who wanted to be shown over the grounds with a view to converting the villa into a hospital for convalescent officers. It was admirably suited for that purpose, he told the General as he left.

The General was disturbed at the thought of having to give up his villa, and the loss of his portrait painter also bothered him. He could find no satisfactory way of filling in the time between eleven and twelve every morning. One day while he was in the lookout tower he received a visit from the chef. Truffles and Malossol caviar and Miss Graves's Earl Grey Blend tea and the kind of pâté foie gras that the General was so fond of were difficult to obtain. There was, of course, the pâté which came from Strassburg and which most people considered good enough, but the General would not eat it. The pâté foie gras he liked was flown in from Czechoslovakia by plane and processed by the chef at the Ritz in Paris. Monsieur Auzello, the director of the Ritz, had written to explain that on account of conditions in Czechoslovakia no more was being received and there were only six jars left, which he was forwarding. After that, the chef said glumly, it was the Strassburg pâté or none.

From that time on, the General telephoned Señor Lopez every morning between eleven and twelve.

The Indian had only half heard and half understood the conversation between the General and the chef, but Anselmo knew it was some trouble about food, and he became very hungry. Before the week was out, Mlle. Borotra came to the tower complaining about the Indian. He had gone out into the country and come home with a sheep which he had slaughtered in one of the washtubs in the laundry. Then all by himself, with the dogs in a ring watching him, he had eaten it, the whole sheep including the head, which he had chopped in half. It took him four days, Mlle. Borotra said, and when he finished there was blood all over him, all over the dogs, and all over the laundry.

A slow angry flush mounted in the General's face as he listened to the story. When it was over he accompanied Mlle. Borotra back to the villa. His riding whips were kept in the music room. Anselmo stood beside him and looked on with interest while the General tried first one and then another. Suddenly the Indian felt the lash across his face. When the whipping was half over, the General leaned against the piano to rest, and Anselmo, waiting stolidly for him to finish, saw a sudden twitching in his left cheek. The General ran upstairs to his bedroom and the Indian silently went after him. When Anselmo got there the General was reaching up into the air with both arms, as if the room were filled with water and he were trying to swim away.

The attacks of the *grand mal* which Leonidas Erosa suffered had a pattern, solid and repetitious. The mental state was made up of the hopeless sensation one undergoes just before vomiting, augmented by a peculiar fear which he carried over from childhood. The whippings administered by his father, who was a great believer in corporal punishment, had been subject to a sinister protocol. He was called into his father's room and questioned; there followed a period of waiting, while the father deliberated about the amount of punishment; and finally came the thrashing.

The thrashing itself was not hard to take. All the dreadfulness was in that period of waiting. He would sink to his knees then, lift his hands above his head, and say over and over: "I will be good, I will be good, I will be good." The same sweaty anxiety overtook him now when an attack was coming on. First there was the fear of Papa's cane. Then he felt as if a thousand fishhooks had been thrown into his bowels and someone were tugging at the thin ligatures to which they were attached. A second later, fear disappeared and a brilliant light illuminated everything for him—what he looked at or thought about was set forth with such clarity that until that moment it seemed to have been hidden by dusty curtains. A new vision took the place of the old dull perception of things.

He looked at the Indian now and suddenly saw him through and through, exact in every detail, like the candid camera photographs in which every pore, every stub of beard is accounted for. He saw the eye, its retina, its pupil, the construction of the lid. The measurements were in his head as if he had just finished drawing them.

Anselmo stood and watched, his hands open at his sides and ready. Then suddenly he rose on his toes and leaped. With the Indian on top of him, the General lost his balance and fell. The giant gardener braced himself, lifted the General and rammed his body into the stone of the fireplace. There was a soft thud, as if one threw a sack of wet sand on the ground. The Indian dragged the General back to repeat the maneuver, but Erosa reached out with both hands and got hold of one of the bedposts. The Indian used his heels to kick the old man's hands loose. Whatever happened, he thought, would be blamed on the disease. He could choke the General or press his face into the pillows. Nobody would know that he had done it.

After a hopeless glance at the Indian standing over him, the General began to turn his head slowly backward. His mouth twisted, and his face became gray. The last signal of the attack, the epileptic cry, came from his throat. His legs shot out, and he hit the glass case of relics, which toppled over and shattered. The long imprisoned smells of wax and of holy objects, of per-

fumed clothes, of myrrh, and of dried flowers, flowed out from it.
The madonna and all the sentimental debris—spurs, riding whip,
gloves, and candles—were strewn about the carpet and did their
ancient services.

The wet and trembling Indian stared at them and heard the
songs of angels. He stood once more in a land of goodness under
a sky of purest blue. All about him were pastures with white sheep
and flowers. He saw the companion of his childhood, the General's
daughter, running toward him in a white dress and ribbons with
a small golden cross at her throat. She put her hand in his. The
picture changed. He was in church and the padre was ringing
the bells. His Indian mother and father, whose faces had been
so long lost to him, were there, and also the General and the
General's dead wife. From the center of heaven the silver madonna
looked down on them. It was all right and good. The picture
changed again and he saw a garden wall and a geranium tree.
Under this tree the little girl had kissed him once and sworn that
when she grew up she would love no one but Anselmo. It was
all as clear as if it were painted on the wall over the General's bed.

Anselmo bent over him but instead of closing his hands around
the old man's throat, he began to apologize, to ask forgiveness.
As if it were a waterlogged tree stump he lifted the clumsy weight
and steered it away from the broken glass into a corner where the
General, still kicking and flinging himself about, could not hurt
himself. The General was bleeding from a small cut on his forehead. Anselmo washed the cut and stayed beside him until he
was sure that the fit was over. Then he went down to the basement
and fell exhausted on his cot.

"Now that the lovely days of autumn are here, a word to the
honored world of the ladies," sang the radio across the hall, in
German. The Andirons had tuned in on Cologne. "For those
ladies who are not fortunate enough to buy a new corset, we offer
the facilities of our repair shop. We are glad to repair your old
corset even if it was not bought in our atelier. To reach our
establishment take street cars No. 7, 16, or 38 and get off at the
Goethe Strasse. Our address is—"

The speaker was interrupted by a band that played "Deutschland, Deutschland ueber Alles." The laundresses turned the radio off and looked worried.

Two days later General Erosa received a telegram from Alfonso Lopez in Paris informing him that all arrangements for his departure had been completed. The General left his villa, and walked down to the lookout tower. He saw Anselmo stretched out on the rocks below and called to him. When Anselmo had mounted the stairs, General Erosa flung one arm around his shoulder affectionately and with his silver-headed cane he pointed out to sea. Soon, he said, a ship would be anchored there, ready to take them away. Anselmo nodded. In the small secret island of his imagination he rearranged his dream so that the murder took place on board the ship that was coming. Like waiting children he and the General looked out over the blue water.

2: *Miss Graves*

THE MANNER in which Miss Graves had joined the household of General Erosa was both unusual and romantic.

On the morning of a day in March of the year 1912, Leonidas Erosa had one of his frequent differences of opinion with his chef. Jacques Vitasse came from the Valley of the Loire Inférieure and was a specialist in the cooking of that region, and besides that a pupil of the great chef, Escoffier. He was a madman in his kitchen and highly irritable outside of it. The General always addressed him respectfully as Monsieur Vitasse or by his title, but Jacques Vitasse, who never looked at him except when he was angry, confined himself to saying "You." He was knock-kneed from standing long hours at the oven which he loved; he was suffering from several other vocational ailments; he drank, and his hands were large and red, and always moist. The General called him "Jacques aux mains rouges," which was the name of a spectacular murderer of the period.

The violent cook ran the house in despotic fashion. He engaged all the servants, he went to market and bought the materials himself, he tolerated no butler in his kitchen nor interference from housekeepers. He was so insolent to them that there was a constant turnover of housekeepers in the household in spite of good food and excellent wages. The only exceptions to this rule were those women who were chosen for the post on account of their youth, their lovely eyes or slim figures, and who, in consequence of these attributes, enjoyed the protection of the General until he tired of them and they found themselves dismissed with flowers, a gift of jewelry, and a dowry. These never went near the kitchen after the first visit.

17

There was a call out again for housekeepers. When the General came down that morning and walked through the foyer of his house, about twenty-five women were sitting there. He walked up and down among them, but they were so hopeless that he retired to his study, rang for the butler, and instructed him to tell the old crocodiles outside that the position was already filled.

Leonidas Erosa was in many ways the stepchild of life. He lived in fear of the attacks of the *grand mal*, he was near-sighted and given to long stretches of melancholia and lonesomeness. But small favors were granted him. In cases of minor annoyances he simply looked heavenward with a weary look, and miraculously something happened. He had become convinced, by the constant evidence of small miracles, that there was a department up above, like the bureau of a minor government official, where Leonidas Erosa was known and looked after. That evening, as he rode through the streets of Paris again, he thought of Jacques with the red hands and of his impertinences. He was hurt. The housekeeper who left was a tolerable companion. The General was lonesome. He looked wearily up to heaven and leaned back in his seat.

The General's carriage was rolling along the Quai d'Orsay. As it turned to cross the Pont Alexandre III, he saw a crowd of people leaning over the balustrade of the bridge and pointing at the water below. Men started running along the bridge and the quay. A woman screamed. Two policemen with a long pole almost ran into the General's horses. The horses reared. The General jumped out of his carriage, threw aside his opera hat and his black cape, and dived into the Seine.

It was a difficult rescue. The General, a fair swimmer, found himself up against a woman who fought him with all her strength. He managed to drag her to the left bank, and when she was somewhat recovered from her experience he had her taken to his home.

When they arrived there he looked at her with wonder. "Leonora!" he said. He covered her hands with kisses, and he asked her why she had never written to him.

She stared at him with bewildered surprise, and assured him that her name was not Leonora.

"You are ill, my darling," he said. He had her taken to a room, called for a doctor, and sat at her bedside most of the night.

He asked her where she had been. He tried with endless questions to bring her to an admission of her identity. Like an accusing judge he pointed his finger at her and said, "Where were you on such and such a date?"

And she answered coolly, "I was the governess of the Cumberland children in Gmunden on the Traunsee"; or "I was home in Royston, Hants."

In her lodgings the police found an envelope containing money to pay for her funeral. The woman's name, they discovered, was Elinor Graves. She was English, and had been employed in Paris as a governess. The envelope also contained detailed instructions about what to do with her body. She did not wish to be buried in France. Her remains were to be shipped to a small village in Hants.

On the next few pages in the General's book of life one observes the constant appearance of Miss Graves, properly dried and out of bed, walking in the garden behind his house, on his arm, listening to long talks on the beauty of life.

On one of the first days that she was able to go out he drove with her to the Restaurant Robinson, the unique establishment in the suburbs of Paris which has its tables up in the branches of a big tree. One climbs to its six small pavilions up narrow wooden stairs that are like ladders. The kitchen and the rooms of the small hotel are in a building near by that is painted red, white, and blue the faded color of a French flag. The young waiters climb around in the tree like monkeys up to the uppermost tables. To the highest, food and wine is sent in a basket on a pulley.

The proprietor came in person to lead the General to the pavilion on the lowest and stoutest of the branches. He bowed deeply to Miss Graves and smiled at her as to an old acquaintance. He cooked the meal himself, and the General held Miss Graves's hand and said, "Isn't there anything you remember?" She shook her head.

Wisps of her red golden hair touched his cheek. He kissed her hand and called her Leonora again. She loved the restaurant, she thought it quite unusual, but she said her name was not Leonora, and she said she was certain that she had never been at the Hotel Robinson before, with him or with anyone else. From where they sat they looked into the windows of the small hotel. In one of the rooms was a dog, in another a woman lay on the bed with bare feet and a man was combing his hair, and in a third was a boy practicing on a violin.

Leonidas Erosa declared that it must be an illusion that he had taken her for someone else. Because she could not have forgotten. . . . She smiled with the politeness of first acquaintance and withdrew her hand to eat. On the way home she fell asleep with her head on his shoulder.

Miss Graves did not explain her reason for wishing to leave the world and the General did not ask her. He suggested a motor trip to the Côte d'Azur, hoping that it would wipe out the unpleasant memory of what had happened. To this, as to all his other suggestions, Miss Graves agreed.

The General had six automobiles, and for touring used a large green Panhard, a car distinguished by a faulty starting device and an inaccessible carburetor. The roads were very bad and mechanics rare. The General's chauffeur was obliged to carry along an extra set of front and back springs, the small ones in the tool boot, the large springs mounted under the running board. The luggage was on top of the car, confined inside a small fence and tied down with heavy straps. A vulcanizing outfit, two pumps and two jacks, and a length of stout rope were stowed away under the front seat.

The chauffeur drove out of Paris by a roundabout way, down the Champs Elysées, between the Grand and the Petit Palais. As they went over the Pont Alexandre III the General squeezed Miss Graves's hand. She looked straight ahead.

At Grenoble there was a fortunate obstruction in the road and they were obliged to spend the night at the Hôtel Moderne. The General engaged a suite with connecting rooms.

Late at night he knocked at Miss Graves's door. He had drawn the heavy hotel curtains in the salon, saying that he could not sleep, and when she came and sat on the sofa with him, he pressed his claims with persistence. In an effort to create an atmosphere of intimacy he had turned the lights out and lit a candle. He kissed her hand and called her Leonora. He kissed her shoulder and her throat. When he wanted to kiss her lips she put her head down.

"You are like a goat," said the General, "exactly like Leonora." She moved away from him. When her eyes became accustomed to the darkness, she saw that he was dressed in pajamas and a robe.

"Don't go," he said, and pressed her back into the seat. "Don't go until you hear me." He poured out two glasses of champagne.

"Leonora came to us in Biarritz as the governess of my cousin Anibal. He was a little boy then, and he sat in the sand down by the rock in front of where the Hôtel du Palais now stands. Leonora sat there with him. He had a red pail and a small shovel which he always stuck in his mouth, and there was a poodle. The poodle's name was Lothario.

"One day the stupid gardener sheared Lothario, and no one recognized him. The villa echoed with the cries of little Anibal, who thought his dog had died. Whenever the poodle came near him in his new shape he screamed and pushed him away. Leonora got the wool which the gardener had shorn off the poodle and knelt down on the floor of the lobby and made a poodle out of it. It looked exactly like Lothario. She cut a button from her shoe and used it for the eye. The imitation dog lay there for two weeks, the floor was never swept, and everybody walked around the poodle. . . . It was on the day she consoled Anibal that I first kissed Leonora.

"I had just come home from a German lycée, and I remember quoting Schelling the philosopher. He was talking about his love. He did it with hammer blows, but it curiously fitted Leonora. I still remember every word of it. This is how it goes:

"'She was a strange, unique being. One had to love her completely or not at all—this masterpiece of the spirits, this rare woman of masculine greatness of soul, of the sharpest wit united with the most feminine, tenderest, most loving heart. O such a one will never come again.'"

"It doesn't sound like me at all. I cannot possibly measure up to that," said Miss Graves.

"You are her image, your voice is hers, your hair, your eyes, your walk is Leonora. Her hair was red gold, she was vain and distant as you are, and as a prelude to anything she said, she held her head up straight and her lovely proud lips set in cool arrogance exactly like yours.

"We stayed at the Hotel Robinson for a week and then came back to Biarritz. She told me that she wanted to die—the way one asks for a knife to cut bread with. And as casually as that she swam out to sea one day, and when I called to her she answered, 'I will come back, Leonidas.' She was a mile and a half out when I began to be afraid for her. I swam after her with the firm intention not to come back.

"A fisherman picked me up in a small sardine boat. We sailed back and forth over the water the whole night. He sat in front of me staring at his toes. There were two empty bottles that rolled back and forth and knocked together in the bottom of the boat. I have never forgotten the sound they made.

"I have never forgotten the words she said over the water, 'I will come back, Leonidas.'

"We came to the shore in the dawn. I prayed that she would be standing there, but there was only the rock and the sand. I died for her then. But now I am no longer lonesome."

She took his hands and allowed him to kiss her cheek. And she rewarded him with a detailed account of her almost fatal walk into the Seine. It was like a young girl's excited story of her first ball.

"It was lovely after the first moment," she said. "I shall never be afraid of death again. I felt a little pressure in my ears. That was all. The water was neither hot nor cold. It was a pleasant tepid bath. Everything about me changed to an orange color and I felt myself turning and then floating higher and higher. I saw beautiful water plants and at times seemed to hold them in my hands. For the first time I was free of all the cares and worries

that are with me every day. I saw a million small diamonds and
my whole family appeared before me. I was a little child and a
big child, all at the same time. I relived my first great sadness.
All the good and evil things appeared in the same warm room
with the water plants and the diamonds. Then I woke up, just
as from a dream in bed, and a man bent over me and said, 'Respirez
profondément, mademoiselle,' and I saw you. I became tired again
and went to sleep, and then I woke up in your house. I am so
grateful to you!"

The General kissed her long cold fingers and her cheeks, called
her "Leonora," and promised that she would never have to worry
again. Whatever she wanted he would provide for her. The only
thing that Miss Graves wanted was to have a gypsy wagon and
tour England—"to wander through the more secluded spots of
my island home," she said like a travel brochure. It was the dream
of her life. The General offered to turn around and leave France
immediately. They would tour England, he said, from one end
to the other, in the most beautiful gypsy wagon money could buy.
When Miss Graves explained that she wanted to do that alone,
the evening ended abruptly.

The next morning she resented the coquetry of the chamber-
maid and the porter, who inquired how they had rested; and at
breakfast, when the General again addressed her as Miss Graves,
she assumed a look of injury which she added to the governess
look. All the way to the Côte d'Azur she sat as far away from him
as she could on the rear seat of the Panhard.

Although Miss Graves wanted to leave him, the lonesome
General kept her on as a companion. The relationship between
them gradually burdened itself with all the misery of marriage
and none of its pleasures. They had a block of self-repeating household arguments such as wife and husbands have. After coffee was
served they disagreed on the merits of Offenbach, the elder Guitry,
and Calvé. If Leonidas Erosa wanted to plant immortelles, Miss
Graves thought mimosa much nicer. She disputed with him over
the bills for champagne and over the size of the tips he handed
out when they traveled. There were also automobile arguments.
When they were in Paris, all the bridges—the Pont Neuf, Pont

Royal, Pont Louis XVI, even the crowded ones that lead over the Île de la Cité—were used, but never the Pont Alexandre III. When they drove south there was an argument about whether they should avoid Grenoble and take the bad roads instead. The arguments always ended with a neatly set worn speech, the substance of which was that if he had let her alone on the day he drove over the Pont Alexandre III in March 1912, all this would have been avoided.

Miss Graves repeatedly tried to take her life. Gas ranges, open windows, oncoming cars and trains, bridges, and the sea all seemed to invite her. Two of the attempts had been so nearly successful that the General knew it was not a ruse on Miss Graves's part to gain an advantage over him, but an illness as serious as his own. By rescuing her from the Seine he had taken on the responsibility for keeping her alive.

In his private thoughts he addressed her as "Mula," and occasionally he used this word in referring to her. "Tell the Mula . . ." he would say to Anselmo. Or, "Go and see if the Mula can read to me." He also prayed—one, two, or three Ave Marias—after their arguments, the number depending upon the nature of the differences they had had. He used this device to keep a fit of anger from coming on.

A few days after Señor Lopez's final message, the General picked up a pair of powerful artillery glasses and watched a ship out on the horizon. Then he summoned Mlle. Borotra and told her that he wanted his luggage ready for an immediate departure. To be included among his personal belongings were thirty-two cases of Roederer 1928 brut, six terrines of pâté foie gras, and a good supply of private cigars. By noon the halls and corridors of the villa were crammed with trunks, bags, and packing boxes.

He had made his decisions. Miss Graves would go, and his doctor and of course his chef; a valet, and the Indian gardener with the three Great Danes. He would give the Schnauzers to the Andirons.

That day Miss Graves did not come down for lunch. In the late afternoon Mlle. Borotra, who shared with Miss Graves a bath and a corridor on the second floor of the villa, invaded her room with tea and biscuits. Miss Graves had taken to her bed. Her face on the pillow looked old as rock.

"I've had your trunks put outside," Mlle. Borotra said. It was Miss Graves's affair, Mlle. Borotra thought, if she wanted them moved into her room.

"I'm not leaving," Miss Graves said weakly.

Mlle. Borotra glanced at her in surprise. "The General is going . . ." she said.

"It doesn't matter." Miss Graves turned her head away.

For the first time the bitter biting dislike that was always on Mlle. Borotra's face whenever she looked at Miss Graves faded. She pulled a chair over to the bed and sat down. "You don't look at all well," she said. "Forgive me for saying this but there are little affairs that one must put in order at your age. One never knows when the good God will call us to Him. But perhaps you have thought about this yourself."

Miss Graves nodded.

"Is it not most extraordinarily fortunate then," said Mlle. Borotra, "that my nephew is an undertaker and that he happens to be visiting me today. He is sitting downstairs at this moment. His establishment, the Pompes Funèbres de B. Marsan et Fils, is without peer in Bayonne. He has the business of all the hotels and pensions of Biarritz and St. Jean de Luz. His charges are moderate, his service is honest and dignified. He is waiting, as I have said, downstairs, and if you don't mind, I'll call him. It will only take a few minutes."

The nephew came in beaming. He had red, fat, simply designed ears and he looked more like a pig than a pig does. He had apparently got up from the table in a hurry. As he sat down he brushed some crumbs off his vest, the lower two buttons of which were undone, and said, "Chère demoiselle, I regret to see you looking so pale."

Miss Graves was relieved that the conversation could be conducted in English. "I know your business," she said. "I know why you are here, Monsieur Marsan. Let us get this over with." She twisted and pushed herself into a sitting position. "I haven't much strength and I have very little money, but I want to be buried in England."

"In a decent casket," suggested the nephew.

"In a plain casket," said Miss Graves, "without frills or fancies."

Monsieur Marsan pulled a tape measure out of his pocket, asked her pardon, and bent over her. As his face came close to hers Miss Graves detected the smell of cognac.

"You are," he said, ignoring her expression of disgust, "chère demoiselle, if I may make this free observation, very stately, as all Englishwomen are. Our stock sizes will not do at all. The casket will have to be made especially for you." He made calculations on a sheet of paper. "Before I can quote you a price we must think about the lining. Shall it be satin or satinette? Satin is more durable, satinette is cheaper."

"You may use cotton," said Miss Graves. "No one will see it. But a good quality of cotton."

"Satinette then." He showed her a price he had written on the piece of paper.

Miss Graves nodded.

"Now about shipping the body to England," he said, as he pulled out of his pocket a small continental timetable. It had an orange cover decorated with a clock face that showed twenty-four hours instead of twelve. "I am deeply grieved that you cannot come and inspect our establishment. Papa was with the firm Oban and Cie. in Davos and it is from there that we have our great transport experience. We have had clients to send to all parts of the world—shipments as far as Cairo, Moscow, and once even a Maharajah all the way to India, not to speak of routine cases to New York, Berlin, and Buenos Aires. Once we even shipped a horse. That is, ma chère demoiselle, a confidence which I would like you to keep. Strictly speaking, we did not ship the horse ourselves—a taxidermist and a veterinary were involved in that. We acted in a consulting capacity. The man who had owned the horse was very fond of it and spared no expense. It went to America in a casket, specially built, of course, and imagine— with an extra compartment for saddle, blanket, bridle, and stir- rups." Monsieur Marsan raised his eyebrows and observed, "Some

men keep women and some keep horses." He giggled. Then he
looked at Miss Graves and became serious. "Yes," he said, "the
horse went to America. America is a curious place. Have you been
there, mademoiselle? I have. Papa sent me on a sort of tour du
monde. I worked for a while with a firm of undertakers in Miami,
Florida, to learn about American methods. From there I went to
Switzerland. I like Davos much better. Not so much competition,
enough business for everyone. It's a big affair, mademoiselle—the
tubercular crowd up there all of them in extraordinarily fortunate
circumstances. It is astonishing with what ease they detach themselves from this life. Even the young with red cheeks go."

Mlle. Borotra opened the door and asked whether Miss Graves
wanted anything. The young man shook his head. The door was
carefully closed again.

"My beloved Auntie has often spoken of you to us. Poor
woman, we buried her sweetheart. When she was young she
wanted to marry a mechanic but Papa and Mama did not agree
to it because she could also have married a young man of very
good family who was at St. Cyr. He became a flier, one of the first.
The mechanic married someone else, and two days after the
wedding of the mechanic, the cadet was killed in a plane accident,
in a Farman double-decker. You know our avions were not much
good then. Since the cadet was almost one of the family and
engaged to Louise, we took care of the funeral arrangements.
They all come to us sooner or later, no one escapes. Though I must
tell you frankly, ma chère demoiselle, there are few people who
possess the courageous instinct to leave the banquet of life at the
proper time and without looking back. And those who have this
courage are mostly English."

Miss Graves, who had had her eyes closed all the while, opened
them and sat up.

"But to get back to our problem," said the young man. "There
are two ways to ship the body. The best, the shortest, but also
the most expensive, is by way of Calais-Dover. Via Le Havre-
Southampton is cheaper but there is four hours' difference. I don't
suppose you care in this instance about how long it takes?"

Miss Graves said that the length of time was immaterial.

"Via Le Havre-Southampton. Good." Monsieur Marsan occupied himself the next few minutes with timetables and costs of transportation, taxes, laissez-passers, visas, and permits.

When he had finished Miss Graves said, "That is all then?"

"No," he said. "Unfortunately no. There is another problem. How are we going to get the cadaver to the depot? The body cannot walk to the train. It is in consequence necessary to transport it there in a carriage, and the charge for this is four hundred francs."

"That's a lot, isn't it?" Miss Graves said. "Why, a taxi is only—"

Monsieur Marsan lowered his eyes discreetly. "Our problem is that we cannot take a taxi."

"I won't pay it," said Miss Graves.

Monsieur Marsan shrugged his shoulder. "Chère demoiselle, if you insist, of course. I know a good man who is always happy to make some little money and I think it can be arranged that he will take the casket and put it on a pushcart and bring it to the train himself. He must obtain a special permit for this from the police for which there is a charge; and you must take into consideration that it may rain. I doubt very seriously whether this good man is in possession of a tarpaulin large enough to cover up the box. You must not forget that this is an extraordinarily large affair. Imagine a large casket and, besides, the shipping box that goes around it, and how will it look? It will look awful. People will not take their hats off as he passes. It is like delivering a trunk. No one will have much respect."

After a weary look at him, Miss Graves said, "The carriage then. But I will not pay a cent more than three hundred francs."

"The least I can do for it, chère mademoiselle, is three hundred and fifty francs. Not a penny less."

"Very well," Miss Graves said.

The nephew got up and brushed one more crumb from his waistcoat. "We have it all settled now," he said. "I will be here tomorrow with a typewritten estimate. I am going back to Bayonne now. Incidentally, Bayonne is the place where the bayonet was invented. That too is an item of interest to us. Au revoir, chère demoiselle."

That same afternoon General Erosa was called to Paris. When he came back three days later everything was in order for the departure. The yacht was waiting in the Port de Refuge, a half hour's drive from the villa, and on the dock, together with other supplies to be taken on board, were the thirty-two cases of Roederer, the pâté foie gras, and the cigars. The General started to go to his bedroom to change his clothes, and came upon Miss Graves's trunks still standing in the hall outside her door. He bellowed for Mlle. Borotra, who appeared almost immediately, with the Indian gardener at her heels.

"She isn't going," Mlle. Borotra said, pointing to the trunks. In a sudden fury the General opened Miss Graves's door. She was sitting in a chair, dressed in black, her hair done very carefully, her hands folded in her lap and her eyes closed. Beside her, resting on two chairs, was the coffin.

"What's this?" asked the General, tapping the black box.

Mlle. Borotra told him about her nephew and the arrangements he had made for Miss Graves's interment. The General brushed her explanations aside.

"Miss Graves," he pleaded, "you can't stay here. If you do I won't be able to leave."

Miss Graves did not answer.

"Get me some brandy," said the General. In his efforts to make her swallow some, half a tumberful was poured down the front of her dress. He handed the bottle of brandy to Mlle. Borotra and pushed her out of the room. Then he turned back to Miss Graves. "Look," he said with insistence, as if he were reading a telegram to a dumb person. "We'll have a doctor on the ship. The sea air will be good for you. You can sit in a deck-chair all day, wrapped in a warm cloak, with blankets around you. You'll be yourself again in no time."

Miss Graves opened her eyes and said, "All the arrangements have been made.

"We will make other arrangements," the General said. "We're sailing for Casablanca today."

"But the undertaker—" said Miss Graves.

"Oh, there must be an undertaker there."

Miss Graves looked as a child does when it thinks it is being lied to. "Very well," she said, "but I like this coffin. I'm quite satisfied with it, and I want to take it along."

The General threw out his arms in exasperation. "You can't take a coffin on board a ship," he said. "Besides, where would we put it? Not in your cabin and not in the salon. This is a miserable tug they have sent me and there's no room for anything. We'll all be sitting on top of each other as it is."

Miss Graves held both her hands out to him and he took them. "Dear friend," she said tenderly "I am so much trouble to you, but I won't leave the coffin behind." Then she closed her eyes and gasped for breath.

The General took Anselmo out into the hall and told him in Spanish to pick Miss Graves up and carry her down to the car, which was waiting at the front door of the villa. When they returned to put this plan in action, Miss Graves's chair was empty and the window behind it was wide open.

With his heart beating wildly the General leaned far out of the window and saw a woman's shoe, then Miss Graves herself crawling slowly up over the plaster decorations.

When the General called out to her, Miss Graves turned and looked back, with her hand on the head of Poseidon and one arm braced against a dolphin's back. The crown of a tall palm tree swayed in back of her, and the ground was far below.

"Dear Miss Graves," said the General, addressing himself to Poseidon because Miss Graves herself had crawled on, and from where he was all he could see was the one foot without a shoe. "Please come back!"

"I know what you said to the Indian," Miss Graves called to him; her words echoed sonorously by a plaster sea-shell.

The General looked up into the heavens, searching for his patron saint and cursing quietly. But then he remembered how thin and frayed the string was by which Miss Graves had so long been attached to this life. He threw his arms out to her. "We'll take the coffin," he said. "Come back!"

"I don't believe it," said Miss Graves. She saw the Indian at a window close to her, and said that if he came any nearer she would jump.

A moment later she screamed and moved suddenly back against the wall. On the head of the dolphin a small green salamander had appeared. In the brief moment that she had shrunk back from the reptile, the Indian had put his powerful arms around her and pulled her back into the room. There was color in her cheeks, her eyes were shining, and she looked quite well.

"All this would not have been necessary," she said primly, "if you had let me alone that day in the Seine."

3: *The S. S. Monte Cristi*

It was raining; a lukewarm rain ran down over the façade of the Villa Amelita and dropped from the pine trees and the mimosa. The cavalcade from the villa to the yacht *Monte Cristi* started.

The two German laundresses, Emma and Anna, cried their sorrow into two aprons. The General embraced them both, stuffed some money into their hands, and told them that he was giving them the Schnauzers. As if he were leaving a hotel de grand luxe, he went along the line of his employees with additional gifts and embraces, handshakes and pats on the cheek for every servant—good or bad. He passed the line of assistant cooks, scullery maids, gardeners, parlor maids and housemen. He made a little speech in the entrance hall of the villa, thanking them, announcing that they would all remain in his employ and that Mlle. Borotra would be in absolute charge until he returned, which he hoped would be soon.

The valet, with an umbrella, stood at the door and shielded the General as he stepped into his car. The first car started off, with the three Great Danes. It was followed by the one carrying Mlle. Borotra, Miss Graves, the General's doctor, and the curé. In the third car came the Indian, the valet, and the chef with his cook book and scrap book of menus. A truck brought the latest picture of the General, the most prized personal possessions, sixteen carpets he was especially fond of, the cigars, and the six jars of pâté de foie gras. Following this was a limousine from the firm of Marsan and Cie, undertakers, which contained the coffin of Miss Graves; and last came the General. He rode alone and his eyes were filled with tears. He looked out of the back window of the car and watched his beloved pink villa disappear in the greenery and the curtains of rain. A few hundred feet past the gate of the villa, he picked up the speaking tube from the side of the car and ordered the chauffeur to drive to the Hôtel du Palais. The rest of the cars went ahead to the Port de Refuge.

At the pier, the doctor helped Miss Graves out of the car. She wanted to walk but he thought it better to carry her up the gangplank. She weighed only ninety pounds. Her stockings were twisted around her thin legs like spirals of black gauze. She was taken below to her stateroom.

Up on deck, between two ventilators and the hatch over the engine room, a carpenter still hammered on three large stalls for the dogs. The Indian walked the Danes up and down on the pier, chasing them away from the mountains of baggage and the huge blocks of ice that were being slid into the boat on a wooden chute.

When the General came on board, he had on his arm a young and beautiful woman, who smelled of Elizabeth Arden's Blue Grass.

"This is Señora Lopez," he said to Mlle. Borotra. "She is a distant relative of mine. The Señora is the wife of Alfonso Lopez. She is coming with us."

Mlle. Borotra went down to Miss Graves and wished her a pleasant journey. Mlle. Borotra sat with hands folded; when she heard the siren she dutifully dabbed at her eyes with a Spanish lace handkerchief. She took Miss Graves's hand tenderly and kissed her. "Poor dear," said Mlle. Borotra; and she left.

The General and the curé sat in wicker chairs and looked at the water. The Indian brought the silver casket and the General gave the curé the last good cigars—two of them instead of the usual one. He also gave him an envelope with a gift for his parish. Then he clapped his hands and told the Indian to fetch the chef. Jacques Vitasse arrived with his cook book and the recipes, and they decided what to have for dinner. Gradually the ice and baggage melted away. The dogs were put into their kennels. The curé blessed the ship and prayed for good weather, then he took his departure.

At about seven, the engines began to turn, the pressure on the ears started, the chandeliers in the cabins, the dining room and the stairhall began to tinkle, a draft slammed the doors in all the corridors, and the palms in the winter garden trembled in their pots. All this would go on as long as the voyage lasted.

The General waved goodbye from the bridge. The dogs in their wooden cages howled and scratched, their tails sticking out like the branches of a tree in the autumn wind, and the siren of the *Monte Cristi* howled with them. A fishing boat showed them the way out of the harbor. A customs official at the dock saluted and then folded his hands behind his back and became smaller and smaller.

The *Monte Cristi* was in great need of the curé's prayer for leniency from the elements. She was a yacht with bad habits. She was narrow and nervous and in a heavy sea she acted like a horse clearing a fence. After she jumped, she lay on her side and it seemed that she would never straighten up again. She was never in the hands of anyone very long; she was built in Kiel for a Dutchman who named her the *Duyfken*, or Dove, sold to the Khedive and resold to an Englishman. She hung around the Dalmatian coast for a while and then, during the First World War, she became a patrol boat. The French Government changed her from steam to motors and at the end of the war she was sold for a small sum to a Belgian motor car manufacturer.

The man who built her must have loved to cruise through the rivers and canals of his native land. The *Monte Cristi* was like a small destroyer. Only in a few places was there evidence of a desire for comfort—a frugal winter garden with colored glass dome was wedged between dining saloon and lounge, a little private elevator connected the promenade deck with the foyer below, and there was a stairhall with a gilded piano and two thirty-foot Byzantine columns. The signs on all the doors were still in Dutch. The present owner had had new linoleum laid in all the corridors, and the whole ship smelled of paint, of bilge water, engine room vapor, and the new linoleum. There was regrettable absence of comfort everywhere. The suites succeeded in producing the effect of a third-rate hotel or institution. The hard, tasseled brocade curtains of faded gold at the portholes, the mahogany bed, the chair, the dresser, made it all very sad and somber. The bed was three and a half feet wide and the mattress on it a pad of dead horsehair with buttons added for complete discomfort.

The charter of the boat was seventy pounds sterling a day, plus running expenses and salaries for the crew.

The captain looked as if he had been in violent proceedings all his life—a ladies' man in sweater and cap; a sticky, sunburned fifty-year-old whose name was Tannenbaum. He was only five feet four, and he had a box to stand on at each end of the bridge. He lived with his raffish crew and in great style, down in the sub-minor world of the *Monte Cristi,* where the portholes were never opened while she ran, and where the smells of the ship above were augmented by that of wet laundry and fuel oil. As they left the harbor, he stood on his portside box beside the General, shouting orders through his dirty hands.

Half an hour later, when they were well out of the harbor and the General had gone below, Monsieur Vitasse came to his cabin and made a terrible scene. "Be careful," he said to the General, "be careful! You are carrying this joke too far. Come and look at my kitchen—and at my cabin. I have been put with the Indian!" He screamed and threatened, and it was agreed that he should have a cabin up on deck, along with the guests. He disappeared saying that he could promise nothing for dinner.

At about eight, they dined. The glasses danced on the buffet and made music, the menu was written on a small card as at a hotel, there were flowers in a low vase so that one could look over them. General Leonidas Erosa thought that it was as good as could be expected. He hated ice cream and when he read that for dessert they had a Bombe Africaine, he thought about his apples.

Leonidas Erosa was fond of apples. He ate them in place of dessert and they were selected with as much care and worry as were his vintage wines and the rare cigars he smoked. His favorite apple came from the Tirol and was called the Calville apple. It grew on the sun-warmed foothills of the mountains around Meran and Bozen. In order to have its skin a uniform sulphur yellow without spots, reddish marks, or roughness, the apple was grown inside a paper bag. The upper part of the apple had a bumpy surface, the meat was firm and snow white—it was handled as carefully as a sick bird. Taken from its paper bag, it went into a sheet of tissue paper, was wrapped in cotton, put into an individual stall in a large box, which in turn was heavily wrapped, cushioned in excelsior and shipped to France. The apple sold in the fruit shops of Paris for five francs.

He came out of his thinking when the woman on his left leaned across him to speak to Miss Graves, who sat on his right.

Miss Graves had asked Señora Lopez whether she had ever lived in England. With a Spanish gesture of regret, Señora Lopez answered:

"Oh—I know this English life. It's terrible! Quail shooting— you know. You see the dogs, you walk, you shoot, you tramp all day long behind a man six feet tall, and then you have dinner: beef or a joint and vegetable marrow—and then you listen to a bishop in knee breeches, who smokes large Corona cigars with the coffee. If you don't like that, there are horses. No thank you. The British life is not for me."

She leaned over as she said this, and the General studied the flawless white skin. His eyes wandered down her throat to the décolletage, to the loose folds of her dress. She was very young and her hair was as black as a gramophone record. It seemed very comfortable to him now, with the rain outside beating against the windows.

The steward filled the glasses. He seemed to fill Señora Lopez's continually. He bent down, smelled her hair, looked at the lovely shoulders and the décolletage, and with a trembling hand he wobbled over to the glass, filling it with an uncertain stream. He knocked a glass over as he withdrew and apologized longer than necessary. He was a very young man.

"This weather," said the Beauty, "makes me feel like spitting in somebody's face."

Miss Graves sent one of her governess looks across the table, and the General said to the steward:

"Bring Madame Lopez a face to spit in."

The steward bowed, smiled—the mood of the voyage was established. Friends were friends and enemies were chosen.

The other man at the table, Dr. Fontana, quoted from the last book he had read.

"'Her eyes were green as alkali, her hair was red and sat on her like a beautiful helmet.'" The doctor was talking about Joseph Conrad. "His men are wonderful," he said, "but his women awful. Of course men of the sea are like that."

"His women were all good, I think," said the Beauty, who had the alkali green eyes. "Not having known any bad ones, he never could write about the good ones with conviction."

She leaned back, her dress stretched across her abdomen and straining at her shoulders. The steward, who seemed to work only between the General and Señora Lopez, bent over and dusted the table. Then he leaned between them again and placed on the table a silver dish with two beautiful Calville apples. He said that the Indian had given them to him. The General called for Anselmo and the giant gardener came in silently as if he were barefoot. The General smiled at him, and spoke in the heavy Spanish patois in which they conversed. "You wonderful friend! What would I do without you and how did you think of them? I will give you a bull for that—when we get home."

The Indian kissed the General's hand and left.

The Beauty said, "Let me do it," and peeled the apple.

He watched her hands. It all seemed good and filled with fine promises.

Coffee was served in the salon. The doctor played the "Rondo Capriccioso," Miss Graves sat upright next to the piano, and the General sat on a chair over the back of which the Beauty had hung her sable jacket. In their conversation he made himself a simple, lonesome man and aired his views on life and love.

They went to bed at midnight. The General kissed Madame Lopez on the forehead. "Until tomorrow then," he said, and also kissed her hand.

In his cabin, the valet undressed him and drew the short, awful curtains of gold brocade in front of the porthole. The General lay scratching the thick, black hair on his chest. He heard some noises in the stateroom at the right, the sound of bottles being put on glass shelves and the opening and closing of drawers. He asked the valet, who was taking the links out of his shirt cuffs, to tell him who had the stateroom next to him. The valet said that to the right was Miss Graves, and to the left the doctor.

The General leaned back and said three Ave Marias. Above him the ceiling of his stateroom was one large work of art, a vulgar spread of paint, resembling in technique and spirit the work one finds on the inside cover of cigar boxes. This ceiling had been added while the yacht was owned by the Khedive. It was mainly in gold and electric blue. A fat woman, with black hair, in a veil, lay on a couch, with a horn of plenty spilling its contents on a Turkish carpet. The carpet was shared by a lion, and a Moor stood in back of the couch waving a fan made of blue ostrich feathers. The background was taken up by an Egyptian landscape with pyramids. Two obese cherubs whispered into the ears of the reclining nude. . . .

The General said to himself, "How naïve . . . to put Miss Graves next to my cabin. I should have looked at the cabin plan."

The next morning, at sunrise, the dogs were let out of their cages for an hour, then caught by the Indian and locked up again. A sailor threw buckets of water on the deck. He had his trousers rolled up to the knees, and was barefoot. He stopped scrubbing and pressed himself against the railing each time Miss Graves appeared at a military clip, walking the well-worn track around the deck. The sun had just come up. She was in a tweed skirt and sweater. The captain greeted her from his starboard box, and the doctor came and joined her.

He told her that he loved England—that he had spent several months there, visiting the cathedrals. Later they remarked about the beauty of the English morning, the morning at sea, the color of the sea, the quaint sailor with his bucket. They stopped to pet the dogs, and they relegated Señora Lopez to the unsavory realm of movie stars, cocottes, and Balkan nobility.

Señora Lopez appeared at eleven, and immediately after her the General. They greeted each other with ecstasy. They admired the calm sea, the Spanish coast. Arm in arm they walked all over the deck, like two birds looking for a place to build a nest. At the stern of the boat, a cabin boy had a line out for a fish, and a man in wooden shoes threw some garbage overboard. The Indian gardener, Anselmo, his face eagerly waiting for a little more phrase about the apples, was told to bring two deck-chairs and to get the steward to serve luncheon to them out there.

The General ordered a bottle of champagne; then he took off his shirt and undershirt and sat in the sun, and the Beauty went to her cabin to put on a bathing suit.

They ate and drank and looked out on the thin ribbon of foam which the *Monte Cristi* trailed through the sea. He kissed her hand. She turned and gave him her intense look from the lips to the nose, to the forehead, and then down to the eyes; he bent over and kissed her, and she stroked his hair. After this banal statement of things as they were, they looked out to sea and the General wondered whether there was any more wine in the bottle. He clapped his hands and the steward filled the glasses.

The day was uneventful. The evening meal was served in relative silence as the General and the Beauty looked at each other and held hands. Afterwards the General had some champagne sent to the upper deck. They sat close to each other in the wicker chairs and later, when everyone else had gone to bed, they began to walk all over the boat, arm in arm. They even went down to the engine room—and there, in an adjoining office, under a lamp with a green shade, they found a cabin plan of the boat.

The General studied it. "I don't know this boat very well," he said to Madame Lopez. "Here am I," he said, and pointed to the large stateroom; "and here is Miss Graves, and here are you, and here is the doctor. The chef complained about his quarters and he has this cabin. I wonder if there is an unoccupied cabin on this ship!"

The captain came in and the General asked him whether any of the cabins were empty. The engines made a good deal of noise, and the General had to shout. The captain closed the door of the engine room, and the General shouted again—was there an empty cabin on board?

The captain pointed toward the stern on the plan. "Here, 14 is vacant," he said. "Nobody is in 14."

The General thanked him, and so did Madame Lopez. They resumed their parade around the deck.

It was about two in the morning, and after the third bottle of Roederer, that the General said: "I wonder whether that cabin really is empty." They strolled down arm in arm. The General tried the door; it opened easily. The Beauty switched on the light.

The cabin was not occupied—but on the bed reposed the coffin of Miss Graves.

Like two lost children, hand in hand, they walked to the galley, where the General, whistling his favorite tune, the "Golondrina," fished a bottle out of the icebox. The Beauty made two sandwiches which they silently ate on deck.

4: *Casablanca*

"But—monsieur!" said the customs official. "You are not a simple voyager, you are a floating warehouse; you are loaded with a thousand things which are not allowed to enter the port without the payment of proper duties."

The official, Monsieur Ssommi, sat at a respectful distance opposite the General. He looked like a benevolent mandrill, his two blue eyes so close together that they almost met on the bridge of his nose, his very red lips bedded in a curly pitch-black beard. He watched the General eat.

Miss Graves stood at the ship's railing and looked across the water at the shore and the white houses.

The Beauty sat with hands folded and said to the General in Spanish: "Be patient, listen to him, he has to do his duty. When we land we will give him some money, and then he will go away."

The official, who understood Spanish very well, looked down at his manifests and notes, and then, as if he had never seen anyone eat breakfast before, he looked on while the General finished three eggs and started to cut up a steak.

Since nobody asked him anything, he began to nod his head ominously, and pointing at the stack of papers in his lap, he said with the French gesture and face that is used to launch difficult undertakings, "Ah, it's not going to be easy, alors—"

Again he was ignored. The Beauty studied his eyes. "Look at him," she said to the General, "he looks like a monkey."

The General looked up, out of his plate, and said, "Mhm," and the official blushed under his beard.

While the General lifted the silver cover off some very hot toasted slices of bread, speared them and pushed them around in a sauce, among kidneys and slices of truffles, the official began again.

"There is," he said, "an import tax of 5 per cent ad valorem on merchandise not of Moroccan origin. There is besides a 2 per cent fee for registration; there are, besides, many things that come under special taxes—on woolen things, for example, is a tax of 55 francs per quintal. You have, Monsieur, enough long-haired carpets to fill the corridors of the Louvre. These are subject to a duty of from 42 to 70 francs the square metre. And the perfume— there is a tax of almost prohibitive size on that. I see here, Monsieur, that you have thirty-two cases of champagne, pâté de foie gras, and over a thousand cigars. Permit me to inform you that our tolerance cannot extend beyond ten cigars, forty cigarettes, or a hundred grams of smoking tobacco or snuff—women and children cannot be included in this benefit."

Miss Graves unexpectedly came to the General's rescue.

"Do you expect," she said in her stilted governess French, "the General to throw a black suit into a carton, tie a string around it and go ashore?"

"Ah, no," said the official.

"They are extremely generous here. Don't forget the ten cigars," said the General.

The yacht was at anchor outside the harbor of Casablanca. The General wiped his lips with a napkin and looked at the official with such weariness that Monsieur Ssommi had to stiffen the muscles of his jaws to suppress a yawn.

The General then yawned himself, got up, and walked to the railing of the ship where he looked toward shore and then glanced heavenward, intoning a small prayer for deliverance from this boring individual.

At that moment a compact municipal craft, brightly painted and beflagged, its brass sparkling in the morning sun, detached itself from the gray stonework of the Grande Jetée that protects the outer harbor of Casablanca. With furious explosions the little ship headed for the *Monte Cristi*.

Aboard it, waving welcome and totally unexpected, was the General's cousin, Anibal Erosa, of the Venezuelan branch of the family, who was Consul General of his country in Casablanca. Next to him stood the Commandant du Port, and the President of the Syndicat d'Initiative of Casablanca; a few feet to the left and rear of that official was the secretary of the Automobile Club of Morocco and the chaplain of a regiment of the French Foreign Legion.

Anibal Erosa could have been the younger, phlegmatic brother of Leonidas. He was devoid of imperial moods, a man of frugal appetites, and he had much less money than his cousin, but was compensated for this by a lesser affliction than the *grand mal*— he walked occasionally in his sleep.

The Consul talked in loose, drowsy sentences; his eyes were bedded in soft, gray folds and his face was like a somber room hung with old draperies. He seemed made to dwell in darkness and was an habitual visitor to the Cinema Roi de la Bière.

The Venezuelan Consul was the first one to come aboard. He walked slowly with outstretched arms into the outstretched arms of Leonidas Erosa. The curtains of his face slowly parted, and the two men embraced each other, first to the right, then to the left.

The rest of the visitors were introduced; the gentlemen bent over the hands of the two ladies.

The anchor winch whined; slowly the heavy chain rose dripping out of the sea and climbed up on deck. All the way back, at the stern, the forgotten customs official leaned against the deckhouse in reflective mood. He watched the boulders of the Grande Jetée pass by as the *Monte Cristi* sailed into the outer harbor, and he was almost pushed into the water when the steward came running past with two buckets of ice in his hands.

The Commandant du Port seated himself next to Madame Lopez, crossed his legs, and smiled nervously. Her beauty impeded his speech—he was not a man of the salons. For a while they both looked as if they were posing for a photograph of the happy married life. Suddenly he uncrossed his legs, jumped forward and opened the conversation with a long drawn out "Aaahh!" which was addressed to a silver tray in the hands of the steward, from which the Commandant took a glass of champagne for himself, and another for the Beauty. She looked into his eyes and said, "Chin chin." He touched her glass with his, they both drank and then sat in silence again.

She came to his rescue with a charm bracelet, which she wore on her right arm. With a slim finger, she fished one of the miniature emblems out of the collection and showed it to him. "Ah," he said, "a little hat;" next came a hobnail boot, a souvenir of an Alpine excursion in the Dolomites. The Commandant relaxed while the Beauty recited the history, approximate date of acquisition, and name of the donor of each small token. By the time they had gotten through the hat, hobnail boot, horn, drum, casserole, concertina, grape, and monkey, the Commandant was completely at home, and was working his right hand along the back rest of the sofa.

The President of the Syndicat d'Initiative exercised his English by going through the fruit trees of Morocco with Miss Graves:

"Ah, oui—apples, yes, we have apples."

"Have you pears?"

"Oui, pears also."

"And apricots?"

"Certainly, apricots."

"Oranges?"

"Ah, oui, also."

"Lemons?" said Miss Graves.

"Lemon—is—citron—no—?"

"Yes, citron."

"Yes, of course, lemon trees."

"And figs?"

"Yes, and almond trees, and dates. We have in the Oasis of Marrakech eighty-six thousand palm trees with dates. The greatest reputation among dates have those of Tafilalet; they are the biggest, Madame, but they are less fine than those from the south; the Algerian, the Tunisian ones are more delicately flavored. Ah, there are interesting things to see, the drying of raisins, the extraction of oil from olives, the distillery of perfume from flowers. . . ."

The Beauty's bracelet was used up. The Commandant had slipped into a careless position and began to anoint Madame Lopez with compliments. The General clapped his hands and called for more wine.

The Venezuelan Consul, who was leaning on a doorpost with both hands hanging down in the pockets of his trousers, straightened himself. He took one large hand out of its pocket, reached for a glass, raised it, and drank the health of his cousin. Then both of them went out on deck, where they leaned over the railing and looked at the water between the ship and the Quai.

Three touring cars stopped alongside the yacht, and in the petit port a submarine was leaving. "I had everything for you, Leonidas," said the Consul, "everything was ready for you. I had a villa, servants, I even sent out for a few antiques. You would have been very contented. There is a small chapel on the place, the padre who came with us is stationed there, it's only three hours from here. But suddenly—the climate becomes foul—overnight everything is different—the administration becomes a black market of despair—it's no longer comfortable here! The problem now, dear Cousin, is not only how to get out of here, but how to get out quickly. I myself expect to leave for Lisbon soon. I will be transferred to Panama—everything is upset."

Suddenly one of the chauffeurs who stood beside one of the touring cars was wet by a wave. The backwash of the submarines set the *Monte Cristi* in motion. The hawsers with which the yacht was made fast sank down into the green water, and then came up dripping, and stretched between the Quai and the *Monte Cristi* with the sound of new leather being twisted. Glasses were broken in the salon, and everyone got up. As soon as the rocking stopped, the Commandant invited the ladies and the General to a tour of the city. He offered his arm to the Beauty and walked down the gangplank beside her, just as a detachment of French Marines arrived alongside the yacht.

The soldiers came to a halt and presented arms, while the Beauty and the Commandant, along with the elegant, bronzed Chaplain of the Foreign Legion, entered the first of the three cars.

Miss Graves and the representatives of the Syndicat d'Initiative of Casablanca and of the Automobile Club took the second car.

In the last sat the General and his cousin. The cavalcade drove unmolested past the gates of the customs house and the barriers of the harbor police, up the Boulevard of the Fourth Zouaves and into the Place de France.

"The soldiers you saw at the boat, dear Cousin," said Anibal Erosa, "were not a guard of honor. They were on their way to intern the *Monte Cristi*, her captain and the crew. Without the little fiesta which I had arranged on board, there would have been some delay in getting you and your party off."

Leonidas Erosa availed himself of the most buoyant Castilian phrases to express his gratitude to his cousin. They looked at each other, shook hands, and smiled at each other.

At the Place de France, the Consul leaned forward and told the chauffeur to let the others drive on. He stopped the car and stepped out. Pointing at the grandiose edifice in front of them, he said: "Here is where you stay, Leonidas—one hundred and fifty rooms, baths, bains douches, cuisine renommé, Templo de la Gastronomía—cave fameuse, American bar with dancing and winter garden. Very good beds—but since yesterday nobody in this hotel has slept. Every trunk and bag is packed, yet no one is leaving."

In the doorway that led to the bar of the Hotel Excelsior, the Consul met a man who stared at him, and barely returned his greeting. "I have a little difficulty recognizing people today," said Anibal Erosa to his cousin. "This one also metamorphosed last night—you don't know who is who any more."

The other cars returned.

Over a luncheon of stuffed olives, an omelette with artichoke bottoms, lobster ravigotte, a pilaff of sweetbreads, fresh figs and almond tarts, the Commandant suggested to the Beauty an excursion to the Oasis of Tiznit. The extremities of the Moroccan climate were discussed by Miss Graves and the Secretary of the Automobile Club. The Consul had a private discussion with the General, and left, together with the dignitaries. Miss Graves went to her room, and the General and the Beauty went to the Cinema Roi de la Bière to see an American film which Anibal had highly recommended.

"They make nice girls in America," said the General, who sat with the Beauty's hand in his, in the third row. On the screen the hero kissed the girl's hair, her ear, her neck, and in the audience the General squeezed the hand of Madame Lopez.

The lovely girl on the screen called the hero "Sweetheart," and he addressed her as "Chicken." They kissed with lips apart— it seemed everlasting.

The General took Madame Lopez by the hand and they went across the Place de France to the hotel.

During the late afternoon, Anibal Erosa came back. He said, "At one time I could obtain almost anything I wanted, over an aperitif, and for a story. My greatest asset, dear Cousin, is not the ribbon of a Knight Chevalier of the Legion of Honor, but a reservoir of dirty stories unmatched in the diplomatic corps. But in spite of my repertory they refuse to let your chef go. He is a French subject and they need him in the army. Also your doctor. And your valet is held because his papers are not in order. As for the Indian gardener, he has no papers whatever.

"If you had come a month ago, or even a week, dear Cousin, it would have been child's play; but now it is very difficult. The French are not so bad—they will let you out, although it will cost money. But the Americans don't want to let you in. At the American legation everything is wrapped in miles and miles of red tape. They are extremely careful these days."

The cost, said Leonidas Erosa, was no object. The loss of the doctor and valet he did not mind so much—there would be a valet on the ship, and he had never found a doctor who could help him anyway. But he would not sail without the Indian and the chef.

"What in God's name do they want with poor Vitasse? He suffers from every known ailment, he is fifty years old and knock-kneed; the army could not afford his cooking—particularly the French army. What nonsense!" The General leaned back in his chair and sent one of his weary looks to heaven.

"Ah," said the Consul, "then we better start with Mister Bullock right away—it will be like pulling teeth."

Over his absinthe the Consul told a story of red tape.

"A friend, a man connected with the Havas Agency here,

decided to get out—that was two weeks ago—wife, two sons, maid. He had let his American citizenship lapse. She is native American, well connected. They telegraph Sumner Wells. Answer comes, everything O.K., passage paid, everything ready—American Consul gets a cable: 'All right, get them off'—followed with instructions by air mail—Secretary of State stamp, everything in order. But the Consul is short fifteen inches of red tape—has enough for Mr. Bloch, and Mrs. Bloch and children, but not enough for governess—they have no Indian gardener. They are attached to governess, will not leave without governess—governess cannot go, on account of the missing red tape.

"He comes to me. I say to him, 'Go and buy red tape in a store—you need more than fifteen inches anyway, you need a hundred yards.'

"'No,' says Mister Bullock, 'regulations forbid, etc., etc.—we must have red tape made in the U.S.A.'

"'I know where we can get red tape made in America,' I said.

"'That's not good enough,' says the Consul after conference with his chief; 'it must come from Washington, it must be official red tape. Sorry, regulations are regulations.' In the meantime, the steamer waits. My poor friend, his wife, the children are at the Consulate all day, waiting with red tape in their hands, which they bought themselves. The Consul finally goes and has a two-hour conference with the American Minister. When he comes back, he says: 'All right, we will use your red tape, but remember if you get sent back all the way from America on account of this red tape, it's not our fault.'

"The governess at least was an English subject, but your gardener—what is he? You say he came from Ecuador, he is an Indian. That makes it difficult, my dear Cousin. I have brought a paper here, which both he and you must sign."

"He cannot write or read," said the General.

"Please don't tell me any more about him," said the Consul, and asked for a menu.

"To come back to you. . . . I have found a ship that sails for America tomorrow. It's not the *Île de France*; it's small, it leaks, it stinks; you will eat rice and lamb every day. It's slow, and they have a wine they call Mastick, and a Greek brandy which tastes like turpentine. But I advise you to take it, if we can get passage."

"I will not sail without my chef and my gardener," said the General.

"I am having supper with the Commandant du Port tonight. Perhaps something can be worked out," said the Cousin, and took his hat.

From somewhere came an awful ticking, the next morning, like the sound of a cheap alarm clock. Long fingers of sunlight reached suddenly all the way across the pale green wall, and then shrank back to the Venetian blinds whence they came.

The General put the palms of both his hands down on the unfamiliar covers of his bed, and felt the texture of a blanket. He sat up and read, stamped into iron gray wool, "Hotel Excelsior." He looked around the room and at the luggage. He had never in his life gotten up without having someone in attendance. But now there was no valet. In his room stood half a dozen trunks; he had no idea where anything was. He sat marooned and lost in his bed. He took the telephone and called the Beauty. There was no answer. He lay back and fell asleep again.

At eleven the Cousin called and said that everything was progressing nicely. Monsieur Vitasse had been taken from a detention pen to the military prison, and his case would be given immediate attention.

"Dear Cousin," cried Erosa into the telephone, "I might as well be in prison myself here. I cannot get up. My trunks are locked. For heaven's sake get the valet out. If you can't get my own valet, get me somebody else, anybody with two hands and two feet." The Cousin promised that he would see what could be done and the General sank into his pillows—with another weary look to heaven.

Finally he called for Miss Graves, who opened the trunks, laid out his clothes, put the buttons in his shirt and the links in his cuffs, placed everything on his bed, and left. The General had to bathe himself, and he dressed with difficulty.

Somewhere outside his window, down below in the street, was the music of a reed instrument. The lonesome tune was the proper music for the mood of Leonidas Erosa. He slipped into his coat— his suspenders hung down outside his trousers. Unshaven, he went downstairs, wandered through the corridors of the hotel, and lost himself among the tubs of the palm trees in the winter garden. Miss Graves found him there, looking very old and as if he had come out of a storm. She took him behind a screen where she arranged his clothes, combed his hair, took his feet in her lap and tied his shoelaces properly. She ordered breakfast for him and she told him that the Beauty had driven with the Commandant of the Port to visit the Oasis of Tiznit. The Beauty had received a new addition to her charm bracelet, a small golden palm tree. The Commandant had given it to her, saying, "I hope you will count me among the number of your friends."

The Cousin arrived at noon. He embraced the General and announced with great elation that he had found an excellent man, a secretary, valet and major domo in one, a discreet, able, hard-working individual, willing to go anywhere, willing to do any and all work.

The Consul turned, and a little man with a flat head, the top of which was criss-crossed by several strands of hair, jumped to the table. His name was Plaschke; he was a refugee hotel man from Lwów. If Herr Plaschke had been a dog, he could not have shown more pleasure at seeing the General. His face seemed somewhere down near the floor, he continually moved backwards with small, apologetic shifts from one foot to the other; inside of him a desperate motor seemed to be running.

The General looked at the pockmarked ex-hotelier who shrank away from the table and bumped into a palm tree.

Herr Plaschke could leave immediately as the private secretary. "He's a little nervous now," said the Consul, "but he will be all right once the ship is under way."

Herr Plaschke was engaged and the Consul dispatched him immediately on an errand, to the agents of the *Xenaide Ybirricos*, on which the General was to sail the next day.

"Come with me," said the Consul. "We will go to my hotel

where we can talk quietly. We will have luncheon there—the cooking is excellent."

They drove up the Avenue du Général d'Amade to the Place Lyautey. Anibal Erosa pointed the buildings out to his cousin—the Cercle Militaire, the Palais de Justice, the Palais de Subdivisions—which are grouped around the Monument à la Victoire. The Consul said, "They have been more than intelligent here. There is a glorious audacity in almost everything the French have done here. I don't think any other nation has ever colonized with such elegance. They have given their best here, they have shown an understanding, even an affection for the natives. They are the only people who have made a sincere attempt at giving the black man something that comes near to real equality. Apropos of that, I have a note from the Commandant. Your Indian will be released, and I think also the cook—they are examining him this afternoon.

"You will be surprised when you see my little hotel," said the Consul. "I live there on account of the proprietor, who is a very fine man and my friend.

"I lived for a while at the Excelsior, and then at the Hôtel Transatlantique, also at the Majestic. I don't know whether I should tell you this—I cannot stand bars on windows, or locked doors; besides, I detest pajamas and sleep in nightshirts. I could stay at all these hotels if I allowed them to put bars on the windows, or to lock the doors. It has happened, they tell me, that I come downstairs in my nightshirt, and walk around, and then I go quietly to bed again. It happened once during a ball for Lyautey. It was not a costume affair, and therefore hilarious for everybody except me. It's not amusing to hear about it the next day.

"In my little hotel I have several rooms, and a private terrace that leads to a roof on which there are no obstacles. It is surrounded by other buildings so that I am quite safe when I walk out there in my sleep. The proprietor says that I come down occasionally in the middle of the night in my shirt, and smoke—I sit at the bar, he asks me questions and I answer them, and then I return to bed without any help. He tells me I even knock the ashes off my cigar, and he says my answers are always correct. Now you know my affliction, and here we are. Herr Plaschke lives here too, he has seen me at night several times, and I must say he never seemed amused by it. He never told me—the proprietor did."

The Hôtel de Famille was the property of an Assyrian. Here, during meals which lasted three hours, Anibal Erosa transacted his private business. The sad, immense face of the Consul assumed an air of peace and expectancy as soon as he was seated. The table was close to the kitchen, half hidden by a screen, and the approach to it was further complicated by a bent wood hat rack and a serving table. The Consul General himself sat with his back against the wall. His waistcoat pockets and the inner pockets of his coat bulged with documents, notes, and papers. He put both his hands on the dirty tablecloth, and after he had snapped his fingers several times, a waiter came to the table, leaned on it with both hands, cocked his head and listened to their order.

"I had a rotten night," said the Venezuelan Consul to the General. "Oh, I hate to have rotten nights! He's a nice man, the proprietor, as I have said, but he is paid for it through the nose. And of course he runs a hotel, and the people who run hotels these days don't care what they do—the hotels are all filled, anyway, no matter how they treat their guests. The sheets in this hotel smell of people; sous les bras, you know what I mean. There's only one bath outside the one I have—and the noise . . . I have Germans next to me, two of them, those two there, sitting next to the door."

He pointed at a boy and a man.

"That lovely blond boy with the blue eyes, you see there, he can't be more than fifteen. You know the foresight and the solicitude of the Nazis is fabulous, beyond belief. . . .

"That boy there is a gift from the Fuehrer to one of the important chiefs here—an excellent arrangement, which works several ways. First of all, the three hundred and some wives that the chief has in his harem hear of it and unite in furious jealousy—very good for the Nazis.

"Secondly, the story gets around and causes talk outside, the chief loses face, and there is disturbance outside—and that, too, is good.

"They do everything so beautifully, one almost envies them. The boy has a sort of duenna with him, the dignified man on his right—a Herr Professor and Gestapo agent in one. Notice the beard and the golden pince nez; look at the neck and the sleeves and you can see also that he has muscles like a butcher.

"They use the boy to tease the Glawi with. They never let him stay very long. When something needs a little hurrying, or particular attention, and he is not sufficiently co-operative, the boy is taken away. They let him come and visit again the moment the Glawi behaves.

"The boy is very well mannered, very well educated. The Glawi is taking German lessons on his account. He reads Goethe in the original now."

The Consul tucked his napkin under his chin. The old draperies in his face fluttered as he buttered his bread.

The rizotto, made with mussels, lobster, lamb and chicken, and saffron-colored rice, was soaked in an extraordinary brine. The General ate well.

Herr Plaschke arrived, loaded down with several pieces of luggage. He was still nervous and danced around the table with bows and disarranged coiffure. He asked for permission to move the coffee cups, so that he could unroll a large paper. On the paper he had loosely sketched the superstructure of the *Xenaide Ybirricos*. He pointed out the quarters available to the General.

The captain's cabin, the first officer's and the doctor's cabins, and the officers' dining room had been set aside for living quarters; the bridge of the ship as a private promenade deck, with a lifeboat reserved for the General and his party. The price of the suite was written on a small piece of paper which Mr. Plaschke showed privately to the General. He said he could not read the sum, and asked how much it was. The price was twenty thousand pounds.

Leonidas Erosa looked at his cousin. The Consul shrugged his shoulders and said, "Usually they ask you how much money you have, and take all of it—and then they forget half of the contract."

The General asked about Anselmo, and Herr Plaschke said

that Mr. Anselmo was at the hotel with the three dogs; that furthermore, as soon as the General decided, the provisions from the *Monte Cristi,* the wine, cigars, and personal effects of the passengers would be transferred to the *Xenaide Ybirricos,* without demand for payment of the customary taxes and duties that are assessed on merchandise leaving Morocco. Also the coffin of Miss Graves, which was packed with the thousand cigars.

In spite of the midday heat, Herr Plaschke insisted on getting back to the hotel, while the Consul telephoned to Bullock, the American Consul, and to Blow, the Minister, about the Indian. The General's new secretary-valet, almost overcome with apology, and performing a nervous mazurka that took him several minutes, during which he overturned a chair, finally came close enough to the General to tell him that he needed some money.

The General gave him two bills as an advance on his salary—which had not been discussed—and the perfect servant ran out to buy quantities of apples, pears, oranges, the famous dates of Algiers, tangerines, lemons, and olive oil. From the fruit shop he ran to the Magasin Freissinet in the Rue Commandant Provost, where he bought three folding chairs, and other conveniences for the long voyage.

The chef appeared at the hotel on the morning of the day the ship was to sail. For once he was subdued, and for a while almost respectful. He thanked the General for having brought about his release; he did not like what he had seen in the stockade in which he had spent the night. When the General told him that they were sailing for the United States, he had nothing but praise for that undertaking.

"Ah, l'Amérique," he crowed, "that is a land—formidable and interesting. There is a boat that goes there, the fastest and most luxurious, the chef of which is a distant relative of mine. The name is *la Normandie.* America is greatly indebted to France. There is the matter of the Marquis de Lafayette—there is a great story about that; and also about the Panama Canal—it is Lesseps who has started that gigantic affaire. . . ."

"I regret to inform you, Monsieur Vitasse," said the General, "that we will not stay there very long, only pass through on the way to my home."

The chef was agreeable to anything that day. He bowed and said, "Command, I follow!" and he went to get his luggage on the ship.

Miss Graves and Señora Lopez went aboard at eleven with the General, whose last act was to entrust a bottle of brandy to the Cousin, for the doctor who was left behind. The Indian ran up and down along the pier to give the three dogs their last exercise.

Plaschke remained in hiding while the *Xenaide Ybirricos* sailed out of the harbor. He watched the houses of Casablanca and the Grande Jetée melt into a misty watercolor. In the frame of the porthole, sky and land swam along in green, gray silence, and, when the coast was gone, Herr Plaschke pasted the stray hairs down on his flat skull and ran upstairs, to show himself and to set the table. As the good servant that he was, he placed the knife of the General, who was left-handed, where other people have their forks.

5: The Good Samaritan

Don LEONIDAS sat in a citron yellow, brand new folding chair, which Plaschke had acquired in Casablanca. The chair was on the bridge of the ship. The seat and back were made of canvas, and the General, with his fingers interlocked and folded over his stomach, gently rocked back and forth, pushing the chair back with his legs and recovering again through the weight of his body. In a wide-brimmed straw hat, Señora Lopez walked up and down in front of him. She was dressed in a trailing lustrous crepe de Chine dress, with large red roses blooming on a gray background.

"As I have said before, dear friend," the General said to Madame Lopez, "I will stay anywhere, but not in America. Not a minute longer than I have to will I stay there. Particularly not in New York. I have a horror of the place. I am constantly afraid the buildings will fall on me, I detest elevators. It is filled with dubious society, you keep one secretary busy with declining invitations alone. You suffer ten different climates every day, and they have only two vegetables, the names of both of which are green peas.

"Besides, chére amie, America is the ruin of any good servant you may have. I brought a valet there once, many years ago, who was a very good man until he met an American valet in the hotel. He was hopeless from that day on. No, thank you, we shall pass through as quickly as possible."

As if a costly beautiful shawl slid off a piano, Madame Lopez stepped over to the railing of the boat and said into the sea, half audibly: "Whatever you think best, Swit-hart, my love. . . ." On the days that followed she spoke more and more English and mentioned New York several times.

At breakfast, on the seventh day out, Plaschke informed the General that the *Xenaide Ybirricos* had an extraordinary passenger list, made up for the most part of professionals: literary men, editors, photographers, and doctors. There was also a Rumanian undertaker and family. And although it was so crowded that men and women used the same toilet facilities, there was a corner of the ship with a small piano, a table with a goldfish bowl, some chairs and shaded lamps, where a trio of handsome women had established an exclusive night club with chemin de fer, baccarat, and chambres séparées.

On the mast at the stern an acrobat sat most of the time. He wore an orchid-colored tricot, and usually sat with his arms folded and his legs swinging. Occasionally he exercised. Plaschke said that the acrobat never washed himself; the water stank and all the people washed in one room. The acrobat dipped a stick with cotton on it into Eau de Cologne and dabbed around the eyes with it. The costume he wore, he had inherited from a friend who had fallen. "You see this costume?" he said. "I got it from Demetrius, I have had it for twenty years. It has never been washed, it has never been cleaned, it has never been away from me." Everybody was glad, said Plaschke, that he sat alone up on the mast when he wore it.

"Look up, Chi-cken," said the General to the Beauty, pointing to the top of the mast. The acrobat sat in the morning light, arms folded, legs swinging. "That, Chi-cken, up there, is you. You are the graceful one, the acrobat, the tightrope walker."

"Yes, Swit-hart," she said. She leaned against him, the alkali eyes soft and satisfied, wandering from his nose to his forehead and to his lips.

"And I, I am the clumsy net, but always beneath you. If anything happens, Swit-hart, if you fall, I shall be there, always, always."

"You are my king, Swit-hart, you are my love." She embraced him and pulled his ear softly. "Have a candy," she said, and pushed a silken pillowlike bonbon into his mouth.

"For the first time in my life," the General continued, addressing himself to nobody, "I am a little homesick. For the first time in my life I have a desire to go to the Hacienda Miraflores, to the house of my father—to the place where I was born. I have never had this feeling before. . . ."

He sat in his canvas chair and rocked back and forth. His thoughts were of his father's house. In his mind's eye he walked up to one of the old trees that stood around it, and across the long forgotten patio. He was about to enter the house, when his folding chair broke under him.

For days, Miss Graves had told him, "Don't rock," but he did not listen, and now the chair was collapsed so flat that one could put it into an envelope. The General sat helpless on the deck.

Madame Lopez and a sailor tried to help him up. Miss Graves helped, and the first officer helped, directing the operation; everyone was sympathetic, nobody laughed.

The General tried to walk. He limped up and down a while. The broken chair was removed. The expressions of anxiety left the faces of the group around him. The officer said that besides the ship's doctor there were four doctors among the refugees, including Professor Nauheim, the former head of a famous clinic in Charlottenburg; but it seemed that the General was undamaged. He kept on walking along the rail. Madame Lopez offered her arm with vehement solicitude, the people disappeared, and a lady who had been asked up for tea with Miss Graves descended to the depths of the ship where, over the lukewarm soup in the chipped enamel plates, she reported on the glories of life up above and on the accident. From then on the General was known below as "the gentleman who got hurt." This entered more easily through their ears than his own romantic name.

Madame Lopez, in the natty hat and the fiesta dress with the large roses, was like a mother with a monstrous son. She wandered up and down with the General. He was pale now, and his hand was wet. He stood still at the port side of the bridge and leaned on the railing. The Beauty stood next to him. He took her small hand in his great, moist paw, and she whispered:

"Swit-hart—I am so fortunate to be with you. I am happy wherever you will go."

She bathed her eyes in his, squeezed his arm, made her animal sound of pleasure; then she kissed him on the temple and said: "Swit-hart!"

He waited until she looked at the sea again. He could never speak to her of anything not wholly within the province of her pleasure, her manifest desires, as long as her eyes were on him. He talked to her small left ear, looking at the row of little buttons which held the fiesta costume together at the neck, and he hoped she would not turn until he had finished.

"One morning," he said, "you will wake up and walk out on the balcony outside your bedroom in wonderful surprise. You will not believe it is real. You will find yourself on marble stairs among fountains playing. You will see birds of Paradise and the most beautiful mountains in the world.

"Of course," he said, "chére amie, it is only temporary. The very moment the trouble is over—the hour the war ends—we shall sail back. I think we shall go to Italy first. The Italians repair things quicker than anybody, no matter which side they're on. We shall go to the Lido, or to the Borromean Isles, or to Capri, and there we can wait until the rest is in order. I am certain that it will take years before one can go back to Paris and expect any kind of comfort. When they are through with the enemy, they immediately start fighting among themselves. The next place to go to is Germany. Even if they lose the war, you may be certain that within six months the Stephanie in Baden Baden will be in order. You will get anything you want there long before you can in Biarritz and Cannes."

"I'm glad you are feeling better," said the Beauty.

Below them the refugees that ate at the first sitting milled about—up for air after dinner. They stood in close groups and talked. The rusty ventilator turned a deep, bloody red—like a last bit of enamelled, bright red fingernail. The sun slowly sank into the ocean. The horizon faded into pale blue, then deepened into indigo. The refugees below were suddenly a gray lot. Over their heads a small bird flew and disappeared in the darkness.

Plaschke came and smiled with all his teeth; in the dusk they looked like the keys on an old piano. He stood in the open door, bowed, and said that dinner was ready. Leonidas Erosa took his hairy hand from the long, white fingers of Señora Lopez and went in to dress.

The gangway that led from the bridge to the General's quarters was badly ventilated. A stairway led down to the refugees, and from below came a warm, sweet and sickening smell of rats and ship's cooking. The General ran to his cabin door.

The *Xenaide Ybirricos* sighed and groaned. A sailor came and closed the portholes. The General sat for a while, washed his hands and looked into the mirror; then he grew very cold. The first warning of an attack had come on. Plaschke stood behind him, and there was a smell like the corridor outside. The General began to swallow hard; he took on the look of the condemned man. But then he heard the rustle of the Beauty's dress, and he went in to dinner.

The sea was rough. Plaschke spilled soup; when the rice and lamb came and he passed it to the Beauty, leaning over the dish, he too began to swallow hard, and suddenly left. The steward finished serving. The General drank two full glasses of champagne, but it tasted like melted snow-water. He suddenly had the sensation of falling backward into space. The ship turned and settled like a drunken person trying to sit down. With handkerchief pressed to her lips, Señora Lopez left.

The steward put an orange on a plate before the General and then helped Miss Graves out of her chair. The General was alone. For a while he looked at the orange, which moved to the edge of the plate and then ran halfway round the rim. He looked hopelessly around for someone. He stood up and tried to go to the door. He grasped the back of the chair; the chair was attached to the floor, the seat was revolving. He held on to it for a while, swinging in half circles with the motion of the boat, and then suddenly, along with the orange that had rolled off the plate, he fell to the floor.

His throat contracted, the epileptic cry issued from him, but nobody heard him. He shifted back and forth on the floor, floundered and struggled, got his arms out from under himself, and kicked and twisted. . . . Later, when he came to his senses, he was surprised to find himself there and got up. He felt a pain in his right hip and remembered the broken deck-chair. He was very thirsty.

He lay on his bed in the cabin for half an hour, and Madame Lopez came in. She had an expression of terrible disgust. She was pale and dishelled, her face shone, she smelled of cold cream— and she begged to have Sultan, the Great Dane who was her favorite, taken out of her cabin. The dog refused to come out from under her bed, where he had been ill.

The General rang for Plaschke. The steward came instead and went into the Beauty's cabin, where he bent down on all fours and talked to the dog. But he came up saying that the dog did not choose to move and that he could do nothing about it.

Madame Lopez decided that she would sit up all night. In a cerise-colored housecoat, with a book, a bottle of perfume and two handkerchiefs, she established herself in the salon. She pulled two chairs together, put her long legs up and read a yellow paper-bound volume.

The General stared at the ceiling. There was nothing for him to read. The *Xenaide Ybirricos* had no library. Among the refugees were several who had books, but these were mostly in German. There was only his Bible. It was therefore a most fortunate accident that Miss Graves, who occupied the ship doctor's cabin, happened to try to get into her berth just as the ship slid down over a mountain of water and lay on her side. Reaching out for support, she clutched at a bookshelf attached to the wall of the cabin over the bed. The shelf almost came off. It was loosened enough so that a small volume wedged between the wall and the bookcase, fell down on her bed.

The book was bound in purple leather, and its title, *The Good Samaritan*, made her think of the General. She took it across the passage to him in a moment when the ship stood on an even keel. She straightened his pillows, washed his face, and then she fixed the lamp for him and said good night and left.

He opened the little book and assumed the calm mien of goodness and peace, the look of tolerance in which one reads good books.

The first page of the small volume was filled with gold illuminations. The title was repeated in gay, uncommon type. On the second page there was an announcement that only five hundred copies of this work had been printed and distributed to a select group. On the third page the story began.

The first letter was an elaborate, illuminated "L," the first letter of the name Lydia. "Lydia Carteret," it started, "was lying face downward in her bed, perhaps it would be more accurate to say abdomen downward—" Having read this far, the General sat up in his pillows and looked at the cover of the book again. He went back to the first page and began again.

LYDIA CARTERET was lying face downward in her bed, perhaps it would be more accurate to say abdomen downward, for her face was turned sideways upon the fluffy pillow and her dark brown, heavy hair, fluffier than even the pillow, framed her features attractively. It was a winsome face of delicate modeling, rather than a strictly beautiful one, which she had turned toward the door of her room, as if attending half apprehensively, half eagerly for the entrance of an expected caller. The cheeks were just a trifle lacking in color to attain the exacting standards of beauty; in fact, she was quite pale, and the expression of her dark eyes and the drooping curves of the pink lips seemed to indicate a strain undergone in a half sleepless night.

It was past ten o'clock in the morning, two full hours later than her customary time for being up and about, seeing after her small but elegant establishment. This itself was extraordinary in a young woman of exemplary and methodical habits, and for her butler, who stood at her bedside, it was nothing short of epoch making. He could not recall having seen his mistress in the role of an invalid before, in spite of her assurance that it was "nothing to fret about." But the little circles beneath her eyes, her posture upon her stomach so carefully maintained, the sigh and grimace of pain that accompanied even the slightest movement she made, all combined to make the trustful servant feel that this was nothing short of tragedy.

The butler had compiled a cup of chocolate and some toast. Mrs. Carteret managed, without too much pain, to raise to her elbows without otherwise altering her prone posture. But it had proven almost impossible for her to nibble and sip at the refreshments unaided in

this position, and as she was determined to partake of the light breakfast, she allowed the butler to feed her morsels of buttered toast
between spoonfuls of chocolate.

Sitting beside her pillow for the purpose, he carefully attended to
this task, alternating the bits of crisp toast with the liquid, in little
trips from the tray to the lips, which Lydia Carteret held level by
throwing back her head as it rested upon her elbows. The butler had
grown suddenly almost completely silent and his mistress saw that his
handsome face was darker than usual.

His eyes turned from hers, but as Charles reached for another spoon
of chocolate for the absorption of his mistress, and she turned from
his glance to look downward, opening her lips for the sweet beverage,
it seemed to her that from the corner of her eye, she caught the gaze
of the servant and she followed the course of his. Her gaze sank and
an answering flush in her cheeks arose. She had not, until that instant,
observed that her position, half lifted up on her elbows, had resulted
in certain exposures of her person to which Charles had not been
accustomed.

The loose bosom of her sleeveless night gown had fallen away
from her chest and all the treasures of her soft torso were visible to
the butler's eye, as far downward as the waist in front. Charles felt
vaguely ashamed. He knew that he should not peer at these lovely
things, so unconsciously exposed, those sweet projecting white
hills of flesh, especially because they were the property of his
mistress.

The *Xenaide Ybirricos* was on her side and the General's watch
stood almost a hand's length from the wall, as if the chain were
a rod. He poured himself a glass of champagne and went back
to page 8.

The accident had occurred several days ago. Mrs. Carteret had
suddenly wearied of the cozy but pent-up little apartment and decided
to go for an outing to the Palisades, which loom so cozily in the sunlight, several hours crossing on the other bank of the broad Hudson.
She had never been there in the course of her family's short stay in
New York, but she knew that several blocks further to the north, past
Columbia College, and the memorial to General Grant, there was a

pier from which river steamers went across the water. Thither she went and in due course found herself on the pier.

A large cockroach came over the edge of the book and the General shook him off. He fell on the floor, where he seemed to have trouble with some of his legs. Two more were sitting near the lamp. Leonidas Erosa chased them with impatience, and continued. . . .

They crossed the mighty river and landed on the other side. Lydia Carteret left the boat after most of the passengers had gone. She got aboard a small railway that ascends, crawling up steep winding inclines, toward the wilder scenery above, from where, on clear days, one can enjoy a superb view of New York. In summer it is cooler here and in winter it is free from fog and warmer than the city below.

Leaving the train, Lydia Carteret bent her steps toward the woodland which she soon reached. Fond as she was of nature untrampled, she found even the deserted road too much of a memento to civilization, so she clambered up a bank and entered the forest itself.

This was evidently, on Saturdays and Sunday, a favored spot for picnics, for empty cans and charred wood and a broken bottle marred the corner of the clearing. However it was pretty there, despite the previous presence of vandals, and she was tired. She determined to rest for a while. She sank upon the green thick grass beneath a silver birch.

If what goes up must come down, what goes down has often been known to go up, even faster. This was the case with the unfortunate excursionist. With a sharp scream of fright, she bounded to her feet. She reached at the rear of her slight muslin skirt and turning her head, she saw that the rusty handle of someone's lost pocketknife protruded, hanging from the rent fabric. It was not only hanging from the fabric, it was caught in her wounded flesh. She started to withdraw it. With another cry of pain she renounced her effort, for the vicious weapon was so deeply imbedded that its slightest movement hurt her.

She heard a crackling sound and hurried footsteps as a man hastened into the glade. Frightened, first by the sound of twigs breaking beneath his robust boots, for she had not seen anyone in all the course of her wanderings in the woods, she breathed a sigh of relief as she noted that this was a man of obvious respectability.

"Oh, I've stabbed myself," she cried, unable in her pain and fright to wait for any formalities. "I've sat upon some kind of a knife which was lying open in the grass. I'm afraid its lodged pretty deeply. It hurts terribly—and I can't get it out." There were tears in the dark eyes which she thrust appealingly in her helplessness upon the new-comer.

"Take hold of the handle to steady it," bade the man with a brusque efficiency that inspired confidence. "Quiet now—it's probably nothing serious. Let me lay you on your face in the grass, it will not be as painful. I'll remove the knife immediately. Luckily I have a vial of good germicide in my pocket."

As he spoke, he grasped her, and overjoyed at finding succor sent, she mastered her tears and her little moans, and she lay there, still, awaiting the withdrawal of the blade with clenched teeth. Only the handle and perhaps half an inch of the blade protruded from the rent in the gauzy skirt. The man at once took hold of the handle and began gingerly to lift the fabric over the weapon. He reached beneath the skirt to grasp the knife and held it immovable while he lifted the pierced garment up and off from it.

Even amid her pain, her anxiety about infection and her relief at the presence of this heaven-sent man who evidently knew what to do, Lydia quivered a bit. She fathomed the idea of the man who had come to her rescue. He wished to detach the skirt entirely from the knife so that he could more carefully and with less pain remove the blade than would be possible by wrenching it out without being able to see just how it was imbedded. She knew that in another moment she would feel her skirt upraised and her person would be revealed more thoroughly to this strange man's gaze than it had ever been to any man's eye, save that of her husband, and that in her predicament and dismay she could still find cause for trepidation and dismay, leads one to agree with her husband, Frank Carteret, that she was not what might be termed brazen.

The stranger drew the pierced fabric of the skirt upward like a little tent, and off over the handle of the knife—and even the casual observer, looking at his not unhandsome face, which poor Lydia could not at the instant do, would perhaps have detected a light in his eye which was not wholly heavenly in spite of his errand of mercy.

There remained a most modern and enticing undergarment to be attended to.

A cockroach came again and walked over the lampshade, casting a huge shadow on the ceiling of the cabin. The General followed him with quick glances, annoyed at the interruption.

On this hot day it was simply the filmiest of combinations which she wore, a combination of pale lavender, through which her alabaster skin gleamed most enticingly. Long ago she had eschewed knickerbockers, agreeing with her spouse that they were not alone unpleasant to the eye, but in the summertime, they were nothing short of silly.

"May I come in for a moment, Swit-hart?" said Madame Lopez, after she had quietly opened the door.

In a simple, familiar motion, the General made room for her beside him. He put the book away and turned the light out. Like a householder who stands in his vegetable garden and counts the fruit on his trees, looks at the honey of his bees and runs his hands through the wool of his sheep and across the warm, moist muzzles of his cattle, he availed himself of the soft, cushioned comforts of her body. In the dark, muted quiet afterward, Leonidas Erosa embraced the Beauty and said that he had thought it over, and decided that he'd love to stay in New York as long as the Beauty wanted.

6: The Salamander

THE CITADEL of gracious living at which the General stopped after his arrival in New York resembled the Villa Amelita in Biarritz in several respects. It was the best, the most ornate hotel inside and out. It stood in solitary grandeur and with long established reputation among lesser, newer hotels. At its doors was a park, and as they had done at the lookout tower in Biarritz, here too the members of the General's household appeared at the revolving door of the hotel with the regularity of figures on an old-fashioned clock.

The swish of the Indian's sandals, the soft footpads of the three Great Danes, were the first sounds in the corridor of the hotel. While it was still dark in the city, they came out of the door and trotted to the corner, where the Indian carefully looked in all directions. He was afraid of cars, and although the streets and avenues were deserted, he waited until the signal light changed and until the hotel's sidewalk man, who was busy hosing, shouted to him, "All right, go ahead." He ran as fast as he could across the street, the Great Danes rocking beside him.

As in Biarritz, he had found a place here beside the water, where he sat among yesterday's dew-soaked newspapers, bottles and candy wrappers.

The dogs each turned around several times, folded their hind legs under themselves and then collapsed in front. They placed their heavy heads on their front paws and gazed at the Indian.

Anselmo looked into the dirty water and waited for the sunrise. He sat upright as a candle until the daylight set the reflection of the hotel into the muddy pond. For a while the Great Danes strained for the geese and ducks, and then the dogs and the Indian ran back. The streets were still empty but the Indian waited for the signal light and until the sidewalk man, who was now busy polishing brass, shouted, "All right, come on."

For the duration of the General's stay in New York, the Indian lived on the roof of the Palace Hotel. He slept away most of the daytime in the greenhouse where the hotel's florist revived the tired plants and the palm trees that were used in the public rooms below. To wash himself, he held his head under a hose; and he slept in a corner, where the hotel's housekeeper had placed a bed. He owed these arrangements to Miss Graves, who came up to visit him and the dogs every day. She had also taken Plaschke with her to buy the few things the Indian needed: shirts, two new suits, and shoes. His food was brought up to him. During the day, when he was awake, Anselmo stared for hours down into the zoo. At night he sat in the greenhouse with the dogs around him. He watched the golden rooster on top of the Heckscher building ride past the stars and the moon in the beautiful blue of the New York night. He beat on the zinc-covered table in the hothouse and sang the four notes of an old lament over and over. The smell of earth, the sight of the palm trees and the rooster, made him feel at home; the noise of the city below was like the waterfall in his native valley, and the roar of the animals in the zoo like the jungle of Ecuador.

At eight, Mr. Plaschke pasted the sixteen strands of black hair across the flat top of his skull, and, with the aid of a mirror, carefully placed his bowler over them.

He came down the corridor, spun the door, and leaning forward with his short legs moving fast, he ran about the city on various errands for the General and the chef. He bought the clothes and linen for the Indian. He came back in time to take the mail to the General.

In a Queen Mary toque and a grey tweed suit, Miss Graves appeared at the hotel's door at nine. She walked fast and far, accompanied by a little dog. She ran three times around the lake in the park as if it were the promenade deck of an ocean liner. She seldom looked left or right. She avoided the zoo because she could not bear to see animals in cages. She suffered for horses—even in the morning, for the tired, lame hacks on the bridle paths whose mouths were torn by Sunday riders. The park, to Miss Graves, was as sad as the city in which it stood—a place of birds fallen from their nests, of weary, lonesome people; and when she saw a soldier or a sailor, young and walking alone, her eyes filled with tears.

Monsieur Vitasse seldom went out. He spent most of his time in the kitchen with the hotel's blue ribbon chef. They respected each other, exchanged culinary memoirs, decried the eating habits of Americans, and spent evenings visiting gatherings of such societies as the "Friends of the Stomach," "The Hundred Pure," or an exclusive club of kitchen aristocracy which called itself "Les Escargots de vingt et un." The chef had occasional consultations with the General concerning the Hacienda Miraflores. They made out lists of the provisions and the spirits that were to be taken along, and the chef went to the wine merchants and food dealers to buy them.

At eleven, the door was swung by the inside footman, and the doorman outside gave one of his best salutes as Leonidas Erosa stepped out into the sunlit square in Charvet tie, a green Homburg, and usually in double-breasted flannel with white stripes, and a bamboo cane.

He looked across the plaza up and down the avenue. He drank in the lukewarm air. The plaza was almost like Paris in May—a little cramped with trees, fountains and statuary, the lamp posts a good deal smaller, but there was an occasional grocery boy on a bicycle, a pretty girl with a hatbox, French sailors, Canadian and British soldiers, nursemaids, nuns, a row of cabs, and occasionally a grotesque couple with three black poodles.

A statue of a man in uniform and on horseback means Bolivar to most South Americans. On every sunny morning, Leonidas Erosa mentally took his hat off when passing the golden equestrian statue which stands at the entrance to the park. The monument of one of his heroes made the neighborhood particularly sympathetic to the General. He was too nearsighted, even when standing directly in front of it, to read that it was the statue of General Sherman.

After paying his homage to the statue, he walked on, and on days when the trees swayed and the papers flew about, he stopped and sat down to observe the play of the wind in young women's skirts.

Swinging his cane he walked through the zoo, where the policemen and attendants saluted him. He turned past the bird-house and walked down Fifth Avenue. His route varied as soon as he came to Fifty-Ninth Street. He visited an occasional art dealer, he walked into antique shops, but most of his time was spent examining the windows in which he saw women's shoes, fur coats, lingerie, tobacco, delicatessen, fruit and candy. The exhibits of Wadley and Smythe and of Schling retarded his promenade, and he was often glued to the partridges, the caviar jars and lobsters in the window of Shaefer's market. From there he proceeded to one of the good restaurants in the neighborhood, where he waited for Madame Lopez. The Beauty left the hotel in a cloud of perfume, in a flower print dress that was like an evening gown. She wore a veil and long gloves. They sat a long while studying the menu, which Madame Lopez read to him. They selected with care, ate and drank slowly, and came back to the hotel with warm cheeks at about three.

The General's apartment consisted of most of the eighteenth floor of the hotel. The rest was occupied by a foresighted German industrialist, Doktor von Despard, who had left the Fatherland with most of his money at the time the trouble started.

To the common run of the hotel's guests, the President and Resident Managing Director of the Palace Hotel Corporation, Conrad Magnum, was a golden myth, a name and title embossed across the ivory-tinted stationery of the hotel. To the distinguished and rare tenants of the eighteenth floor, he was actually existent.

He greeted the General with the elaborate ceremonial of a potentate. To Herr Doktor von Despard he offered a warm, moist hand. Occasionally, he even invited him to a Herrenabend, in a small private room close to his office, where protocol was thrown to the winds. At these small banquets, the two sat facing each other across a wide table, and over the carcasses of geese, hares and ducks, they revealed their qualities to each other.

The manager had set an elevator aside especially for Leonidas Erosa and Doktor von Despard, and although they daily used this conveyance together, the peculiar etiquette attached to elevators was rigidly observed by members of both households.

As the passengers entered the car, conversations were broken off, the eyes were fixed on the back of the elevator man's neck, on the Adam Medallion overhead, or played catch-as-catch-can with the numerals that flitted past in the shaft. No facial expressions were worn. On emerging from the elevator, while they fished for keys, changing handbags and small packages from one hand to another, they resumed the laughter, argument or talk left off above or below.

On one of the rides down in the elevator, the General stood in back of Frau von Despard. He noticed her neat auburn hair; she smelled clean and fresh like a linen closet, and white as linen was her skin, her softly padded hands; she had lovely bulges here and there. He smiled into her blue eyes as he left the elevator.

Over the table at the Ermitage, he said to the Beauty, "Strange race, the Germans. Every twenty or thirty years they break out of their borders; they overrun the land like a plague, they murder and plunder and ruin what they can't take, and then suddenly they go back again, and for the next twenty years they are admirable neighbors—orderly, good people, and some of them extraordinary scientists, inventors, musicians, and philosophers. Take Doktor von Despard. Plaschke tells me he is a distinguished chemist. He walks and stands too straight, his neck is red and thick, but he seems a nice man; and Madame Despard is a very fine woman."

"I will tell you how I feel about Germans," said the Beauty. "In time of war I detest them. In time of peace they don't exist for me."

Casagrande, the wine waiter, pulled the table, and the General, breathing as one who lifts a heavy stone, got up, buttoned the two last buttons on his waistcoat and, nodding to a few people, left the restaurant with Madame Lopez. They walked slowly and arrived at the hotel just as Herr and Frau Doktor von Despard came back from a walk in the park. On the way up in the elevator, the Doktor stood in back of the Beauty, and the General behind Frau von Despard. The Beauty went into Room 1818.

The General smiled and walked into Room 1820, where Plaschke undressed him. Don Leonidas slept an hour every afternoon. He lay on his bed with arms folded and stared at the ceiling. He thought that for a man like himself the Frau Doktor was the right woman to marry. First of all, on account of her linen-closet morality, she would have the cool hands of a nurse; she would be wife and mother. Without any make-up on her face, she was a very handsome woman, and her face had only one expression, that of absolute honesty. He disturbed himself with visions of her anatomy. He said to himself, I would like to see her in a large bed, her body glowing in white linen, a bed with curtains. He knew the classic majesty of such women, of the wide planes, the soft navel, the rouged aureoles of their soft breasts, and the caressing pressure of their thighs. In such women all promises were fulfilled, yes, yes.

In Room 1842, Frau Doktor sat at the open window knitting with the cool hands. The Herr Doktor rested on the sofa, his hands clasped behind his head. He was thinking about the Beauty; her perfume was still in his nose, her raven hair a memory in the palms of his hands, as if he had actually touched it. He worked out in his mind an exotic tableau. He saw her nude, covered with black lace, a white Borzoi dog at her feet. He was about to think of the details of her body when the Frau Doktor said "Papa," a signal she always sent ahead of her conversation.

At the word "Papa," the tambour inside him rolled a drum and the disorderly emotions of Doktor Despard marched back to their black barracks, taking the Beauty, the white Borzoi and the lace blanket with him.

"Papa, you like the Spanierin?" said the Frau Doktor. "She is sometimes very elegant, one cannot say otherwise, and her eyes are very beautiful, Spanish, dark—and young—about twenty-five, I think. The other one, the old one, they say, is crazy. She eats nothing, she lives on champagne, and weighs only ninety pounds."

"Also," said the Doktor, "that is not possible."

"That is what Plaschke told the Fräulein," said Frau Doktor.

The Herr Doktor spoke a precise English, he had a fad for using the word "also" frequently. He employed it in its German meaning, which is "thus, so," or "consequently."

"Also," said Doktor von Despard to his Frau, every day except Sunday at two, "I am going to go spazieren for an hour in the park. Are you coming, Mama?" Carrying his cane in his folded hands at his back, he wandered off. On the days that she went with him, the Frau Doktor walked a little to the right and half a foot behind. Doktor Despard shared the opinions of Miss Graves about the park.

"Also," he observed, "this awful Dreck, this awful dirt, these bottles, these cigarette butts, these people lying around in broad daylight, and everywhere these dirty wild children and Negroes.

"Also, I must say, Mama, in Berlin, you remember the park and the people in it? It was a pleasure to go spazieren there. One met one's kind, and the walks were swept clean, the grass green and not walked on, and the animals with room to run around. Even the birds are dirty here—look at these filthy pigeons. Also, I must say, in Berlin it was otherwise. And remember Unter den Linden, Mama? Also that was something else than this Park Avenue of which they are so proud—nothing but houses in a straight line. Trümmerhaufen, Mama. Also, am I right?"

"Gott, ja, Papa, you are right, absolutely," echoed Frau Doktor. "Spazieren gehen ist no pleasure here."

This led into a revery on the beauty of life in Berlin, and the only restaurant in the world, which for the Herr Doktor was Horchers. "Also, there they sit now, the swine, the Goering, the Goebbels, the Himmler, drinking the last bottles of my Steinwein. I wonder if we shall ever eat there again."

Such sad talk passed between the Herr Doktor and his Frau only when they were alone. Dr. von Despard hated the word "refugees." With new acquaintances he hurried through the formulas of greeting to establish the fact that he was not a refugee. As soon as he could, he made it clear that he was a German living abroad, a man of vision who had seen the evil days coming when it was still possible to pack one's trunks without haste.

Occasionally he could not avoid meeting a former Berlin acquaintance, such as Geheimrat Doktor Erich Yohalem, a pale little man, once a brilliant jurist, witty, debonair and elegant— now quickly aged, so sad and indifferent that he forgot to have his hair cut. A yellow and white wig, it hung down the back of his head, and made him look like a mouse that had just been taken from the river.

When it was impossible to avoid him, when it was too late to turn into a path or cross to the other side, the Doktor extended a roaring greeting to him. The Geheimrat always spoke of Berlin. At every such meeting, he unpacked his worn memoirs. The Doktor became impatient and once he said to him, "Also, Herr Geheimrat, I must say I like it here. And why shouldn't I? I don't have to be homesick for Germany, I am an Aryan."

And so that there should be no doubt whatever about this fact, he took the knife that hangs so loosely in many a German belt and used it. "Also, Herr Geheimrat, I attended a meeting of the Nazi Party as far back as 1933. I talked to Goebbels several times. I found the good Doktor a little too emotional. I decided to leave your beloved Berlin, I came here in the spring of 1934, on board the *Europa*, Herr Geheimrat—a good boat, excellent food and service."

He switched from the past to the present, speaking of life in New York as if it were a foreign city for Geheimrat Yohalem; of restaurants, of the theatre, of his wife, his child and the Kinderfräulein, and when he was certain that the portrait was finished, he gave the Geheimrat a cigar, invited him to dinner at an unspecified date, and then let the sick, sweating little mouse run.

The Herr Doktor and his wife took most of their meals up in the apartment. Except for the promenades and the visits to the bank and the doctor, von Despard sat at the window of the corner living room, a still life of contentment and respectability.

He wore a flowered dressing gown and red slippers on which Frau Doktor had embroidered the heads of two stags in petit point. On the windowsill was a thin long pillow, also especially made by the Frau Doktor, so that Papa's arms were comfortable when he leaned on it while looking out. On this pillow usually slept a black cat, an ordinary cat whom he called Muizerl, and on a table next to his easy chair were a pair of high power Zeiss field glasses, with which the Herr Doktor studied the bird life in the park during the day and the activities in the hotels and apartment houses after dark. A dog of which he was very proud, a giant Schnauzer, slept at the foot of his bed.

They had a little boy named Kurt who spoke the local jargon. Kurt was put to bed at eight by the Fräulein, and afterwards the Herr and Frau Doktor went to visit, to a movie, or to the bar of one of the neighboring hotels for a drink. Several times a week they made a long promenade, a loop that began at Fifty-Ninth Street, passed the windows of all the shops down Fifth Avenue to Radio City, and returned by way of Broadway or Seventh Avenue.

On these tours they wore light, coffee-colored, rough woolen coats called Lodenmäntel, which they had bought in Munich and which seemed indestructible. They walked arm in arm, the Schnauzer with them, the leash of the dog taut like a metal rod stretched in front of them to the neck of the tireless animal.

On such a walk the Frau Doktor would stop before a sable coat or a chinchilla cape at Bonwit Teller's or Saks and say that it would be good for the "Spanierin"—as they called the Beauty— but too gaudy for herself. Somewhere along the route the Herr Doktor would say, "Also, for Christmas, das Christkind I think is going to bring you a mink coat, Mama," and he pointed to several models. He liked ankle length capes with yardwide sleeves.

Frau Doktor always said, "No, Papa, I have told you I want no mink coat. When I think of all these poor animals that have to die, then I don't want a mink coat. They love their life like you and I, and when I think they are killed because a foolish woman has to have a mink coat . . ."

"Also, Mama, I would not worry about these minks." The Herr Doktor, who was very fond of educational movies, described a mink farm. "They are raised like chickens," he said, "on beautiful places in a beautiful climate that agrees with them. They are fed on cereals, milk, nuts, and raisins. They run around and play, when they are old enough they get a smell of something, and it's all over, no fuss."

"I know," said the Frau Doktor, "just the same, I don't want to look like the Spanierin. She must have a dozen different fur coats. She walks out like I don't know what, with a gold chain around her ankle. I like the old one much better, Miss Graves. She wears plain suits, English; she is very elegant, like a Baronin."

"Also, the old one is crazy, Mama. The hotel manager told me she has a coffin down in the baggage room. She takes it with her wherever she goes."

They had arrived at the window of a restaurant. Tilted so that it presented itself fully to the onlooker was a bed of ice, camouflaged by a row of whiskey bottles. Bright lights shone down on cheese cakes and reflected themselves in the glossy skins of a backdrop of salami. In the center of the block of ice was a pyramid of blue plates, each occupied by a boiled lobster cut in half, bedded in cole slaw. A claw held up a celery stalk or a red, white and blue shield which announced a five course dinner for seventy-five cents.

Half buried in ice, to the left and right of the pyramid, were live lobsters, their claws locked with small wooden pegs, their feelers moving about and the small mandibles of their lower jaws constantly in motion.

"That," said the Frau Doktor, "is why I don't like to eat lobster. Look at it! It's disgusting!"

The Herr Doktor, who was very fond of crustaceans, observed, "Also, they don't feel anything, it's all reflex."

"How does anybody know?" said his wife. "They can't talk. I heard them cry once when I saw a man throw them into boiling water."

"Well, anyway, it just takes a second," said the Doktor, and they walked on.

When they returned to their apartment after one such walk through the city, they found little Kurt still awake. He sat on the floor and announced that he had had a terrible time, that he could not go into the park any more, because a playmate, Jennie Lindemann, had a pet lizard and he had none.

"Jennie Lindemann," he announced, "has a lizard. She puts it in her hair and lets it crawl on her face, she lets it touch her teeth and put its head up one of her nostrils and then the other. You can also put it into the fire and nothing will happen to it. Lizards can walk around in fire."

"Also, that's wonderful," said his father, "but you have a cat and a dog to play with. And now go to bed—march off!"

"She has two dogs, Papa," countered Kurt. "Besides, I would give away the cat and dog if I could have a lizard. They're only a quarter and you can get it where I got the turtle."

Kurt stood beside his father's chair. He whined a while and twice repeated his complaint, and then his mother said that if he went to bed right away and went to sleep, perhaps Papa would buy him a salamander the next day.

The Herr Doktor looked at his son and leaned forward as if to get out of his chair, which was always the beginning of trouble, and Kurt went quickly to bed. In his room he talked to himself in the dark, loud enough so his father could understand that Jennie Lindemann had a lizard, that he hated the dog and that he wouldn't go into the park until he had a salamander.

"Why can't the child have a salamander?" asked the Frau Doktor in the squashed tones in which she started arguments. She always referred to Kurt as "the child" in such discussions.

The Herr Doktor answered over his left shoulder. "I don't see why the Lausbub must have everything he asks for. Good God! What is he going to be like when he grows up? Kurt wants a salamander! Kurt wanted a turtle, Kurt got a turtle, what happened to the turtle? The cat got it and killed it."

The Frau Doktor looked at the back of her husband's neck, the place on the left where a small scar shone in memory of a painful boil, and then she looked at his thick red ears, one of which stood away from his head, shaped like a spoon; and then she got up and silently went to bed.

The next day, while the Herr Doktor was out, the salamander was acquired. It came from a souvenir and amusement emporium.

Kurt selected him from a hundred others; he cost a quarter. The saleswoman put the small reptile in a paper container such as is used for ice cream. She punched holes in the top, and gave advice on its care and feeding.

"I wouldn't show the salamander to Papa until he is in a good mood, Liebling," said the Frau Doktor. "We'll keep him behind the curtain in the bedroom, and only you and I and the Fräulein will know where it is. Of course you can take him to the park and show him to Jennie Lindemann."

Kurt sat in the taxi and looked at the salamander. It was an elegant small creature, emerald green, with quick, liquid motions of body and head. On the side of its face was a red spot.

The Frau Doktor asked the hotel for a soup plate. She did not wish to use her own Meissen china. This they filled with water and put the salamander in it. Kurt emptied half of the turtle food in the water, and put the plate in its secret place behind the curtain.

The salamander stayed there until a day when the Herr Doktor came home in a good mood. He laughed at the table, and, just as the soup was served, Kurt came in with small steps carefully carrying the plate, his salamander afloat in it. The water was in motion and the salamander was washed up on the edge of the plate. He slid over the rim of the plate and fell on the table. The Herr Doktor picked him up and gently placed him on the back of his hand. The salamander lay still with its legs curiously bent; he seemed very feeble. Kurt announced that he had had him for three days and that he was bigger than Jennie Lindemann's.

For a while thunder and lighting played around the eyes and mouth of the Herr Doktor, but he swallowed it. He smiled and allowed Kurt to light his cigar. He examined the plate and said, "Also, you're not going to keep him in that plate. Salamanders need a kind of garden, a terrarium. They must have a moist place but they don't live in the water. He should have a rock to sit on at least, and be in a cool place." He ate a few spoonfuls of soup.

"Also, really, whether the salamander is wet or dry doesn't matter," said the Herr Doktor after a while, with a look at his wife. "The poor animal is half dead now, and he'll be eaten by the cat anyway." Also, it was sad that in this house things had to be done behind his back.

The salamander was removed and the dinner ended in silence.

After dinner, down at a table in the Café de la Paix, the Herr Doktor, fortified by two brandies, said, "Also, this phenomenal love of animals you profess makes me laugh. For example, look at that salamander. I don't know how long he has traveled around the edge of the soup plate trying to stay up. Any moment the cat might come and get him; all because Kurt must have a toy. I don't subscribe to this American system of child raising. Do not talk to me about mink coats and lobsters again. I am not pretending to be a humanitarian, but I wouldn't dream of sub-jecting a small helpless creature to torture just because you can't refuse your Kurt anything."

The waiter came and brought the bill. On the way home, Frau Doktor cleared her throat several times and at last said, "I wouldn't ask anyone to do anything I wouldn't do myself."

"What has that got to do with the salamander?" asked the Herr Doktor, stopping in front of the awning of the Essex House.

"Well, speaking of animals and torture, what about me? Have you ever thought about me? You worry so much about your animals, how about thinking of me?"

The Herr Doktor stood still. "Also, what has this to do with the salamander?"

"I am talking about the dog and cat. Who has to clean out the cat's box?" Frau Doktor was almost in tears. "Not Fräulein. I wouldn't ask Fräulein to do it. I do it myself. And it's your cat. You brought the cat home."

"Also," said the Herr Doktor, "it's the first cat I liked. I never liked cats and this one is different. I found it half starved in the park. But I told you, Anna, if you didn't like it you could give it away."

"Ja, I remember, I said I wouldn't give it away, because maybe the people who would get it wouldn't take care of her properly. I wanted to have her put to sleep."

"Oh," said the Doktor, "just a minute. The cat has as much

right to live as you have. She loves life as much as we do. It has a lot of character, that cat."

"And as for the dog," continued the Frau Doktor, "he's your dog, and who has to take him out and suffer indignities in the street? You never take him when he has to go out. How do you think it feels to stand there with the leash in your hand on the Fifth Avenue waiting until he moves on? If I were the mayor of this city, I would forbid all dogs. It's disgraceful and unsanitary!"

"Also, all you have to do, Mama, is call for a bellboy, and give him the dog to walk. That is what we live in a first-class hotel for!"

"Yes, and every time I do that, I have to give the boy a quarter. I'd rather do it myself and keep the money."

"Heiliger Gott im Himmel!" said the Herr Doktor.

The maroon and gold doorman saluted as they entered the mirrored hall. The Herr Doktor had another speech ready, but just then the General and Madame Lopez entered the foyer. The four people smiled at each other and silently rode up. This time Doktor von Despard stood in back of Madame Lopez, stiff-lipped, his eyes like those of a frightened horse on the lovely back décolletage of the Beauty, his nostrils filled with the sinful allure of her hair, her clothes and her perfume.

The passengers smiled again at the end of the ride and went to their rooms. The next day, before he went down to the broker's office, the Herr Doktor looked at the salamander and said, "Also, he is still alive."

He took the salamander's plate and placed it in a shady spot in the serving pantry. He was gone a long time. When he came back he found the Fräulein lying on the sofa. The salamander was in her hair, lifting his short legs and stalking about.

"He's trying to build a nest," explained Kurt.

The Herr Doktor had a box under his arm. He undid the string and wound it up carefully for future use. He folded the wrapping paper and put it away, and then he opened the box and unpacked a terrarium the size of a cigar box, a paper bag of dirt, some stones and small plants, all bought at Bloomingdale's. He was busy for an hour arranging an appropriate landscape for the salamander. He broke an old flower pot into small pieces with which he lined

the bottom of the terrarium. Next he arranged a hill of gravel
on the left, constructed a cave opposite this, the entrance to which
he hid in the shade of a miniature fern. He made a depression,
lined it with white sand, and filled it with water. It was shallow
so that the salamander could comfortably hold his head above
water. Over the small world he placed a sheet of glass held down
by two metal clamps.

The salamander was grateful; he ran about, visited the cave,
dragged his body with his long tail after it through the water,
and then he pasted himself on the glass, his soft scaleless belly
weaving in and out, the ends of his fingers like tiny wet pearls.

The terrarium was placed at the second window of the living
room, and both father and son enjoyed watching the salamander
and feeding him.

One day the Fräulein heated some chocolate for little Kurt in
the serving pantry of the apartment. She walked out into the hall
to talk to Herr Plaschke, and while she was gone, Kurt tried to
find out whether the animal could really walk through fire. He
carried the salamander into the pantry; he moved the pot; but
when he looked into the blue flame, he changed his mind, held
the cold animal close to his nose, and put him back in the terrarium. He forgot to put the cover over it, and while he drank
his chocolate the cat reached into the glass case and took the
salamander out. She held him dangling from one claw and examined him with curiosity. She gave her paw a quick twist and
he fell to the floor. The cat jumped down to him, slowly pushed
him to the border of the rug, and tossed him against the wall,
where he lay still.

The Fräulein, who had gone to fetch a napkin to wipe little
Kurt's mouth, walked through the room and screamed when she
saw the cat and the salamander. Little Kurt ran to the window
and kicked the cat, which fled up the back of the Herr Doktor's
chair. The salamander came to life, ran to the windowsill, waited
there for a moment, breathing hard, and then, in two lightning
moves, he was on the outside of the building and gone.

Little Kurt climbed up and stood on the thin pillow. The Fräulein held him while he leaned out of the window, looking for his salamander. But he had disappeared in the vast symmetries of the hotel's brickwork.

On the evening of the next day, the elegant mood of the Palace Hotel was disturbed. A few minutes after five, Mr. Greenspan, the hotel's tailor, whose workshop was at the bottom of an airshaft, returned to consciousness and found himself lying on the floor.

He stood up and reached for his head; he felt his shoulders and his neck. He thought at first that someone had clubbed him and taken his money. But then he noticed that the room was much lighter than usual and, looking up, he saw the sky through a wide hole in the glass ceiling of the shop. The work table and the pressing machine were covered with pieces of glass. Under the upturned clothesrack he saw a leg, and a moment later he found under the clothes the slightly clad body of a young woman, who was dead. With his tailor's mind, he fixed his immediate attention on the dresses that were on the rack. Three of them were smeared with blood, and a tailleur was stained and also torn. Mr. Greenspan started to tremble. He read the names on the tickets that were attached to the clothes, and then he called the front office, sat down in his chair and fainted.

The next morning, as Miss Graves with her little dog came out of the elevator, she was greeted by Mr. Magnum, the manager, who requested her to follow him to his office. The housekeeper had a maid bring in the tailleur. The torn and stained garment was spread out on the table while the housekeeper recited the lamentable details of the young girl's suicide, after which the director offered the hotel's apologies, and the assurance that the garment would either be replaced, or else Miss Graves would be fully reimbursed for the loss. Miss Graves was surprisingly indifferent. She said that she understood that such things happen; she said the suit was old, she had wanted to give it away. She thanked the manager, took her little dog and walked into the park, toward the lake.

At the north side of the lake stood a mounted policeman beside his horse. He always saluted Miss Graves, and sometimes talked

to her. He left his horse and, pointing into the water, he told Miss
Graves that early in the morning a patrolman on his rounds had
found a woman's body floating face down in the water near where
they stood. He pointed out a rock on which the woman had left
her coat and her pocketbook, and he said that after an emergency
squad had failed to revive her, the police had pronounced her a
suicide.

The robust, bronzed man stood with his legs apart, his cap
moved back on his head, the fists stuck into his sides. He said
that too many people did it; the rate was especially high among
members of the Police Department. Hardly a week went by without a policeman killing himself. Occasionally, he said, they hang
themselves, or jump; most of them use their service revolvers.
He said that if he ever did it himself he would use poison—
arsenic, he said, or cyanide—it's the quickest and cleanest. You
take it, you lie down on your bed, and it's over like that. He
snapped his fingers, got on his horse and rode away. Miss Graves
and the little dog walked back to the hotel.

The windows of the hotel which faced the park were unusually
large; they reached from the ceiling down to within three feet
off the floor.

Miss Graves stood in the living room of the Erosa apartment.
It was nine o'clock. She walked slowly toward the open window.
The park was in a purple haze, framed in the flickering lights of
the houses along Fifth Avenue, Central Park South and West,
and a Hundred and Tenth Street. A ribbon of the small lights
of cars moved slowly around it. In the last deep ultramarine of
the beautiful Manhattan sky, the stars appeared.

It was the blue hour, the time of danger. A warm wind moved
the curtain. Miss Graves pushed the hair from her temples and
sat down on the window sill. She sat like an acrobat on his trapeze.
Straight below, where all the lines of the building converged, the
street had been opened. Around a ditch swung red lanterns attached to iron staves. It was like a grave.

The scandalous moment arrived, the invisible hands tugged at
her, trumpets blared in her ears, and the street seemed to come
up like a train rushing into a dark tunnel. She had one of her

feet on the window sill, she leaned out, as if to take the hands of someone waiting in the night.

With a sudden backward jump and a cry of surprise, Miss Graves was in the room again, three feet from the window. Her eyes were fixed on the window sill. The salamander had appeared there.

She turned and saw Leonidas Erosa standing at the end of the room.

"You promised me, you promised me," said the General, his hands held out towards her, "you promised me never again to . . ." His face was ashen. "I came into the room a few moments ago. I stood here in terror. The distance was too great. I was afraid to call out to you. I hoped for a miracle. I was too scared to pray."

Miss Graves looked ashamed and bitter; her mouth was shut tight. She breathed like someone about to begin a violent argument, and as if to show the cause of her failure, she brought the salamander from the window and placed it on a silver humidor, under a lamp, where the General could bend down and see it.

"Tiens—tiens," said the General with his nose almost touching the salamander, "look who has come to visit us. I shall never forget what you have done for me, Tio." The salamander raised his head. He looked up, his small tongue appeared, he opened and closed his mouth. "Look," said Don Leonidas, "he is talking to me. Ah yes, Miss Graves, I can hear him."

And as if the salamander were a Spaniard who had only recently learned English, the General spoke for him: "Listen what he says. He says, 'Look at my fine uniform, what you think about me, eh? Such a leetle animal, and the heart so big, is going tick tock now, can you see him pounding? I ran so fast to save that wicked old woman, and now I want to go sleep.'"

"Is fine, Tio," said the General on behalf of himself. He opened the silver box, took out a few papers, and put the salamander into it. "Only for tonight, Tio. Tomorrow I get you a new home, with banana trees, a little cow, and a wife, no?"

He took Miss Graves's hands. "Tomorrow," he said, "I will take my hat and the little uncle in there, and I will have a jewel made for you, just like him, and you will wear it every day—so you will never forget again.

"I am well acquainted with death, Miss Graves," he said, holding her hands. "I die almost every three months, and then I wake up, and I am here again. Oh, how happy I am to be here again. No matter where or how I wake up. I say an immediate prayer of thanks. A running child, a flag waving in the wind, a grapefruit, Miss Graves, fills me with ecstasy. I am so very grateful to walk about once more in this beautiful world. Perhaps I love life as much as I do because it is paid out to me in miserly fashion, in fearfully little fragile instalments. I stand here in constant fear that the next day may be my last one. You have no idea, Miss Graves, how very precious the hours become. I have a kinship with the condemned. As for the day on which I really must go, I pray that the good God send me back—that I awaken, no matter how and where, but here again. I cannot imagine a paradise more complete and beautiful than this world. I wish I could make you at least a part of the smallest of my joys. I have never seen you smile, Miss Graves. If anything worries you, tell me and I will attend to it. But I have asked you a thousand times—I have of course instructed my bankers and made provisions, in the event that . . ."

"Please . . ." said Miss Graves. "Dear friend," she said with watering eyes, "you are so kind! I am so much trouble to you!"

He made a motion to kiss her, and then said: "Just like a goat—you always put your head down when I want to kiss you."

7: The Jews Are to Blame

LITTLE KURT tore his cap from his head and offered an enthusiastic good morning to the General, and the Frau Doktor smiled, as Don Leonidas entered the elevator.

The General stood facing the Frau Doktor and little Kurt. He carried his cane and bowler in one hand, and a small, perforated box in the other. He would have shown the salamander to the boy, but little Kurt started to talk to his mother in German, and for the last ten floors on the way down, the General confined himself to the banal routine of examining the Frau Doktor from head to foot.

Stepping out of the elevator, he bowed, and let the boy and his mother pass. The General found himself following the Frau Doktor down over the red carpets of a corridor. He came out of the side of the hotel through a door which faced the park a block higher up, and of whose existence he had not known. The General turned around, to orient himself. In order to get to his jeweler he had to walk back and halfway around the hotel. But the good things of life are all within easy reach in this neighborhood, and Don Leonidas had to walk only five blocks.

The jeweler was an American by the name of Garfield, who had bravely lettered into the right-hand corner of his window, "English spoken here."

Under a quartz lamp, in the private atelier of the jeweler, Don Leonidas placed the small box on a table. Softly whistling, he called Tio out of his box. The salamander ran across the table onto the drawing pad, where he stopped, looked up at the General, and assumed his usual pose of alert immobility.

"That is how I want him," said the General.

Don Leonidas produced a magnifying glass framed in tortoise shell, the size of a butter plate, and through this he looked at Tio and gave a jewel-drunken order. It sounded as if the Lord were busy with the creation of a new animal.

"Make him a nice body, pliable and elegant. Take particular care with the skeleton; make it of gold, and flexible. For the sides use flakes of emeralds, for the belly little plates of ivory. At the ends of the fingers place small pearls. Give him good eyes—take care that they shine—and on each cheek he gets a small ruby. Make him nice."

When the designer had measured and sketched Tio, the General put him back in his box and left, walking back up to the plaza to his florist.

Stokowski, the florist, hopped to the center of his humid establishment, to greet the esteemed client. His coquettish hands danced a ballet of disdain as the General opened the box. On seeing the salamander, the florist shrank back into a bower of forced apple blossoms. When he came out, he waved his hand toward the door, saying: "I have exactly what Your Excellency is looking for." Walking out of his shop, he pointed through the plate glass of his show window at an elephantine brandy inhaler, a foot and a half in diameter, flecked with blue and rose tints and landscaped with mosses, a dwarfed tree and a jade bridge.

The General placed Tio in the glass, and gave several orders for his favorite orchids to be delivered to different addresses while Stokowski wrapped fleecy material around the inhaler and placed it in one of the cochineal blue boxes that were his trademark.

Holding it in both hands at arm's length, Stokowski, who was afraid of traffic, ran across the plaza, the General following him. In the lobby of the hotel they waited for the elevator. The nervous florist nodded at clients and shifted from shoulder to shoulder as if his collar itched.

They were inside the elevator, the door was almost closed, when the operator saw Herr and Frau Doktor coming down the corridor. He excused the delay and opened the door again. Herr and Frau Doktor arrived not arm in arm as usual but in single file, the Doktor up front. They were in one of their regular two-week periods of silence which always followed major disagreements. When the Herr Doktor was angry at his wife, he was angry at the world. He marched into the open elevator, executed a resolute about face, and grunted, "How do you do," after his back was turned on the General. Frau Doktor was articulate and loved everybody except her husband at such times. She unswathed herself of a woolen muffler, lifted her sober blue eyes, and smiled at the General.

That evening the Herr Doktor dressed in his made-in-Germany dinner jacket, another indestructible garment, one which he knew he never could replace in the entire world. It was one of the evenings on which he dined with Conrad Magnum. The Herr Doktor kissed his child good night, and grunted good night to his wife. Conrad Magnum's menu was elaborate, the wines good, and the conversation animated. The theme was mostly Jews and hotel-keeping, and the phrase recurred: "Ja, ja, diese Gottverdammten Juden."

At nine the next morning, as he had done ever since the Café de la Paix argument about lobsters, mink coats, the child, the salamander, and the dog and cat, Herr Doktor von Despard took his Schnauzer out himself. Miss Graves, with her little dog, was standing at the elevator when the Herr Doktor came out of his apartment. The little dog's shrill barks, which echoed through the long corridor, became a painful, hysterical sound in the elevator. Miss Graves picked him up, but he kept on barking.

The Herr Doktor held his Schnauzer tightly on the leash. The big salt-and-pepper colored dog turned his head away and faced into a corner. The hair on his back slowly began to rise; he trembled, his red eyes leered upward in the direction of the little dog, but he never looked at him. He roared his anger, which was choked by spasms of fury against the wall of the descending car. They arrived on the ground floor and the Schnauzer pulled the Herr Doktor out of the lift, on his daily route to the cigar counter and the newspaper stand.

Miss Graves was halfway down the long corridor. She put the little dog down to fasten the leash on him. He stood still for a second, then he suddenly turned, dug his hind legs into the red car-

pet and raced back down the corridor looking for the Schnauzer.
He found him at the newsstand. The little dog jumped and
barked; he barked only once. Before anyone could help him, his
throat was in the Schnauzer's jaws. The little dog looked as if he
were wearing a tight ruff. His head was tilted sideways, and he
stared up at a passing woman until she screamed. "My God, isn't
somebody going to do something?"

The courageous Irishman who was the doorman on duty came
in and with his heavily gloved hands separated the two dogs.

The Schnauzer stood with head down, trembling and cough-
ing; his mouth was filled with hair. The little dog, silent, limp and
flat, lay on the marble floor. The veterinary said later that he had
no hope for him.

At four that afternoon Plaschke opened the door of the Erosa
apartment to admit the Herr Doktor, who had called to inquire
about the little dog's condition. Plaschke offered him a chair and
left the room to summon Miss Graves.

While he was gone, von Despard got up and walked to the
window. He saw a table there, and on it the brandy inhaler.
Examining its contents, he saw a salamander sitting on a green
bridge and looking up at him.

Miss Graves came in; she sat down on a sofa, looked at the
floor, and said that the little dog had died.

"Also," said the Herr Doktor, he would make good the loss
and be responsible for the veterinary's bill; also, he was very sorry.

Miss Graves looked over toward where his shoes were, and,
to his astonishment, she said cheerfully that there was nothing
to pay for—nothing to feel sorry about. The dog was dead, the
dog was much better off.

"What is a dog?" she said. "A poor miserable creature with a
collar around its neck, on a leash or a chain—often left alone,
plagued by sickness he cannot talk about, afraid of things nobody
can explain to him, dependent on the mood of his master. His
bark," explained Miss Graves, "was a sign of friendliness—the
little dog had always greeted her with it. The Schnauzer had misunderstood him; he wanted to play, not to fight. My little dog was
lonesome. If they had known each other, they would have played

all day." She had had him only for a month. "The General," she said, looking at the knees of the Herr Doktor, "thinks he can cure all troubles by buying presents. He felt lonesome one day, and therefore he thought everyone else felt lonesome, and he said to me, 'You should have a dog, Miss Graves; you are lonesome. The first dog that looks at you, I will buy for you,' he said. The General also thinks he can buy anything and everything. We walked through the park, and down Fifth Avenue, but fortunately not a single dog looked at me—and so he took me into a dog store where all the dogs looked at both of us. 'Pick one out,' he said. I wanted to buy them all, to get them out of their dirty boxes. I took the one that I thought no one else would take, a little bow-legged Yorkshire terrier. I wanted to rescue him from the bored cage in which he sat. He was not a very happy dog. He could not sleep—he pulled the blankets off my bed at night—I had to walk slower in the park so that he could keep up with me on his short legs. He was always sick because he ate too much—everybody fed him—and he was cold. Most of the time he sat in the ashes in the fireplace. He dug a hole in the sofa, because he was not allowed to dig in the park. . . . And now, all at once, all his troubles are over. I shall buy him a little place in a cemetery. I can now go anywhere I like, and as quickly as I like, because I am free of him."

She looked at the Herr Doktor's shoes again and, getting up, she ended the visit by saying, "We love to be loved by dogs, we love to love dogs, but we don't love dogs— I suppose you don't understand that. I am quite happy the little dog is gone. I had not named him yet."

With two awkward, backward motions, the Herr Doktor bowed himself out of her presence. He went to his room, sat down in his easy chair, and looking into the empty terrarium, he said to himself, also, the old woman is really and completely crazy, that much is clear. Also, he continued, in Berlin, I must say, it was otherwise, when you live in an apartment hotel for almost ten years, you know who the people to your left and right are, you know who lives over and under you. Here, if I did not have a Schnauzer who hates little dogs, I would never have found out that my neighbor has a salamander too. Also, that is only possible in America. He was continuing his speculations on the anonymity of the citizens of New York when the doorbell rang.

Outside stood an old man with a messenger cap, who handed him a large blue box.

The Doktor removed the string and took the cover off. The box was filled with sprigs of brown and purple orchids, small elaborate flower trumpets, growing from ochre-colored stems. The blossoms were bedded in fleecy paper. The Herr Doktor took a card from the envelope that was in the box with the flowers, on which was written:

> Ange et Diable—
> From the pure and gentle man
> who held your hand last night.

The note was written in ink of the same color as the box, and was unsigned.

Doktor von Despard ran out of the door and called the old man back. He stuffed the tissue paper into the box, pushed the cover over it, and handed it to the messenger.

"This is a mistake, this is not for me," he said.

The old man read the ticket. "It's for your wife," he said.

"I don't send flowers to my wife, nobody sends flowers to my wife!" screamed the Herr Doktor, and slammed the door. He sat down at his window and stared into the terrarium.

Suddenly he got up and rushed into the pantry. He came back with a fork in his hand. While the cat watched him, he removed the cover of the terrarium, and slowly, carefully, he used the fork to rake through the ground at the bottom of the glass case.

"Also," he said, "he is not here."

To make sure, he spread newspaper on the table and dumped the contents of the terrarium on it. He examined the earth thoroughly. The salamander was not there.

He went out into the corridor and walked past the door of the General's apartment twice before ringing the bell. Plaschke opened the door. The Herr Doktor excused himself. "Also," he said, "I am interested in that glass you have there, in that salamander you have inside the glass. Where can you get such a salamander? Where did the General get that salamander?" He said he wanted one for his little boy.

Herr Plaschke, who also spoke German, said, "Also, I think the Herr General bought him. He brought him home only three days ago, from Stokowskis, where he buys all his flowers."

Also most probably I am wrong, said the Herr Doktor to himself, as he went down in the elevator. He was a thorough man. He walked across the plaza and into the florist's shop. Mr. Stokowski told him definitely that he did not carry reptiles, and did not like them. The General, he said, had brought his own salamander; three days ago he had sold him the inhaler and some flowers, but no salamander.

The Herr Doktor hurried back. He felt weak in the knees. The leaden waves of suspicion broke over him; the way to the hotel was like a trek through loose sand. He went to his room and sat down in his chair. He stared into the empty terrarium, got up, and walking to the corner window, he took his field glasses and surveyed the park.

Where was she? Where had she been the night before, when he was dining with his friend Conrad Magnum? She was nowhere in the park. He saw Kurt and the Fräulein in the zoo below; he looked into every open hansom cab, including those that stood empty below the statue of General Sherman. She was not along the Avenue, nor anywhere within the range of his vision. It was suddenly simple as a film scenario. He threw the terrarium on the floor and said with a sad smile:

"Also, he has my salamander, also my wife."

With these words he went out into the corridor, walked up and down, and then rang the bell of the Erosa apartment. There was no answer. He tried the door; it was locked. He decided to mount guard there until somebody came. He fled from one end of the long corridor to the other, brandishing the wooden sabre of the cuckold. He came up from the emergency exit, toward the elevator door, as the car stopped and the Fräulein and little Kurt stepped out.

The Herr Doktor took Kurt by the collar of his little jacket, and pushed him ahead of himself through the living room into the bedroom of the Despard apartment. There he said to the boy: "Lies have short legs," and, placing Kurt across his knees, he pulled the small trousers tight and beat him with a thin cane that whistled and bit. "Also where is the salamander?"

Little Kurt screamed, "The cat got him."

"Also, more lies," said the Herr Doktor, working away with the cane. He stopped after a while, exhausted. He said once more, "Also, where is the salamander?"

"The cat almost got him, but he ran out of the window," said Kurt through sobs and tears.

"Also, more lies," said the Herr Doktor. After a third thrashing, he left the boy alone and ran out to the Fräulein, who was picking up the debris of the terrarium. With the cane still in his hand, his voice out of control, he groaned: "Don't lie to me, Fräulein— tell me the truth. Where is the salamander?"

"Also the cat got him," said the Fräulein.

"Also," said the Herr Doktor, "your have all been very well coached, I must say that!" He ran out into the corridor, and, as if it were his own apartment, tried the Erosa door. He kicked it, he shook it, he rang the bell as if it were a fire alarm—but no one answered. And then the unhappy thought came to him that the General and his wife were locked inside.

When this fact penetrated to Herr Doktor von Despard, he went back and attacked the door with new vigor. The Schnauzer barked and the doctor roared, calling the General "Schweine- hund," "Sauhaufen," and "Drecksack." The strong man rammed his shoulder against the door; he tried the six other doors of the Erosa apartment, screaming, "Come out, du Schweinehund, komm heraus, du Drecksack. I will show you, Sauhaufen."

But the ornate doors, like everything in the Palace Hotel, were made of the best materials and stayed closed.

"Also," said the Doktor, "we shall find a way to open it," and he started for the elevator to get the house detective.

His neck was redder than it was before, the scar was shining; he kept his finger pressed to the bell until the elevator arrived and he yelled "house detective" at the operator.

He took the elevator down to the lobby to look for the house detective, who always stood under the leaves of a palm tree, leaning on the newsstand. When you needed him, he was not there.

The Herr Doktor walked up and down the lobby. He went all over the hotel, came back to the palm room, and stood still for a moment, looking around. The orchestra was playing one of the shepherd dances of *Henry the Eighth,* and the Herr Doktor suddenly thought of his friend, the Managing Director General. The office of Conrad Magnum was reached by a decorative marble stairway, which led up to a small balcony overlooking the foyer. There were an inner and an outer office, both equally luxurious— and also the small dining room where only last night they had laughed as if nothing could happen.

The Herr Doktor had never dreamed that he would ascend that stairway in the disgraceful role he now played. He walked slowly, and hesitated several times on the way up. He stood still and held on to the doorpost before entering the outer office. The anteroom was empty and still, but from the Director's inner office he heard the sound of Conrad Magnum's loud and commanding voice.

"You get out of here, right now!" it said.

"Oh no—oh no, you can't do that to me," said a woman.

"Well, I'm sick and tired of this Gestapo stuff around here, and I don't like it. What I do is my business; I don't like scandal passed around this hotel."

"Who is passing scandal around the hotel?"

"You are; you're jealous."

"I am innocent, I swear, I never told anybody."

"I don't believe it. Now get out!"

"How dare you talk to me like that after all I've been to you all these years? You can't just——"

"Don't talk."

"But I swear I didn't tell a soul. I'm absolutely innocent of this; I'd be a fool, I need the job."

"I'll have no more of this."

"Oh yes you will! All right, I'll go, and I swear to you that I'll tell my husband, and you'll be in serious trouble."

"Now don't lose your head. I'll let you stay on one condition: you have to promise me that this kind of thing will never happen again. If I hear a word of this again, I'll just make an end to this situation. . . ."

"Yeah," said Mr. Magnum's private secretary.

The harangue continued. Without revealing his presence, the Doktor walked out on the balcony. There he stood as if thunder had struck him.

The tambour inside of him rolled the drum again, this time a muffled drum for the funeral of his friendship with Conrad Magnum. Despard, a family man who detested scandal, decided to move out of the hotel then and there. While he was thinking about this in shocked surprise, the revolving door began to wheeze and move, and the footman who turned it gave a first class salute as the General entered with Miss Graves. A chauffeur who followed them handed a few packages to the footman; the General and Miss Graves walked past below, talking.

"Also maybe, I am crazy," said the Herr Doktor. For a while such words as "For twenty years, happily married—you and I— dear Papa—liebe Anna," passed through his mind. He stared straight ahead of him, unmoving.

He stood there for a while, enjoying his reprieve, especially grateful that the detective had been away from his post and the Director had not been alone. He savored these thoughts several times.

The revolving door swished in a continuous rhythm. People came in from the street. It had grown suddenly cold, and the guests staggered into the hotel with bright eyes and rubbing of hands. The Frau Doktor came in, wrapped in her blue muffler and wearing the cigar-colored, faded Lodenmantel. She was carrying a package—a plate wrapped in paper—and she passed by below without seeing him. The Herr Doktor subconsciously wrote "ANNA" with the index finger of his right hand in the dust of the marble banister, and then he slowly descended to the main floor with the dignity of a very rich man.

"It's getting cool outside," said the detective.

"Yes, very nice," said the Herr Doktor.

"You like the cool weather, Sir?"

"Yes," said the Doktor, "very much." He walked to the house florist and ordered half a dozen talisman roses, and stopped at the newspaper stand to buy two tickets for the opera.

As they left for the opera, the Herr Doktor's hand rested in the soft white palm of his wife's. He was dressed in his tuxedo, and Frau von Despard had three of the talisman roses pinned to the left shoulder of a black velvet dress. The taxi drove by a moving picture theatre on the marquee of which *Suspicion* and *Frightened Lady* were announced. The Herr Doktor withdrew his hand. Now that he lay again in the secure and warm bed of marriage, more certain of its comforts and of its stability than he had ever been before, he was angry and felt sorry for himself. He thought of the crisis he had been through, the terrible emotions he had suffered—his right shoulder still hurt from the attack on the Erosa door—and with his logical mind he looked for the cause of it all.

It was because his wife had not been home. And why had she not been home?

He asked the Frau Doktor with extreme casualness where she had been, and she told him that she had taken some books and a cake to the old Herr Geheimrat Yohalem, who was ill, and that she had been late because his place had been in great disorder and she had stayed to straighten it out.

As they walked through the foyer and up the stairs to the dress circle, the Herr Doktor said to himself again, "Ja, ja, it is always these Gottverdammten Juden that are the cause of everything."

8: *The Kiss Royale*

THERE WAS a telegram on the silver tray. The Beauty read it. It announced that Señor Lopez would arrive within the next few hours aboard the Clipper. Madame Lopez left the telegram where it would be read by Plaschke, who would tell the General about its contents, and then she went to her Salon de Beauté, and on the massage table plotted her farewell to the General.

The General heard about it at three. The Beauty, he said to himself, had lost a lot since their arrival in New York. She was fairest on the *Xenaide Ybirricos;* she was very beautiful on the S.S. *Monte Cristi;* but in New York her nose had become too long.

He walked across the plaza. A breeze was blowing; a gust of wind pressed a girl against the Sherry Netherland, and while she held her hat, the skirts flew up. She looked like a cancan dancer, for a moment. It would not be difficult to console himself, the General said to himself. He walked through the park to a spot where the statue of the inventor of the Morse code stands. The hand of the statue pointed at a spot on the cement walk, where, in large letters even the General could read, a fearless hand had written with white chalk, "Tonight I will"—then came a space, and then the word, "Mabel." There was one word which the General could not read, because an old lady in a wheelchair sat over that part of the sentence.

The General walked up and down. He read the sentence over again, "Tonight I will"—then came the old lady—and then "Mabel." The General sent a weary look to heaven. He waited around, but the old lady was asleep in her chair. He walked to the fountain and back. While waiting he planned his conversation with the Beauty. "I love you, I will always love you," he said.

97

"Last night when I came home, I tiptoed past your room, so as not to wake you. I wanted to go in and say good night to you, I wanted to sit at the side of your bed and hold your hand and talk to you—about Alfonso. I am very fond of Alfonso."—No, No, No—a note, a box of orchids—she loved chocolates, a box of orchids and chocolates. But he sent her orchids every day. . . . A jewel, then. It began to rain. He walked back to the old lady—it was still, "Tonight I will . . . Mabel." A few raindrops fell on her and she was wheeled away, and the General read the complete sentence. He was satisfied; it was exactly what he had expected. Again he was privileged; the moment the old lady was moved the rain stopped. He looked at his watch, turned, and started back to the hotel.

Madame Lopez met him in the foyer. He asked her where she was going. She said she was on her way to Cartier's, to get something fixed. "It seems," she said, "that all the little things I have are broken."

He took her arm. "Help me," he said, "to pick out a bracelet."

She looked up at him and took his arm. "Chi-cken," he said. "Swit-hart," she said. It was like going to see somebody off on a train. She chose an emerald and diamond bracelet with stones so large that they looked false. Then they went home, and the General asked for a car, and sent Madame Lopez to the airport to welcome her husband.

Plaschke picked up the phone and asked for the Kiss Royale. "The usual wine, the same table, tous comme d'habitude; I understand—Mer-ci, Monsieur Plaschke." With respect and precise inflection the captain who had the early evening watch said goodbye to Mr. Plaschke, replaced the telephone in its cradle, wrote the reservation on a pad, and went back to his private thoughts.

Later that evening the captain had a call from the manager of the Palace Hotel, to intercede in person for a table for one of his guests, Dr. von Despard—a table for four. The captain asked for the spelling of the name and patiently put it down.

An hour later, the doorman kicked a rubber mat ahead of him-

self, unrolling it across the sidewalk until it spelled "Kiss Royale."
Angelo Suroya, the washroom attendant, silently drifted across it,
entered the night club, hung his coat and hat in a closet, and
walked out into the kitchen. There he took a vase of red, white,
and pink carnations out of a refrigerator and carried them to the
bar. He took a long drink of ice water and spat it in a spray over
the flowers, and then he picked them up, loaded himself with
towels, and descended to his washroom, where he gave evidence
of his patriotism by sticking a macaroon of stars and stripes into
the buttonhole in the lapel of his white coat.

Up above, a man polished the parquet of the dance floor.

Two hours later, at ten-thirty, the room was all ready for the
long voyage through the night. The tables were all set, the waiters
had stopped polishing silver and glasses, and the napkins hung
limp from their armpits. They stood talking, picking their teeth
and shifting from one foot to the other. On every table was a large
sign with "Reserved" printed on it. Until Royal Kley and his
Royal Kleypigeons began to play, the drone of the ventilating
system filled the dim room. The long gilded tassels swayed in
the silken draperies, which were like the sails of many ships standing in a circle.

The door to the kitchen was open, and there a pantryman cut
butter into small pieces and pressed on each pat the bitter legend:
"Remember Pearl Harbor."

In back of a screen sat the maître d'hôtel of the Kiss Royale,
eating an Italian dinner and drinking *vin ordinaire* out of a thick
glass like the ones people use to keep toothbrushes in. Signor
Santini was the owner of three apartment houses in Astoria, a
family man beloved by a wife and five sons. After rinsing his
hands in one of the blue, gold-crested fingerbowls of the Kiss
Royale, he got up and walked down to the washroom, where he
talked for a while with Mr. Suroya. He went to the mirror,
arranged his tie, and straightened the three-inch high collar which
he wore to compensate for his bombastic nose. Signor Santini,
who was known as "Naso" to his intimates and as "Cyrano"
to the habitués of the Kiss Royale, was a very neat man. He
washed his hands once more and put some pomade on his black

hair, while Mr. Suroya brushed him off and stuck a gratuitous white carnation into the lapel of his dinner jacket. Then Cyrano mounted the stairs to the foyer of the Kiss Royale.

He entered the cabaret like a conductor walking to his orchestra, his nose in the air as if assuming an unpleasant scent somewhere. He looked over the room and made a sortie to its center, a holdover from the days when he used to speak sharply to this or that member of his staff and make them come to attention. Now help was hard to find, and they all remained in the relaxed positions they happened to be in. He returned to his desk and picked up the list of reservations. Pointing with a quill toothpick in several directions, he read off the names, reserving the already reserved tables for the most particular and select of his clients. As he did this, the first guests entered, and Royal Kley and his Kleypigeons began to play.

The atmosphere of a restaurant at that hour is like the nervous moments before the rise of a theatre curtain. Its moods fluctuate; they are influenced by the day's good or bad news, by the digestion of Cyrano, by the names on his list of reservations, by the weather; even by such details as the biologic upsets of a coat room girl of whom the maître d'hôtel was beloved.

There were eight guests in the room, and their voices sounded as if they were in an empty swimming pool. Small blue stars shone in the ceiling. The music was idling along when Cyrano was faced by four curious people who demanded a table. He was about to say that all the tables were engaged, when the man at the head of the group identified himself as Doktor von Despard. Cyrano clicked his tongue for one of his captains and gave him the number of a table. He looked after them and shook his head—they would never have gotten in at all, in spite of obvious respectability, except for the prestige of Mr. Magnum of the Palace Hotel. This secured them a small table in the part of the Kiss Royale known as "Siberia." That section filled up rapidly after the Doktor and his party were seated. They found themselves bedded among American editions of their own kind, solvent citizens from Detroit, visitors from Des Moines and Chicago. Next to them was a big table at which some advertising executives and their wives were entertaining the dynasties of cheese and underwear. In this quarter the jewelry was as genuine, the wedding bands as wide, and the women's dresses of the same couture as those of Frau von Despard and her friend, Frau Hufnagel.

The Hufnagels were old friends of the von Despards, once having taken the cure in Bad Gastein with them. At that resort Herr Hufnagel, although he was a pure Aryan, sometimes found himself in uncomfortable situations on account of a nose only a little less formidable than that of Cyrano of the Kiss Royale, and he had made it a practice always to carry his American passport with him and always to talk about America. It was Eugen Hufnagel at Bad Gastein who convinced the Doktor that America was the only place to sit out the coming war and to keep one's money.

The Hufnagels lived in a stone and slate mansion in Passaic. Herr Hufnagel was the president of a corporation that manufactured paste jewelry.

Herr Hufnagel asked for the wine card and ordered two quarts of Bollinger which were listed at $15.00 the bottle. In this quarter, despised by the management, sat the best clients of the Kiss Royale.

The ladies examined the room, they looked up at the twinkling stars, and their eyes shone in the tall mirrors. They admired the sails that floated through blue smoke. The voices of the crowd blanketed the music so that it sounded far away, like a rhythmic trouble in the plumbing, like cloth-covered cymbals softly knocked together.

"If it rocked a little, it would be like a ship," said Frau Hufnagel to Frau von Despard.

"Ja, ja, exactly so, like the *Europa*. Remember, Mama, the restaurant upstairs?" said Herr Doktor von Despard.

The service at the Kiss Royale was perfect. The waiter who appeared at their table was tailored exactly to their taste, he might have come up out of the kitchens of Horchers—he was round and fat, and his jowls wobbled when he spoke. He had a nervous twitch in one eye.

"Where does General Erosa sit when he comes here?" asked Frau von Despard.

"Ja, the General's table is over there, Madame," he said, pointing across the room. "The Herr General Erosa comes every night, and that is where he always sits. A fine customer!—like old times—they came no better! You will see him, there," said the waiter.

He offered a menu but nobody wanted to eat.

A table for three was reserved for Erosa. It was on a small platform, the Royal box of the Kiss Royale, out of the draft and not too close to the music. On another platform equally well placed stood the table of the Immortals, a group of the honorary pallbearers at the fall of France, who found themselves driven by Hitler into the traps of Roosevelt, and who greeted each other with extravagant joy. In the protective embrace of a ring of champagne buckets, the grand pensionnaires of the Lido, the Place Vendôme, the Bar Basque in Mentone and the Rock at Cap d'Antibes, sat together again, almost happy, and always grouped around their patron saint, Catherine de Bouvier de Flandres, the ancient mezzo-soprano who had led the cotillion of emotional cripples safely across the ocean, and was known to her intimates as Buffie.

In a wide armchair especially placed for her, she sat with her back to the audience. Most of the time the room was sheltered by a snood of small artificial flowers that was draped from the top of her head to her shoulders. When she turned her head, the complexion of the Kiss Royale changed. Everything seemed covered with a curious gray dirt, and remained so as long as she faced it. A bitter complaint resided perpetually in her face. Her pores were so large that you feared she would be cold inside, but she frequently ventilated the large tub of her bosom, reaching into it to adjust a strap on her underclothing. Her mouth was open, except when she spoke. The hair on her head, moist and warm, was pushed back frequently, and when she turned and looked into the room and her stale oyster eyes dragged over the crowd, the lines of complaint in her face grew deeper. She stood six feet in her nylons and she weighed two hundred and fifty pounds. She had been Bayreuth's ideal Walküre. She was an excellent portrait of her circle—regardless of sex and height—and she turned back to them gratefully.

With talent, diligence and unrelenting persistency, she had pushed her obscene form from the obscurity of a Kansas homestead, up and up, through the capitals of the world, up even past thrones.

Since she had stopped singing, she had become a kind of female maître d'hôtel for her friends, arranging their divertissements. Buffie's new divertissement was the war. She preached priority and patriotism, she wrote articles about great figures, whom she called one and all by their first names. She took three dimensional lessons in elocution and was about to become a radio commentator.

Opposite her sat a woman who had just returned from Reno, where she had rid herself of her husband, a British peer, because there was no way of getting money out of England. She was a wet-lipped idiot with blond hair who strained at the genteel accents of a Lonsdale parlor maid. Between them was a man who had been too young for the last war and was too old for this.

At the right of Catherine de Bouvier de Flandres sat Monie Van Dua, originally Dutch, then English, at one time Swiss, a man of the world whose high good fortune stemmed from the peculiar new geography of the war. He was glad that the properties of the corporation of which he was the head were located in the comparative safety of the Belgian Congo, the Island of Aruba, and in ships that still sailed the ocean.

He was also properly thankful that control of the corporation was vested in him, and that the funds were in New York. It was unfortunate that most of the books had been in a building on the Beuersplein, the Exchange Square in Rotterdam, and disappeared, along with the bronze statue of van Hogendorp, the night the Nazis gave their first lesson in pattern bombing. When the war was over, he feared, there would be a terrible mess. "I am afraid," said Monie Van Dua, looking into his glass of champagne, "about my poor stockholders. I wonder who is left. The entire board of directors, I hear, is in a concentration camp."

Monie's chief complaint was with American cooking. He sipped some champagne, and then turned to Buffie. "God," he groaned,

"I had dinner tonight in a restaurant—I forget the name of it—somebody recommended it. I went there before the theatre. Never go there. Let me warn you, don't ever go there. It had a French name, something very obviously French—I'll find out the name for you. The proprietor insists on sitting with his guests and bringing the chef to the table.

"I said to him, 'Call him doctor, call him plumber, appelez-le un con if you wish, but for God's sake don't call him a chef. . . . Look what he sends me!' . . . He served an abomination which he called his specialty, a Poulet à la mode de je ne sais quoi—a stew if you please, with cheese spread over it, au gratin, like soupe à l'oignon. They think cheese spread on something settles everything. 'Tell him to go away.' I said, 'all the way back to his kitchen where I cannot see him.'

"'Perhaps you like a little Sauce Maison on it,' said the proprietor—absolutely unperturbed. He has the gall to stand there rubbing his hands while the waiter grins like an ape and holds a plate with a glass pot with the famous Sauce Maison under my nose. This Sauce Maison, which you find in all restaurants in this country, and which they will put on your hat if you let them, is something which drives me to utter despair. 'Go away,' I said. Oh, you know it's something awful. And then that Russian play on top of it—you know I was ill during the whole play."

"I must say," huffed Buffie, waving a rolled up program of *The Lower Depths*. "I must say it is unpatriotic—I will go further—I state that it is positively treacherous, it is sabotage, to produce a play like this, at a time when our glorious allies the Russians are embattled, bearing the brunt of . . ."

The wet-lipped divorcée disarranged her coiffure, a strand of her hair fell over her left eye in her gesture of violent agreement. She strained her throat to say: "Reehllie it's awful, Buffayh, isn't thr a Secrtry of smthing, or othr, I mean a soohd of cncrshp o the theatah?"

Another of the old girls at the table of the Immortals unnestled a brooch made of diamonds and rubies in the shape of a hammer and sickle and showed it to Buffie. The house photographer passed. Enlisted in the grim demands of the times, he trained his camera on the scene and arrested it for the morning papers. The owner of the brooch, a bewildered little titled woman, the back of whose head looked like that of a canary with most of the feathers gone, posed for another shot. "Sir Harry gave it to me," she said, "to wear at the Russian Ball. Harry is Chairman, you know," she said, turning to Buffie, "and of course when it's all over you can always have it made into something else." After this she returned to the quiet alcoholic garden in which she lived, in which all things were pretty and the color of liqueurs and pearls.

She had sat there just like this, at this very table, all happy and smiling, and fondling her pearls, on another night when Sir Harry had called her out of the beautiful garden. She had stumbled after Cyrano, to the private office of the owner of the Kiss Royale, where Harry was on the phone, speaking from London, and she had run back to the table, breathless. "Tokyo!" she said, and sat down, wringing her jeweled hands. "Good God, how awful! First Pearl Harbor, then Singapore, and now Tokyo. What will they do next?"

The Immortals sat stunned and silent for a moment, and then they looked at each other and just laughed and laughed, because they knew that the Japanese wouldn't bomb Tokyo.

There was a crowd ten deep standing in the foyer of the Kiss Royale, trying to get in. Cyrano stood at his desk with his nose high in the air. Looking over the herd, he saw an admissible face and nodded to a strong man who guarded the door. The doorman unhooked a velvet cord and let in a white-haired man who looked like a demented Goethe. He pushed a little girl ahead of himself, a silver blonde wrapped in a gargantuan jacket made of white pelts. Cyrano steered them to a ringside table and snapped his fingers for the waiter, who opened a waiting bottle of Bollinger. The man, in spite of being a celebrity, wore a large identification tag attached to a slave bracelet on his left wrist. He unwrapped the girl whom he had chosen for his ninth wife, and looked into the crowd with the same complaining glare as Catherine de Bouvier de Flandres, to whom he waved. He was almost one of the Immortals, but not serious enough. His publicity was bad;

he always married badly. He settled down and later busied himself rolling dollar bills into small pellets which he dropped on the floor for the bus boys to pick up the next morning. It was an idea that his press agent had thought up, and it would appear the next day in all the gossip columns.

The room was almost filled. Cyrano had to go into a dance to get back to his door through the crowd.

In the center of the floor was a human pie slowly turning, a mass of pressed-together arms, faces, elbows, and backsides. Here and there a too-confined couple tried a few leaping steps to get out of it, but they only moved to the edge for a few steps before the pie sucked them in again. A young couple dancing with arms stiff, holding each other at a distance and looking into each other's eyes, were pushed out of the center and upset a table. The rest went round and round. The Kleypigeons never stopped playing. The proprietor of the Kiss Royale had calculated that it would cost him several hundred dollars every time the music stopped: people came out of the beautiful dream, walked to their tables, asked for their bills, and got up before the band started again. So the musicians played like a football team relieved by substitutes, and the music went on and on.

Here and there among the crowd, as if they were afloat on small rafts, sat soldiers and sailors, properly grateful that they were allowed in, their girls' fingers trapped in the warm, moist prisons of their strong hands. They stretched the drinks and avoided the waiters' eyes. They looked at the girls like small boys begging for candy, and their only worry was that the money in their pockets might not be enough to pay the bill.

All around the room, like snow-white lilies in a field, sat young girls—none anywhere in the world so fair, so beautifully dressed, so regal in mood and bearing. Exquisite creatures with perfect throats, ears, hairlines; with the modern, elegant, bashed-in faces, the wide lips, the small noses, and the long lashes. They were, except for the color of their hair, all of a convenient sameness, like the mannequins that stand in the shop windows of upper Fifth Avenue. You could take the long limbs of one, the head of another, and the torso of a third, and assemble another lovely creature from these parts. They looked alike, they spoke alike, and they served themselves of the same mechanisms of lowering the long lashes over their eyes, of looking up, of turning the head slowly, of laughing a careful, porcelain smile. They bent their heads and arranged their lips in compassion; they performed little playlets of injury, their eyes clouding at will; or they sat up straight like cadets at mess. They could hold these poses for unbelievably long stretches, and when they left the room they turned and twisted their slender hips through the narrow passages between chairs, weaving their shoulders like toreadors through the bullring.

They came back with all the small damages from smoke and the warm humidity of the room repaired, the lip rouge lost on the edges of glasses and on the mouthpieces of cigarettes replaced. They were altogether new and young now. They walked with hauteur, the head held high, the face immobile, they wore an expression as if someone outside had just mortally insulted them, had smacked their faces and hynotized them. Elbows held close to the sides, they sat down in one controlled motion, and only then humanity came back to them and they bestowed a smile on the intimates at their table.

Their current Queen was the vocalist of the Kiss Royale, a spun-sugar-haired girl, tall, with small paraffin bosoms half hidden in a veil of bluish gauze. At twelve-thirty, the appearance of Virginia Vanderbilt, née Mary Cornwall, was announced by a blare of trumpets, the darkening of the room, and the shaft of a floodlight. The music stopped, the talk subsided to the sound of oatmeal boiling, a waiter dropped a last tray of dishes on the floor, and a curtain sailed up disclosing the Goddess leaning against a Grecian urn. On the hand of a master of ceremonies, she descended six small steps to the crown-crested microphone. She took the metal rod to which it was attached and tilted it so that the mesh-covered metal box was under her small nose. Her amethyst eyes looked across the crowd to a point on a distant imaginary horizon. An agonized expression came into her face, and she vomited a song of sorrow into the microphone. The little eyebrows formed a gothic roof over the sad mouth.

At the end she let the staff go and threw her arms back. The little breasts heaved, and she tore and twisted at a little batiste handkerchief. The pain of her beauty sank into the hearts of the service men, who let their girls' hands go and stared open-mouthed at Virginia Vanderbilt.

She sang two encores from the current hit parade. But her specialty was folk ballads, and she ended with "Sweet Molly Malone." When she began this song she swallowed deep and waited while the music imitated a wheelbarrow going over a cobblestone pavement. She adopted a look especially holy and winsome, pointed the little mouth, put the little white hand next to her face as if calling into a great distance. Holding the microphone away from her, she dragged out the "o" of "cockles" as long as her breath lasted; and after the flutes had bridged three bars with their wail, she called out "and mussels" and followed with the cry, "alive, alive, oh!" There was a period of doodling by the orchestra, and then the song proper began:

> In Dublin, fair city
> Where girls are so pretty
> That's where he first met her,
> Sweet Molly Malone.
> She wheeled her wheelbarrow
> Through streets wide and narrow
> Crying "Cockles and mussels
> Alive, alive, oh!"

The soft silky tissue of her voice floated out over the audience, unbelievably unreal and more like a perfume than a sound. The unfortunate cockles and mussels were modeled into sweet song. When she was through, the applause rocked the glasses on the tables.

Herr Doktor von Despard applauded for three. He tried to get the check, but Hufnagel put his hand on his arm and said he wanted to pay. Frau Doktor said she did not want to go until she had seen the General. They ordered another bottle of wine, and the waiter pointed to the General's table. "Sure, he's coming," he said; "it's the only table that's reserved all night. He always comes.

Ja, ja, he is coming all right; also how about something to eat—a little goose liver paste, a chicken, maybe some oysters, a Welsh rarebit, a woodcock, a caviar, maybe some eggs and sausages? Also, later maybe?—Nothing now? Thank you. He will be here any minute, the General."

About two in the morning, the crowd thinned somewhat, the dance floor became visible here and there, and the regulars arrived from other places. They ordered and ate, and conversation began. The music played softly. The strains of the "Blue Danube" brought Herr and Frau Hufnagel onto the floor. They danced, Frau Hufnagel wearing eyeglasses, her husband holding her at arm's length with a cigar in his mouth. They moved about in elaborate old-fashioned choreography. He set off with gusto, with one leg in the air, as if he were blindly reaching for the bottom rung of a ladder, and then, unable to find it, brought his foot down sharply on the floor. They hopped and swung in dizzy spins, just recovering at the edge of the floor.

Their success brought out the Despards. When they came onto the floor, the rest of the dancers left and the two couples had it to themselves. Herr and Frau Doktor von Despard had not danced since the crossing on the *Europa*. The Herr Doktor leaned back and swam in delight; he laughed and looked as if a surgeon had laid half his face bare. Royal Kley played Waldteufel and six Lanner waltzes. At the end the dancers stopped to wipe their faces, and everybody applauded them. On the way back to their table both the Herr Doktor and Herr Hufnagel sent wolfish leers to all the Goddesses, who waved at them and smiled.

"He must be here any minute now," said the waiter as he drew the chairs and opened another bottle of Bollinger. "Also, he usually comes earlier. He should be here now. Every time he comes, five dollars for the captain, ten dollars for the waiter. Ein feiner Gast, the Herr General."

The music played softly. The dance floor was a quiet pond. Yellow and blue flames burned under chafing dishes and casseroles, the captains stirred sauces, the waiter served plates of food. Doktor von Despard sniffed the air, and his wife said, "I'm hungry."

Catherine de Bouvier de Flandres was eating asparagus. She held the stalks up, leaned back and swished them into her mouth with a thick tongue. The sailors and soldiers held their girls' hands and began fencing for admission to the love garden. The establishment provided the best possible mood for them; it was purring, blue, tender and expensive. Among a thousand dishonest grimaces were some honest ones. A beautiful girl and a handsome South American began dancing a rhumba to barely audible music. Everywhere heads were together in conversation, foul-mouthed talk beside bitter words, wisdom and clarity next to cloudy drool and blabbermouth and awful confession. The dispensary of joy sailed quietly toward the morning.

Out of a small door near the Despards' table appeared Virginia Vanderbilt in a gold lamé gown, the skirt slit up to the height of her knee. She walked across the room to a table where two men waited for her, neither of whom got up, and sat down between them. They kept on with their conversation. One of them took the girl's hand and patted it, and after a while he turned and said:

"Well, how does it feel?"

"Oh, Mr. Eisig, I tell you, when I heard about it, that I was to sing here, I started to cry, my mother started to cry, my agent even started to cry. And here I am. I have to pinch myself."

"Well, you'll get used to it," said Mr. Eisig, and continued: "So, where was I?"

"The playwright," said the other man.

"Oh yes, the playwright is sued for damages, for the alleged theft of an idea from a girl writer, so he goes to settle the suit out of court and falls for the dame. He ends up by falling in love with the girl. All right, so the girl inherits a railroad and arriving in Chicago she finds that her fortune consists of a junked locomotive and a hundred odd miles of rusty trackage. First she thinks it's a total loss, but the boy finds that it is worth a lot of money, there's a man who wants to buy the junk—a banker who is a cover up for the sons of Nippon. So . . ."

"I know, I know, I read it—you told it to me, I told it to my wife. I told you what I am willing to pay . . ."

The other man took his hand from the girl's and held on to the sleeve of his friend. "Well then, I'll have to . . ."

"Listen slowly," said the other. "If somebody passes you in a Yellow taxicab, and throws you a Boston bag containing thirty-five thousand dollars, my advice is, take it. But I don't pay that kind of money for that kind of a story. Now let's talk about the girl."

They both suddenly looked at Virginia Vanderbilt, as if she had arrived that very moment. The man who held her hand at the beginning began to stroke her arm now.

"This little kid here, she works her head off. She gave an audition and stole the goddamn show. And now, hell, they're all gangsters anyhow, they're all after her. This is the toughest racket. . . . Gee, this kid here is a little artist, she gets out there on that small stage . . ."

"I've seen her, I've seen her."

"I don't know how old she was when they sent her around, but she couldn't have been older than eighteen." The kid nodded. "She's a swell actress. I had a little character woman in one of my shows, she never could do much except say a few intent words, and she used to get three thousand a week. I put the kid in it— she stole the goddamn show. Now, handled right, Sam . . ."

"No dice," said Sam. "I told you what we're willing to pay. Well, I'm going, I'll have to tell the boys."

"Listen, Sam, the boys were here yesterday. They saw her, they like her."

"I know, they saw her yesterday, you don't have to sell her to me."

"Can't we make some deal, for Christ's sake?"

"See me tomorrow," said Sam, "and we'll have a chat over at my office." He got up and left.

On the way out the producer almost ran into a tall figure, a consumptive Samson, half man, half Government, a historic person with bushy eyebrows. He came in with a limping small man who had a round face and a little beard that seemed pasted to his chin.

"I am sure that bye-and-bye some agreement can be reached with a strong France on the Continent," said the Government.

"I agree with you, I am altogether of your conviction." He bowed from his great height to Cyrano, who bowed back to him and took him to a banquette.

Two of the Goddesses smiled and waved at him. He bowed back with Old World courtesy.

The two girls whose men had left the table and gone down to Mr. Suroya stuck their heads together, and the one with ginger hair said:

"That's Bushy, the guy with the head of John the Baptist. Somebody ought to buy him a haircut, or a fiddle."

"Is he important?"

"You're asking is he important! My God, whenever he gets a girl in trouble, a Supreme Court Judge or somebody takes care of it. I met him in Washington, we had a house there, and you know how it was, people move in and out. It was before the war and you couldn't rent it, so we let a relative run it as a rooming house. She calls herself Miss Campbell. She's really a high-class person, and if Chickie—that's Miss Campbell—was a thousand years old, she'd never think of herself but in the real estate business. Honest as the day is long. Never makes any dough at it— real dough, I mean. The cheap girls are at 1406. She's high class, she gets anything she wants.

"She worked for the State of New Jersey for five years, that's how she met the right people. She kisses it real good, it's near the Swedish Embassy. You ought to hear Bushy talk. You know he said to me—he has a beautiful voice—he said, 'I demand life.' He said, 'It's quicksilver, I give myself like an artichoke, everybody can have a leaf.'

"Look at that mattress mouse with the bedroom hair; they think they're dancing in Roseland. But to get back to Bushy. 'I demand life in great style, to the sound of Chinese firecrackers exploding,' he said. Look at him, he's so thin, if you gave him a glass of grena-dine, he'd look like a thermometer. I bet he's got four sweaters on now. He calls me Jacky Wacky. 'Jacky Wacky,' he said, 'you've got a swell little muscle there.' I will spare you the painful details of what comes after. I told him that women always judge men by the size of their ankles, so he takes half a dozen Kleenex and puts them in his socks. Highly unethical—but he tries, God how he tries."

A young man passed by and smiled and waved. "That's Johnny," said the blond Goddess. "Hya, Johnny!"

"Hya, Toots!"

"Oh, I'm just fine. . . ."

"That's Johnny Orbach, a rich boy from Brooklyn. When he got married he gave me all his blue films and he wrote his memoirs under another name on a Remington De Luxe. All the stuff he wanted to throw away he gave to me, a broken bed, a bicycle and an old polo coat with a cigarette hole. He needs that Bronxville attic for the two buckets of dry sand and the ax and shovel; he's an air raid warden. And she's so happy, look at her, the one in the knuckle-length striped ticking. He'll be back; you can see she has no talent, not in this fierce market. He buys dresses for her, he sends flowers to her every day, he introduced me to her. Funny how they always insist that you meet the wife. I was trapped for an hour and a half in the girdle room of the Waldorf with her. He does everything for her, I guess he does her hair too—look at it."

"Also, the turtle soup is for me," said Doktor von Despard, and the waiter put it before him.

"Also," said the waiter, "the boss has a venison somebody shot on his farm, and there is a venison saddle—with Weinkraut— if anybody cares to have that."

"We will have the venison," said the Herr Doktor. "You love venison, Mama. Also for me the lobster. For Mister Hufnagel the Paprika Chicken, for Frau Hufnagel the cold ham with potato salad. No, she takes the chicken. And for meine Frau, the venison saddle with Weinkraut, and for Herr Hufnagel the Paprika Schnitzel."

A Hungarian playwright who sat within hearing said to his companion, "You know, I have eaten six times last week Paprika Schnitzel and Paprika Chicken. Because I am a Hungarian playwright, whenever I am invited they have Paprika Schnitzel, and if they have not Paprika Schnitzel, I get Paprika Chicken. Because I am Hungarian."

Another of the Goddesses at the end of the room said to her escort, "I am certain that one of these head waiters with their benign faces has my diamond clip in his pocket. They swear that they have searched everywhere. Naturally they have searched, or they wouldn't have found it."

She looked at the historic man and said, "You know, he's very interesting. The last time I saw him, he was at Condé Nast's funeral. I've been a bridesmaid so often at that church that it seemed strangely like a wedding—the same old faces, the same flowers, the same place. I had the same feeling when Maury Paul died. What time is it? Oh—it's late, don't go, sit here with me. Let's talk, we always seem to talk. I don't know what you can do except talk; love talk is awful. Look at Mrs. Katzensatz and her chinchilla. It's like pinning thousand-dollar bills all over yourself."

A young, sad man was talking: "Listen, May."

"Yes, I'm listening."

"May, I burned out another bearing. I'm being treated to second-class infidelity. I never thought I'd go through it, I never thought it would happen to me. I wanted to get it over with quick, I thought I'd shoot the bastard, but then I thought, Christ, anybody can shoot. I can hit a field mouse from here to there, you put a Coca-Cola bottle on that waiter's head and I'll knock it off at a hundred yards, but that's not the point. Well, it's my third wife so it doesn't hurt so much. I don't know what she sees in him. Impecunious immigrants don't interest me, and Italians don't interest me at all, particularly when they are titled. The Italians I know all shine shoes. Well, Boston always needs one family to shock it. I went up to see my boy last week. They have three feet of snow in Boston. Now I'm over it, I don't care a damn. I'd be concerned only if my pants dropped off in Grand Central Station. There are a thousand trains leaving New York every day, and I'm not on any of 'em. I had the flu in one room, and she in the other. I left the door open and we talked it over. It's all over as far as I'm concerned. Yes, it's all over as far as I'm concerned."

"I'll have terrific respect for you if you'll just say the same thing tomorrow, John. And what do you want with me?"

"The smile, the big smile, May—smile a little, May. . . . A thousand trains, and I pick the one you're on.

"Christ I'm glad you were on that train. That's how it is. You look for one thing, and then you find something else. If I'd known you were on that train, probably I wouldn't have taken it. Well, we're here, and where do we go from here? The big smile, May—don't look so sad."

"What time is it, John? Let's go."

"My God, because I'm divorcing her, you won't . . ."

They sat silently hand in hand, and the waiter brought two more Scotches.

A Frenchman said to the mattress mouse with the bedroom hair, "There are a thousand women in New York that are beautiful, of those a hundred have heart, of those one has beauty, heart and intelligence, and that is you." The little girl squeezed his hand and looked down.

Two women at an adjoining table had gotten up and walked to the washroom. As soon as they had left, their husbands sat down, and one of them, who was from Pittsburgh, said:

"My God, Charlie, funny how small the world is. Did you see her?" He moved his bulk sideways so that he faced his friend, and pointed to the door. "She just left," he said. "Didn't I tell you about her?

"I was at the American House, Charlie, in Altoona, P.A., when she came in the door, this big, beautiful, handsome woman. I was introduced to her later, Mrs. Trabitsch was her name. She was a widow. You couldn't get anything to eat at the American House that night, it was filled with peace delegates, so I took her arm and said, 'Come on, you and I, we'll grab ourselves something to eat down the street. I know a drugstore there.' We found three vacant stools when we got there, we took two of them. She was a damn good-looking woman, with a military cape. I was younger then. 'What'll you have?' I said. She ordered a club sandwich. She spoke very fine English, so I said to her, 'You know, it's surprising the way you speak English, for a Balkan.' So she said,

'Why, bless your heart, my name is Mabel Davenport, I'm from Butte, Montana.' Well, sir, I almost fell off my stool. I had the feeling, now there's a woman. She had married that fellow Trabitsch, who had something to do with making Yugoslavia. He made it up out of the Serbs, the Croats, and the Slovenians, but at the end it seems that they all hated him and each other, and so he was killed. And for a while she ran the place. Imagine a woman like her running Yugoslavia!"

"Who's the guy coming in?—looks awfully important," said a man to his friend. They sat close to the table of the bushy man with the thick ankles. "I've been through something awful. The next time Pepe introduces me to one of his swell dames, I want to know her height, her age, and what she weighs soaking wet before I commit myself. The last one had a friend. . . .

"Listen: They live in the Village, like ants. They furnished the place on five bucks, they painted an old table, they sleep together in one bed. It's all youth and innocence. You know, the little home girl with the white piqué collar—makes them look like schoolgirls. They live five flights up. I had to stop for air on the fourth, at my age. They always had their heads together, confidantes, and they cooked over gas. They just got through reading the *Sea of Cortez*, borrowed from a proof reader on the fourth floor. First you have to ring the bell, then you have to admire the furniture, my, my—while they open a can of salmon. In the bathroom hangs a douche bag and two particularly pink hostess gowns. There's an empty apartment in the same building right below, they show it to you. How would that be? If you moved in, there's a cold radiator and moonlight—and she shows you to the door, she leans in a dark recess and fiddles with your necktie, people pass by and she talks low. . . . Oh for the joy of the chase, the thrill of the hunt. I had to fight a rearguard action to get out of the damn place. I bow out. I go to Monte Carlo—Monte Carlo is closed. Morocco is being redecorated and I end up here. Hey—waiter—Psst."

"Also who gets the venison saddle?"

"The venison saddle is for die Missis," said Herr Hufnagel.

"The Paprika Chicken for me!" cried Frau Hufnagel.

"Also, you see," Doktor von Despard was saying, "that was a Sozialist, really a Sozialist, the first Sozialist."

"Who?" asked Hufnagel, with a piece of chicken on a fork near his mouth.

"Christus was the first Sozialist. But nothing was kept, not even the Ten Commandments."

"I keep six of them, most of the time," said Herr Hufnagel, and wiped his mouth with a napkin.

"Also, there comes the Erosa," said Frau von Despard. Everybody stopped eating and looked.

"With the Spanierin," she added.

Cyrano ran to the door. "Table soixante-sept," he breathed. "Bon soir, mon Général, bon soir, Madame.—Psst, psst, table sixty-seven. Psst, the wine. . . ."

The maître d'hôtel bowed deeply. The waiter slapped his napkin down on the table several times, arranged the silver and glasses in precise order for the tenth time. Erosa bowed and smiled at several people, and slowly and importantly sat down. With them was Señor Lopez, who walked to the table of the Immortals and shook several hands.

"Ja, das ist der Erosa, and the Spanierin," Frau von Despard repeated. "The old one, Miss Graves, stays at home. She weighs only ninety pounds. She lives on champagne. She is crazy and has a coffin in the apartment. They have besides an Indian to take the dogs out, and a French chef."

"Na, also, I must say I wouldn't be opposed to the Spanierin," said Herr Hufnagel. After staring a while and wondering who the little man was with the General, they went back to their conversation.

The service at the General's table was supervised by Cyrano in person. Leonidas Erosa, the Beauty, and Señor Lopez began with turtle soup and sherry. They ate silently.

A crowd of three very animated people came in smiling at everybody. In the center was a very small soldier, and as they stood deciding how to seat themselves, a young Goddess, with her nose touching the cheek of the soldier, said, "We'll put you in the middle, honey, yes, we love you in the middle." The soldier plumped down between the two girls, who giggled and messed up his hair and put their arms around him.

The soldier spoke to the waiter from under the caresses of their arms. "I tell you what I would like," he said, "I would like something solid to start off. Bring me a dozen Oysters Rockefeller, first."

"Gee, honey, I love you."

"I love you too. I turned around to turn, I meant to tie my shoe-lace, and there you were. I didn't believe it—honest I didn't. I have to be back in Tennessee on Friday—three more days. I want something to eat!" he screamed. "And something to drink!" Then he put his arms around both girls' hips, and leaned back into the soft seat.

"Right away, waiter."

"Yes, sir, certainly, sir, immediately."

The waiter brought the drinks and they tasted them.

"Listen, waiter, sweeten this up for me, make it a little sweeter," said one of the two brides of the soldier.

"So it's you he loves," she said. "Well, I can learn a new game, I learned a new game only last night. All right, forget it. . . . I want your advice on one thing. Johnny gave me this, and after giving it to me he doesn't think it's very snappy, and he said if I don't like it, to change it. So I saw something at Ballou's, it's got a round star sapphire in the center, so big, and whatchama-callits all around it. Should I get that or should I stick with this?"

"What time is it?" said the Englishman to Bushy, reaching for his wallet.

"Oh, it's long past twelve. Don't go—let's have some more to drink. What did you think of the speech? I liked it."

"Sherwood wrote that speech. Unbelievable things are going on. At the beginning of the war, there comes a man to my apartment, shows his credentials, tells me he's from the F.B.I., tells me he's come to investigate Bob Sherwood. I said, 'My God, man, that's like investigating the American flag. He practically ghosted the Gettysburg address,' 'Just the same,' says the man, 'I have to turn in a report on him. What do you know about him? Is he radical?' 'Christ,' I said, 'he's almost as radical as Roosevelt.' 'Has he any enemies?' 'Only one I know of—and he's not in politics.' Can you imagine? It's like the Gestapo."

"Let's go." They walked out, the historic figure straight. The small man stopped at the table of the Immortals and shook hands all around. He spoke in French to Monie Van Dua, and when he was gone Monie said to Buffie: "Beware of Englishmen who speak faultless French. They are either card sharps or diplomats." She wrote it down for her article with a little golden pencil which the Pope had given her.

"Look at the other one, he's so thin," said Señora Lopez.

Her husband got up and went down to the men's room.

The conveniences there were occupied by the Private of Infantry who had come with the two girls, by a rednecked Irishman, and by a sergeant. They all faced the wall, and the civilian in the middle spoke to the sergeant. He said:

"I damn near froze to death last Thursday. I just got back from Newfoundland. Yesterday I go into the office and the boss tells me, 'Go pack your bag, you're going to North Africa tomorrow.' So I say to him, 'Go pack yourself'—but here I am, and leaving tomorrow. They just don't take no for an answer."

The sergeant turned. He looked at the private and recognized him. "I thought the face was familiar," he said. "My God, no more commissions to personalities." They shook hands.

"Listen," said the private, "when we get up front, it isn't the Germans I'm going to shoot at—they haven't done a thing to me— it's one of you sons-of-bitches. I'm going to shoot every goddamn sergeant I see."

"As you were," said a voice from the stairs.

"My God, it's Charlie!"

"What—no music down here?" said the Major. He stepped down and the three men formed a ring, their arms on each other's shoulders. The nephritic oubliette of Mr. Suroya had suddenly become the shining temple of democracy, the sanctorum of the brotherhood of man. They waited until a lone lieutenant commander got through washing his hands, pulled down his jacket and mounted the stairs, and then they began to sing with the washroom attendant. There was no good song for this war, and so they sang an old one.

While Señor Lopez descended the stairs, Cyrano up above was pouring a little champagne in a glass. He tasted it and then poured some into the General's glass, who sampled it and found it right. The three glasses were filled, and the General started the battle.

"I tiptoed past your room last night. I did not want to wake you up, Chi-cken," he said.

She placed her answering shot neatly. "You needn't have," she said. "I wasn't there."

Silence.

They had both thought it would be easy, amusing, painless, and at any rate without tears.

She took his hand; she dabbed at her eyes. "Remember, Swit-hart, when we watched the acrobat on the mast of the ship, you said to me, 'That is you, up there, the acrobat, the tight rope-walker, and I am the net. I will always be there, beneath you, to catch you if you fall.'

"'I shall be there always,' you said, Swit-hart."

"But, Chi-cken, sometime the magic veil must tear. It can't last forever. When it's over, it's over."

"You said you would always be there."

"I don't like ménages à trois, Chi-cken. I have no talent for that. You have promised me that there would be no tears—I can't stand tears—and now you sit here like the Madonna under the cross."

She withdrew her hand and sat straight.

"So," she said, "that is how it is. I shall get a trunkful of the famous Erosa orchids tomorrow, like the little girls you amuse yourself with."

"Yes, it must end sometime," said the General, and he waved for the waiter to fill up his glass.

"Besides, you have Alfonso. He is a nice man, he loves you, he will look after you."

"Yes, Alfonso at least is a human being with a heart. He is kind, he has noblesse about him. He said to me in Biarritz, when we left, you and I: 'Go ahead—go with him. It isn't going to last long anyway. And when it's over, I shall be there, I shall always be there for you.' For that, one must have great heart."

"You are very right," said the General. "Alfonso is a man of understanding and great heart."

Alfonso emerged from the men's room. He sat down, and the Beauty smiled at him. The battle was over. The enemy looked at them and lifted his glass, and silently drank his own health.

The Beauty buried her nose in the soft tips of her sable scarf. The alkali green eyes were hard as she looked at Leonidas Erosa. In her head was a quick and merciless résumé of the last few months. It was efficient accounting with no detail overlooked. She added and subtracted, she calculated what could have been better, what should have been and was not, what had been and should have been otherwise. In the final statement the man, as usual in such cases, came off a good deal better than the woman.

The Immortals left in a cloud of words.

"This was the most beautiful evening I have ever had . . . but the most beautiful evening!" "Where are you going tomorrow? . . ." "We're dining at the Ermitage on Thursday. . . ." "I have only twenty cases of the stuff left, and you can't get any more. . . ." "I'm going to the hairdresser's at three, and afterwards we're going to the Pierre for something for the Chinese, I believe."

The von Despards and the Hufnagels departed. The bill had come to a hundred and twenty dollars, and on the way out they greeted the General and the Beauty with the warmth that comes of the ancient tribal security of membership in the same cave. They smiled, bowed, and waved.

The blue-gray dawn was in the doorman's eyes and ashen face, and in the street outside a dog was almost run over as the taxi swerved to the sidewalk to drive them back to the hotel.

"Also, I had a wonderful time," said Frau Despard to Herr and Frau Hufnagel. They arrived at the hotel just as the Indian came out with the Great Danes. Frau von Despard gave the bellhop on duty a quarter to take out the Schnauzer, and then they went to bed.

The General laid his knife and fork away. He was gray—he felt the first signal of an attack. He got up and walked to the foyer, and the Beauty followed him with her eyes. "Perhaps he will die this time," she thought. Virginia Vanderbilt, who nightly sang the General's favorite, "La Golondrina," sang it now as he walked out dragging his feet:

> I said adieu to all that once I cherished;
> I left my home for some bleak distant shore. . . .

Leonidas Erosa came to the stairs and looked down. "This is going to end badly," he said to himself, and pushed the door. "Now I lay me down to sleep, I pray the Lord my soul to keep. If I should die . . ."

He looked down. The stairs were there in new, sharp, optic clarity, a mathematical clear vision. Six steps down, each one covered with small cork blocks, sixteen across, four deep; sixty-four blocks, a metal strip at the edge, six times, and then a small square.

Suddenly he stood on that square as if he had been pulled down the six steps. "If I should die before I wake, I pray the Lord . . ."

A French Naval officer, whistling, sailed past him up the stairs. Below now, around the corner, were six more steps, and at the bottom stood Mr. Suroya, his hands stretched out as he often stood to protect drunks who came down too fast. "If I should die before I wake. . . . Dear God, hear me! Not here, not now. Once more let me live. . . . I will be good, I will be good, I will be good, dear God."

The stairs were sharp again, six times sixty-four small cork blocks, six shiny strips of metal, a short run, three white porcelain shells that turned, and tiles in even pattern, and then the scream, and the fall, a pain in the leg, and the vises on arms, on legs, on the neck—the merciless hammerlock. The General lay on the floor.

Mr. Suroya, who was competent to deal with the unsavory routine disasters of the washroom, lost his head. He ran upstairs and screamed.

A pimply recruit, a private of the Medical Corps, came down the stairs and took charge. He forced the end of a comb between the General's teeth, so that he would not bite his tongue. He opened his collar.

As the General came out of the attack, Mr. Suroya and the private tried to help him up, but the General had injured his foot.

The private went upstairs to call an ambulance.

Leonidas Erosa lay on the tiled floor, waiting. He fished for a cigarette and tucked it into his holder. Mr. Suroya bent down and said: "A light, Sir?"

"Naturally, I don't want a comb and brush for my cigarette," said the General.

SEÑOR LOPEZ in striped trousers and high collar, accompanied by a beautiful and compact young secretary, came to the Palace Hotel and rendered a financial report. The General received him in the salon of his suite. He signed several documents and listened to him, playing with the tassels of his dressing gown and admiring the long slim legs of the secretary.

At the end of the meeting, before he could say, "I salute you," and bid Lopez adieu, Señor Lopez, who had planted himself out of reach of the General's handshake in the center of the salon, addressed him, turning the large diamond on the ring finger of his left hand with the delicate thumb and index finger of the right.

"I came chiefly in the matter of the chef," he said. "I came to recommend his instant dismissal."

He looked at Leonidas Erosa, who had suddenly come to attention.

"My dear Leonidas, allow me to say beforehand that no one has greater admiration for the talents, the imagination, the originality of Monsieur Vitasse. It has always been an inestimable privilege to eat at your table, dear friend. In his capacity as a cook, I am the first to salute him; for the rest, he is a crook and belongs in jail."

"What has he done?" said the General impatiently.

"He has missed his profession," said Lopez. "He should have been the chief of a band of brigands, instead of just a chief," said Lopez. He reached into his portfolio for the fat dossier on the affairs of Jacques Vitasse.

"Every time you light a cigar, every time you drink a glass of Vichy, my friend, every time you engage an automobile, this robber baron holds out his red hands and takes his tribute. He collects commissions from the vegetables, the meat, the flowers, the hotel. He did it for years in Biarritz, too. He has cost you a fortune."

"You are not telling me anything new," said the General wearily. "These commissions are time-honored prerogatives of chefs and butlers, and who am I to challenge that? That is as it should be. That is no reason to call the man a crook," said the General with every sign of annoyance.

"I have said before," said Lopez, "that I understand your attachment to Monsieur Vitasse. I grant you, also, that he is not a pioneer in this form of exploitation. But there is more, my friend."

"He has been with me for thirty years," said the General.

Señor Lopez searched for some invoices. "Here," he said, "look at these figures."

"You know I don't like to look at figures. Tell me about it," said the General, handing the papers back to him. "Or, still better, don't tell me about it. I detest this kind of shabby affair."

"I will be as brief as possible," said Señor Lopez. "Before we go any further, did you give Monsieur Vitasse authority to buy provisions for the Hacienda Miraflores which are to accompany you on your voyage, aboard the ship?"

"Yes, yes, yes—" said the General.

"Allow me one more question, Leonidas. Did you evoke in him any idea about what you wanted, and to what limits he could go?"

"No," said the General, loud as an irritated child. "I always leave that to him. And stop playing inquisitor, Alfonso!"

"Well, he has prospered vastly on this business, my dear friend. Just for example, do you know that he has bought one thousand wax candles, and sixty cases of turtle soup? Look here!—Ancora Brand, Genuine Clear Green Turtle Soup with Sherry Wine."

"That is extremely wise of him. I am very fond of turtle soup. And as for the candles, you know that the electricity at the Hacienda fails regularly. What is wrong about that? That is fore-sighted.

"I salute you," said the General, getting up and holding out his hand.

"Just one more thing," Señor Lopez, "and then I will go. Surely there is dog food at the Hacienda, with several thousand head of cattle. But let that go—it's not important. What I wish to bring to your attention is the matter of the wine."

He took a bill from the dossier. "Here is an item for twenty-four cases of sherry, Sandeman Three Star, bought at a private sale— so private that only Monsieur Vitasse knew about it. This same sherry is to be had at a dozen wineshops for almost half the price he charges here. The second item is for two hundred and sixty-eight cases of Dom Perignon—I grant you it is rare, but here, please look at this, so I will not be accused later of having invented these charges. Here is a quotation from the owner of a night club— if you please—who has some of it left, and offers it at eight dollars a case less than the chef was able to get it for—and what do you say to that?"

"I will speak to him," said the General. He called for Plaschke. "Albert, get hold of the old maniac. Tell him to come here immediately."

"I'll leave these papers and bills. Just show them to him," said Alfonso Lopez, and left abruptly with the pretty secretary.

"A glass of sherry, Monsieur Vitasse?" said the General as the chef came in.

"You are very kind. Yes, thank you, I will have a glass of sherry," said the chef. He reached back to pull up the chair to which Leonidas Erosa had motioned.

Plaschke brought two glasses of sherry and left.

The General folded his hands and looked at the chef, who brushed the ends of his mustache, parted his beard, and held up the glass. He looked through the pale golden liquid, waved the glass back and forth under his nose, and finally took a sip.

"It's the Sandeman Three Star," said the chef. "It's excellent. We have twenty-four cases of it. I was very fortunate in obtaining it. You can't get it in the open market any more. I bought it at a private sale. A friend was so good as to inform me—Monsieur André Buffoni, the Sommelier of the Kiss Royale."

The General looked quietly at the chef. He agreed that the sherry was excellent. He swung the cord and tassel of his dressing gown in a circle, and said, "I have just had a long conversation with Señor Lopez." The chef moved to the edge of his seat and opened his mouth, but the General stopped him from speaking by holding up his hand. He took the dossier and handed it to the chef. "The notes attached to this," he observed, "are not my own; they come from the hand of Señor Lopez."

The chef looked at the bills and moved forward again, but the General still stopped him from speaking.

The chef, whose purple veins had disappeared in the high coloration of his face, walked knock-kneed over to the window. He held the papers to the light, examined them with small, stupid eyes, and then stared down into the park.

Slowly trimming the end of a cigar, turning it between his lips and carefully lighting it, the General got up and walked to the tabouret on which the giant inhaler stood, and placed both his hands at the sides of the cool glass. Looking down at the salamander, he said, "The manifestations of Señor Lopez have nothing to do with the sympathy and esteem which unite us. Be assured, my dear Monsieur Vitasse, that I detest situations like this one. Allow me to make another observation—I count on your services, I count on having them for many years. The methods you choose to employ, Monsieur Vitasse, are your own."

The General blew smoke rings, and the chef stared at the top of a street car below without seeing it.

"We are sailing for Ecuador in a few days," said the General, pleased with his speeches, and grateful that the chef had listened in absolute silence. "Our Villa Amelita there is as modern as this hotel, and almost as large. It stands, however, in a terrain that is foreign to you. The distances are immense, and the language difficult for you. You will find dealing with tradesmen irksome. It is not like here where you can pick up a telephone, or Paris where you could run across the street for a banquet. I am thinking only of your well-being when I suggest that . . ."

He began again as the chef's ears colored anew. "When I suggest that some of the vast responsibilities that go with running a household as large as this be put on other shoulders, so that you can devote all your time to the work that is the most important— to the kitchen. Let an intermediary worry about the provisions. Let us say Monsieur Lopez—someone who speaks Spanish—could come and . . ."

The chef turned around. He looked murderously at the General.

"I propose the following arrangement," said the General, who was angry himself. "I hate to worry every time I sit at the table and eat, or open a bottle of wine, whether you have received your proper share. You confine yourself to cooking from now on. And you stop taking money from grocers, butchers, and winemerchants! I in turn will make up the difference and add it to your salary. Let me know how much it is."

"You couldn't afford it," sneered the chef. He threw the papers on the floor and walked out of the apartment, slamming the door.

The General sat at his favorite table at the Ermitage. A saddle of lamb was sliced before him. The maître d'hôtel served some barley cooked with tomatoes. But Leonidas could not eat.

Miss Graves said, like a governess to a small boy, "Come now— eat," but he sat vacant-eyed, staring up into the lighting fixtures.

"Now I have done it," he said to Miss Graves. "Oh, the mackerel in white wine, which he makes like no one else; the fricadelles with sauce piquante, the carbonnade of lambic, the chipolata, the calf head en tortue, the bécasses flambées . . ."

She said, "Eat! He will come back, I promise you. He will be at the boat. And don't run after him. Above all, write no letters to him. Act as if nothing had happened. Don't do anything."

"But there is his cabin. You know he is very fussy about his cabin. He picked it himself."

"Cancel that," said Miss Graves; "cancel it tomorrow."

"But then he will never come!" said the General.

"He will come and sleep in a lifeboat—and like it," said Miss Graves.

"You think so?" said the General, unbelieving.

"I know it."

"You really think so?"

She patted his hand and said, "Eat!"

The General was held up at the pier while his party's passports
were examined. From the steel beams of the long, barnlike struc-
ture hung the alphabet three feet high, with "Z" far down the
aisle, an inch high in perspective. Baggage was piled along the
way. In front of the General, at the passport window, stood a
woman who looked as if a painter had started out to do a portrait
of the Beauty and had used Frau von Despard to pose for the last
sittings. It was beautiful in its details—the alkali eyes were there—
but it was badly put together. She had heavy blond hair that hung
down to her shoulders, and wide hips like a peasant. With the
spatulate finger of her powerful hand she pointed at the picture
of a little girl which was affixed to the passport. She was warm; she
raised her elbows, wiped her face, and with the concern that
Europeans have for people in uniform she lifted the little girl
who stood beside her and showed her to the inspector. The little
girl had on a soiled yellow coat, and her hair was matted.

"Mrs. Bosch and infant Hilda," said the man, and made an
entry in the ship's manifest. He smiled an obligatory, benevolent
smile at little Hilda, and then she was let down again, her coat
bunched under her shoulders and her panties showing, and stood
with her head against her mother's right hip. Just then she pointed
down to the letter "Z" and pulled at her mother's skirt. Mrs. Bosch
said, "For God's sake be quiet!" though the child had not made a
sound. She was pointing at four policemen who were coming up
the pier, with another man in their midst. From a distance it looked
as if the policemen were protecting a distinguished visitor from
the crowd. When they came as near as the letter "C" it was clear
that the man in their midst was a criminal. Two policemen held
him by the arm and two marched behind. Just before they came
to the gangway he tried to break loose. He ran for a few feet and
was overtaken. He held on to a girder while the police tried to
drag him away, beating him over the knuckles. The man screamed,
but the only person who came to his aid was little Hilda. She

kicked a policeman in the shin and cried until Mrs. Bosch pulled her away.

"They are in the second class," said Herr Plaschke to the General, pointing at Mrs. Bosch and her screaming Hilda.

"And that man with the police?" asked Erosa.

"He will be locked up," said the steward.

"They are taking him back to his country, to the Argentine," said the inspector.

"A murderer," offered the newspaperman, taking the General's picture. And the party went aboard the S.S. *Céfalo*.

"Remember what I told you?" said Miss Graves, as they walked up the gangplank. She stopped the General halfway up and nodded downward.

In the black body of the *Céfalo* was an opening; a door on heavy hinges hung out over the water and a ramp led from the hold to the pier. Above the clatter of the small wheels of hand trucks pushed over heavy iron plates and the shriek of hawsers on power winches, the General asked, "What did you tell me?"

"About the chef," said Miss Graves. "He's down there."

The General, who had never questioned anything Miss Graves prophesied, walked on. Later they stood at the railing of the promenade deck and looked down at the thin strip of dirty water between ship and pier, where the stalk of a bunch of bananas, an empty bottle, the oil-smeared halves of eaten grapefruit, and all the obscene forms of city refuse bobbed up and down.

"There he is," said Miss Graves, pointing at the chef. He was running across the planks with a foulard muffler around his neck, in a dark overcoat and bowler. He carried a board to which some papers were attached with a large metal clamp, and he held a pencil in his teeth. He ran in and out of one of the refrigerated holds, personally seeing that everything was stowed in its place.

"Now don't wave to him, and don't talk to him," said Miss Graves. The chef had seen the General, and the General had seen him, but neither acknowledged the other's presence.

The Director of the Palace Hotel came with a bon voyage

basket. Herr and Frau von Despard arrived, and the Beauty with Alfonso Lopez and an immense bouquet of the Erosa orchids.

The General had engaged the two suites de luxe of the S.S. *Céfalo*. He leaned against the railing with the Beauty, and at the last minute he tried to persuade her to come along.

"No, Swit-hart," she said, and she pressed his hand. "It is better so. We will visit you."

"Also bon voyage," said Herr von Despard. "Also, I wish I was going. Since I have left on the *Europa*, I have not felt this thrill of sailing."

Frau von Despard squeezed her husband's hand. "Also, Bubi," she said, "one day—on a day just like this, Bubi—but I don't care, it can rain cats and dogs—on a day like this we will all walk across a gangplank and sail home again."

The bow of the ship slid away and the daylight fell into her eyes. Frau von Despard blinked and dried her tears.

"Also, the coffin is aboard, Plaschke told me. And the Spanierin is together with her husband again. Also, Mama, I call it schwein-erei, a household like that. Like animals—you know."

"Bubi, he looked so—he looked so lonesome, the General. With a man like him these things are right; it always depends on the man. Lopez is the bad one."

"Bah!"

"Also, Bubi, look at that ship. Also I would not like to sail on it— for anything."

The *Céfalo* was out in the river. It was gay and awkward, dirty as a tramp steamer except for the large neutral flag painted on its side, its newness underlining the general neglect. It had two funnels, a bridge very high up, and a silhouette cluttered with loading beams, masts, and deck cargo covered with tarpaulins.

"Look, Bubi, look! Also there is the Indian with the three dogs. Also there is Herr Plaschke—wave at him—and the chef at the stern, next to the flag."

The chef was the only one who did not wave. His arms were folded.

"Also, when we sail, Mama, it will be different. I promise you," said von Despard. He walked away with his wife following him, a little to the right and half a foot behind.

The *Céfalo* progressed slowly against an incoming tide. The General and Miss Graves stood on deck and watched the magnificent panorama of New York pass them. They walked to starboard to see the Statue of Liberty, and they waited until the pilot was taken off. Two destroyers passed them and sailors waved, and the little girl in the yellow coat ran into the General and almost knocked him down. The rhythm of the machinery accelerated, the ship began to vibrate and pound, and the water changed to a deeper color.

On a chair like the one Plaschke had provided for the *Xenaide Ybirricos,* but of sturdier construction, sat the General, and Miss Graves was at his right.

The *Céfalo* slowly began to rock. The silhouette of the Atlantic Highlands rose and sank over the hand rail, although there was neither wind nor sea. As the ship's bell rang, two stewards rolled a wagon out on deck. They were engaged in animated conversation. On the top shelf of the wagon, without a napkin under them, stood rows of thick-lipped cups, a pile of saucers heavy as stones, a large can containing saltine biscuits, and a steaming zinc pitcher. One of the stewards poured hot consommé into the cups, the way one waters flowerpots standing in a row, without stopping between cups. The second reached into the can and placed two saltine crackers on each saucer. They kept on talking while one pushed the wagon and the other placed the cups on saucers and handed them out to the passengers. Everybody else was served before they came to Miss Graves and the General. They had two cups left. One of the stewards filled a cup and then turned the battered pitcher upside down. Only a few drops fell out of it. He smiled at the General and shouted to his comrade: "Julius, run down and get some more Kraftbrühe—mach' schnell!"

Miss Graves reached for the cup. At the bottom of it floated the debris that is found in the last helpings of clam broth—a gray, sandy residue. She held the cup up and smelled it. "Bouillon," she said, and gave it back to the steward.

"Never mind more soup, Julius!" yelled the steward down the stairs, and gave Miss Graves's cup to the General.

"Not for me," said the General, "thank you."

"It's good for you," said the steward.

"Thank you," said the General.

"Wait till the sea air gets you, you'll have an appetite all right," said the steward. He mopped the spilled soup from the top of the wagon with a towel, which he wrung out over the side of the ship, and resumed the conversation with his colleague.

"Who recommended this boat to me?" said the General. "It's worse than the *Xenaide Ybirricos*."

"Your friend Lopez," said Miss Graves.

An officer appeared on deck. He came closer, walking loosely with his head rocking back and forth. His hair was cut very short and parted with a wet comb, and he was dressed in a white uniform decorated with the stripes of an admiral. He was a man of unusual format: head, eyes, feet and hands, nose, ears, nostrils, teeth—everything was extra large and very simple in construction. His face was blank and pink, and he had pale blue, water-clear eyes. He advanced toward people searching their countenances as if he had lost something and they knew where it was; then he waited for a signal of friendship and, at the least encouragement, pointed his lips and then parted them, smiling like the full moon. He took the person's hand and wrapped it in his own as in warm dough. With his head wobbling, he asked questions in a resonant, warm voice, and answered with patience, after a long look out to sea, the nautical conundrums which are addressed to all ships' captains.

When he greeted the General, he assured him that everything would be done to make the voyage agreeable. He informed him that he and Miss Graves were to sit at his table; then he bowed, shook hands, and left. "Gulbransson," he had said, introducing himself; "Captain Kasper Gulbransson."

The dining room of the *Céfalo* was amidships, two decks down, the low ceiling held up by iron columns that were painted brown and gold. Old mahogany and brown leather swivel chairs were fastened to the brown floor, and this tedious and practical color scheme was relieved by olive green linoleum, emerald chintz curtains, and two Kelly green doors that led into the kitchen.

The captain got up as they came in, and bowed. The General sat to his left and Miss Graves to his right.

In the center of the room, on the first day of sailing, was a cold buffet, and everybody helped themselves. Plaschke came just in time. "No dead fish for me, Albert, please," pleaded the General. "Just get me some cold chicken, a slice of Virginia ham, a little green salad." He had a demitasse afterward up on deck.

In the afternoon, just as the General got up from his sleep, the wagon with the cups came again—the same cups in which the consommé had been served. Now tea was offered in them. The General and Miss Graves were sleeping, and it passed them by.

"Oh, God," groaned Leonidas Erosa that evening, when Miss Graves read him the dinner menu: Herring Salad; Scotch Broth; Grilled Fresh Pork Tenderloin or Cold Roast Goose with Celery Knob Salad; Cold Rice Pudding with Fruit Sauce.

"That Scotch broth is the bouillon from this morning with barley thrown in. Is there anything more revolting than a salad made of herring? I am going to starve to death on this ship," said the General. "I hated rice pudding even as a child. Oh, where is Vitasse?"

"The chef is eating in the second class. He has a cabin in the second class," said Plaschke.

"Go and tell him," said the General, "that I want a bottle of champagne in my cabin, and—you know, Albert—something simple: a little turtle soup out of the can, just warmed up. That is all I would like to have."

Plaschke came back with a bottle of Dom Perignon and a message from the chef, which said that the provisions were in the hold of the ship and the hold was locked and would not be opened until next morning.

Monsieur Vitasse was in the galley, sitting in a cozy corner which was the combination office and dining room of the cook. He waited for the chief cook to finish dishing out the food for the passengers who ate at the second sitting.

Adolfo Guzman, the chef of the *Céfalo,* was a specialist with leftovers, an economical garrison cook. He was a sergeant in that army in which Jacques Vitasse was a marshal with every campaign ribbon and the Legion of Honor pinned on his chest. The chef had made that clear immediately in the way he had walked through the kitchen, the fashion in which he had listened to the apologies of Herr Guzman and looked into his inadequate iceboxes. Iceboxes were the love of Monsieur Vitasse. One of his pronouncements was, "The icebox is more important than the oven."

Adolfo Guzman had opened the greasy doors, one after the other, of his refrigerator, and had recited the contents: "Beef, for boiling. We have boiled beef on the menu every Tuesday. And pork," he said, "they love pork roasted. Veal for steamed Kalbsbrust on Wednesday. Goose and chicken for the captain's dinner. Duck I don't have. Here is lamb, for stew, and the vegetables. And here"—he pointed at a tub in which beef was marinated—"this is for Sauerbraten on Thursday, with potato pancakes."

"Ah, yes," said Vitasse, "a kind of Bœuf à la Mode."

"Sausages they also like." He showed garlands of sausages up on hooks. "Hams and bacon on Monday. Before we get in, we have a Beer Evening—you know, music and beer and sauerkraut—mit ham and sausages."

"Ah, oui," said the chef with understanding. "Choucroute à l'Alsacienne. Very nice, very nice." He wiped his hands on Mr. Guzman's apron. He was getting hungry.

"You know, of course," said Vitasse, "in cooking, it is not the material but what is done with it. A bad cook can ruin the best food—a good cook perform miracles with practically nothing."

"Ah, yes," agreed the chef of the *Céfalo.*

"May I have a casserole, Monsieur Guzman—may I make a little dish, for you and me?"

"But certainly," said Guzman.

"And for my friend, Herr Plaschke?"

"I am honored, Monsieur," said Adolfo Guzman.

"Good." The chef put his hand on the shoulder of his colleague. "Now, while I go to get some wine from my cabin, I want you to prepare the following: One pound of mushrooms, some sweet butter, one shallot chopped, one cup of brown sauce. I see you have that there on your oven. One-half teaspoon of chopped parsley. You have all that down, Monsieur Guzman? Eh bien. As for the meat, I will cut it myself when I return."

The chef went to his cabin and returned with a bottle of the Sandeman sherry and a bottle of champagne. A table was set in the corner of the kitchen, the oven was cleared, and two casseroles waited there for Monsieur Vitasse, who removed his coat, rolled up his sleeves, and tied a borrowed apron around his middle. He expertly cut a beef tenderloin in large dice, put it into a casserole of hot fat for two minutes, drained off the fat and removed the meat from the pan, while he simmered the clean and dry mushrooms in melted butter in the second casserole. He added salt and pepper with an elegant swish, poured the right quantity of dry sherry out of the bottle, without bothering to measure it in a cup, and sprayed parsley over the dish.

"Tarragon," he said to Adolfo Guzman, "and chervil." He shook the casserole back and forth, violently, mixing all the ingredients with quick jerks.

Mr. Plaschke appeared, sat down quietly, and unfolded his napkin.

"Dinner is served," said the chef.

Adolfo Guzman ate as if he were in church. They mopped up the sauce on their plates with pieces of bread. After the bottle of champagne, Mr. Guzman offered brandy. It was sticky and sweet. Monsieur Vitasse drank it like medicine, holding his breath. He directed the conversation to his illustrious past, going back to his apprenticeship in the kitchen of the great Escoffier. He talked of ovens, and particularly of iceboxes, and of the people he had cooked for. Adolfo Guzman, who was the natural son of the proprietor of a German Rathskeller in Buenos Aires, nodded continually in agreement and took all the lessons to heart.

The General was sitting alone in the bar, with a glass of the same bad brandy. Everyone had gone to bed. There was only the dreary counter stacked with dirty glasses, and a glaring light on a loading beam outside. The bar was toward the stern of the

Céfalo; its terrace faced the superstructure which housed the second class.

A small sad-eyed man measured the deck with clattering heels. When everyone else was in tropical suits, he wore uncomfortable dark clothes. He came in and sat down at the opposite end of the room and rang for the steward. He ordered a small beer and sat with it for an hour, amidst the creaking of the ship's plates, the pounding of the engine, and the ship's bells' monotonous ringing. He chased a fly from his beer with both atrophied hands, paid the steward, and sat quietly until the General asked him about the ship.

"All I can tell you," said the emaciated man, "is that I was warned not to sail on her. But then, one is warned about everything these days and nothing happens."

"I don't see what else can happen," said the General. "The service is abominable, the kitchen is foul, the captain seems to be a halfwit, and I am told that we have a murderer on board."

"The captain is a fine man. I also thought he was a fool, and a Nazi, too; but on the way from Portugal, when we were stopped by a German submarine, he stood behind this door with a gun in his hand while the first officer, who is the Latin type with dark hair and skin, took his place and spoke to the Boches in Spanish. And those two stewards who serve the consommé stood ready with guns too—they are Swiss. It looked bad, but they let us go. Curious," said the Frenchman, "how even a boat suffers from the depressing formulas of this war.

"This mysterious ship, which sails under the flag of Argentina, never touches an Argentine port. She is owned by a syndicate in New York. Her captain, who was born a Norwegian, has Swedish papers. I am a Frenchman who left my country with a Portuguese passport. Alors, I was glad no one asked too many questions of me, and I will do the same for them." He disclosed that his name was Laguerrie and that he had been at one time the proprietor of the chairs in the Luxembourg Gardens in Paris, from the rental of which he had amassed a comfortable fortune.

Later, when Plaschke came to tell him that it was after twelve o'clock, the General said, "The old maniac could have come and spoken to me. I am so hungry I can smell his cooking." He sat on the bed and scratched himself. "Have you seen him, Albert?"

"Yes, I have seen him, General."

"Did he say anything?"

"No, Your Excellency, he didn't say anything."

"I especially sat there alone last night for an hour," said the General to Miss Graves the next day at the luncheon table, "so that he could come and speak to me while no one was around; but he didn't come."

"You mustn't go and see him now," said Miss Graves. "Let him stew in his own juice."

Captain Gulbransson pointed his lips as if he were about to kiss the General. Tapping with his spoon at the edge of his soup plate as a signal that he was through, and looking into the faces of his guests, he began to sing the praises of the S.S. *Céfalo's* cuisine.

The captain had started off with one of his cook's specialties—a thick purée of lentils in which slices of sausage floated half submerged.

"Since I stopped smoking and drinking, I eat much better," said the captain. "Everything tastes so much better. My advice to young men is never start smoking and drinking. You don't enjoy your food if you do. I lost weight when I went ashore, eating in restaurants, throwing my money away. I said to myself, why spend your good money when you can live so much better on board?"

The steward bent over the table with a thick porcelain platter of meat covered by another brown sauce.

"Taste this Sauerbraten," said the captain. "Only my mother, who was German, made it better. You won't get a Sauerbraten like this anywhere in the world. And the potato pancakes—taste them —like snow! They melt in your mouth."

The potato pancakes were soggy, large, gray-blue, and crisply fried at the edges. The General fiddled around with his knife and fork. "It's always that way the first day out. Wait till tomorrow," said the captain, consoling Miss Graves and the General.

Miss Graves picked up the menu and read: "Quesos Surtidos, Galletas de Sodas Tostadas, Frutas Frescas en Temporada."

The General wanted nothing. He held up his hands and ran out of the room.

"Give me the cheese," said Captain Gulbransson. "A nice ripe Liederkranz and the soda crackers."

Miss Graves took an orange. She went to look after the Indian, whom she found eating in the crew's quarters. The dogs were established in a kennel over a hatch near the bow. They moaned when they saw Miss Graves. She gave the orange to Anselmo and petted the dogs.

The General, who was undressed for his afternoon sleep, said to Plaschke, "Have you seen him?"

"Yes, Your Excellency, he spends most of the time on the top deck," said Plaschke.

On the day that the *Céfalo* passed the windward channel between Cuba and Haiti, and was off the Morant Cays, the sky turned yellow and brown, and the wind began to plow the water, to howl, to shriek, and to slam doors.

A blow like the first punch of an aggressive fighter sent the *Céfalo* reeling. Her bow rose high out of the sea. The storm washed the waves up her portside, blasted them to spray, and sent sheets of water across the cargo hatches. And this horizontal rain rode far out over the dark water at the starboard side of the ship.

The *Céfalo* had two separate, sickening motions. She dipped forward, and, when her stern came up, she added the clumsy, exhausting maneuvers of an elephant trying to lie down on its side.

It lasted for two hours. At seven, the storm subsided as suddenly as it had come. The noises of the wind and the sea died down, the yammering and creaking of the steel plates came to an end, and the General got out of bed, dressed, and walked on deck. The sky was aflame, preparing for the sun's setting. Anselmo let the dogs out of their cages and dried them. The stewards mopped the decks and unfolded the deck-chairs, which had been folded up and tied to the railings when the first storm warning was received.

Plaschke, who had persuaded the chef to cook something for the General, served it like a thief on a small table in the bar.

"I have been subsisting on orange juice, tomato juice, Cornflakes, and cream and eggs. My insides are like those of a baby," he said, wolfing his food down.

He drank a full quart of Pommery, and when the special coffee was served in a thick cup, but with a brandy fifty years old in an inhaler, he was again a happy man. He sat looking out over the ocean with his eyes half closed. He was in this happy mood when Captain Gulbransson came into the bar.

The captain asked the General whether he would join him in a beer. Erosa, who was warming his brandy in the palms of both hands below the level of the table, silently lifted his glass, showed it to the captain, and thanked him.

The jovial captain beamed several times at the General. He seemed drunk, or very tired; all his motions were slowed down. He refused brandy, said he never touched anything stronger than beer. A woman passed and waved at the captain. He waved back at her and told the General that he should have stayed for the "get together evening." He himself had danced with this lady half the night. He turned and looked into the mirror next to the bar, and said to the General, "She said to me yesterday, 'Kasper, you have such beautiful eyes, they make all women dreamy.'" He stuck his elbow in the General's side and laughed until the tears flooded his pale eyes.

He said that in the morning she had put one foot over the high doorsill of his cabin and beckoned like the Lorelei, and held up a small box camera to take his picture. "You see?" said the captain, and got up.

He looked into the mirror once more, and patted his short blond hair. He was often photographed, and he was so fond of his uniform, with the four stripes on each sleeve, that he always held his hands down in front and miraculously stopped his head from wobbling. The constant motions of his head seemed a sign of happiness, like the wagging of a dog's tail, like singing or whistling; they stopped when he stopped smiling.

He turned to the General. "I came to tell you something . . . I came to tell you something . . . what was it I came to tell you?" He looked into Erosa's face, searching and worried, with his head still. He lifted a huge stein of beer; and while drinking from it, while putting it down, and while reaching with the lower lip over the upper to retrieve the foam, he looked constantly at the General.

The General said something about the storm, and that helped Kasper Gulbransson. He was in his native element. He smiled again and his head wobbled. He began to tell the story of the worst storm he said he had ever been through. First, he said, there was a fog so thick that you could make figures out of it and carry them away. He modeled figures with his hands. "We had a plane on board," he began. "The fuselage was up forward, the wings and control surfaces below. Cement was stored next to the plane —tons of it in paper bags; they were slippery like a parquet floor. We got out of the fog and ran into this terrible storm. The ship almost capsized, and the cement sacks shifted, moved over onto the wings of the plane, and wrecked the control surfaces.

"I confidentially took my first officer below, and we decided to fix the plane. We worked all night. We did a good job, and after we had straightened everything out, we painted the injured and repaired parts. I ran upstairs to match the samples of paint with the fuselage on deck. After it was finished, nobody could tell that it had been broken. But the next night I could not sleep; I was tormented by the thought that the plane would take off and crack up in the air. I had a nightmare—the plane crashed and everybody aboard was killed, and I was to blame. Dishonor and jail followed. I woke up covered with sweat. We were making port the next day and so I had a midnight conference with my first officer. We worried about what to do. It's insured, said the mate, so we went down into the hold with an ax, and broke the parts we had fixed all over again. I felt sorry for those poor people who had waited for that plane down in the Straits of Magellan, counting every day. It was insured, all right—but the new parts took eight weeks to ship. The man from the company came aboard; we shook hands with him; I sat him behind a small beer. It was very hot and very unpleasant."

"Perhaps it would have flown after you repaired it," said the General.

"Perhaps," said the captain, and ordered another beer. His head stood still again. "Now, a coffin is simple to repair," he said. "Besides, this time it's not my fault. Your man, the Frenchman, wouldn't listen to anybody. He was in the refrigerator hold below while we loaded, and he knew exactly where he wanted everything. This time, the champagne cases shifted, and moved over onto the coffin."

The General was concerned. "No damage to the wine?" he asked.

"Nothing hurt," said Gulbransson, "not a case split open. Only the coffin is a little damaged."

"Don't worry about that," said the General.

"We'll take it up on the top deck tonight, when nobody is around. I have a couple of sailors, one an expert locksmith and the other a carpenter, and they will fix it so it looks like new. By the time we dock, you won't know it from a new one."

Now the jovial captain took some brandy and a cigar. He enjoyed both. When he was in the middle of the cigar, he turned to the General and said, "The shipping box that's around that coffin is broken. We'll have to make practically a new one. The cover of the coffin is split down the middle, and two of the feet came off, also a handle."

"I suppose," said the General, "the best thing would be to throw it overboard."

"You come up and have a look at it when it's fixed—you won't know it from a new one."

The husky second class passenger, Mrs. Bosch, afire with the painful patina of a new sunburn, replaced the straps of her white lastex bathing suit and rose to her knees from the mat on which she had been lying. Pressing the upper part of her bathing suit against her ample bosom, she sat back on her heels, shielded her eyes with her free hand, and asked the chef what time it was.

She shared a space on the top deck, in back of the second funnel, with Monsieur Vitasse, who was dressed in an armless gray flannel gilet. The chef's face had become as red as his hands. She repeatedly rubbed his shoulders and arms with a sunburn lotion, and asked him in return to apply it to her back, which he did with less enthusiasm than he would have put into larding a filet mignon.

Monsieur Vitasse was immune to the allures of women, even to racy, ample, and sensible ones like Mrs. Bosch.

In spite of the acrobatic séances which Mrs. Bosch performed, on a large Turkish towel spread over a mat beside the chef's chair, Monsieur Vitasse remained frigidly polite and gazed out over the sea, shaded by a white loose hat such as babies wear. He changed the position of his legs and sat plotting and planning amid the automatic drone of intake and exhaust ventilators, the strumming of the wind in the rigging, and the damp, gobbling sound of the pucks of shuffleboard games.

It was the hour of the morning when the clatter of the consommé cups came up from the promenade deck.

Mrs. Bosch rolled her heavy golden tresses into a lapis lazuli turban, placed a loose striped skirt over the trunks of her bathing suit, and hung a four-strand necklace of gilt and purple beads around her bronze throat. She got up, fished with one of her strong feet for a rattan sandal, and called for her child, Hilda— the sweet-faced, neglected little girl who ran about the ship in her dirty yellow coat held together by a safety pin. The child was left alone all day, but every morning at the bouillon hour Mrs. Bosch asked the chef to keep an eye on her, and he complied.

Mrs. Bosch descended a narrow passage to the crowded pantry of the bar steward. A windowless narrow cabin built under the stairs, it contained the steward's bed and lockers for his clothing, and the reserve stock of films, cameras, souvenirs and sunburn lotion which he sold. On a little table, neatly covered with a napkin were a cup of the first class bouillon and a few crackers. Mrs. Bosch nibbled daintily at the soda crackers and gratefully partook of the bouillon, which was not served to passengers traveling second class.

The two stewards with the bouillon wagon, out on the first class deck, were smitten with sudden benevolence for the passengers, for many of whom this was the last day on board. For once they had nothing to say to each other. They were in clean uniforms, each carried a napkin over his arm, and they fell all over each other with solicitude. They poured the bouillon out of the battered zinc pitcher as if it were the rarest wine, and whenever a few drops were spilled in the saucer, they carefully wiped it dry with the end of the napkin before handing the cup to the passenger. In their guttural Swiss German, they addressed all the passengers by name. When a child's hand touched one of them, he bent down with a smile, placed his hand on the little one's head, and embellished everything he said to it with interest and affection.

Afterwards they collected the empty cups with broad smiles, and with the little fingers elegantly held away from the rest of the hand. They stopped at each chair like doctors on a round of visits —said pleasant things, inquired after the health of the passengers, and made guesses at the hour of the ship's arrival in Colón. Then they ran to their pantry to add the tips they had collected, and in brotherly fashion divided them.

The bar steward was not subject to this sudden change in sentiment. He disliked the passengers every day and even on the last day. In his pantry, now, he was leaning against Mrs. Bosch, who had finished the bouillon and stood with her back to the wall. The steward's right hand lay in possessive fashion near her left shoulder, the heel of the hand over the collarbone, the fingers and the thumb caressing her throat. His hand slipped up on her throat to hold her jaw firmly; he pressed his knees into her, and slowly and expertly kissed her.

"Psst . . ." said the General impatiently, sitting at his table outside in the bar. He snapped his fingers several times and hissed louder.

Mrs. Bosch whispered to the steward to go and see what the guest wanted, but the ardent steward, breathing heavily, pressed her against the wall again, and in two brief short words offered to do for the General what he had so successfully accomplished with Mrs. Bosch herself the night before.

Leonidas Erosa looked like absinthe. He was pale green in the light that filtered through two and a half feet of the emerald-fringed awning over the terrace. He sat at his small table in the open part of the bar and watched the stevedores below knock away wooden blocks and remove the plum-colored tarpaulins from the hatches. He clapped his hands again and said, "Psst . . ." but nobody came.

Miss Graves passed with the little girl on her hand, and after her came the amiable Captain Gulbransson with a dark-haired woman whose voice was like that of Señora Lopez. She was introduced as Mrs. Farah. She had a small box camera, and she wanted to take a picture of the captain and Don Leonidas.

The captain's rump was encased in a newly washed gala uniform, snow white, stiff and glossy at the seams. It stood away at the hips, the elbows, and the sleeves as if it were wired. The trousers rode high above the white shoes. Captain Gulbransson put his arm through the General's, but held one of his own hands with the other, so that the gold braid on both sleeves got into the composition, as well as his richly braided cap.

"The disheartening things about travel on ships," said the General, bowing gallantly over Madame Farah's hand, "is that one always meets the nicest people at the end of the voyage." The lady admitted to a like sentiment and asked the captain to photograph her with the General. They stood together facing the camera. The only consolation for not having met her sooner was that Leonidas Erosa could feel that she was heavily corseted.

She wanted to photograph the murderer next, she said. The captain's face wobbled cheerfully. To the General he said, as if inviting him to the zoo, "Come and see the murderer. We have a murderer on board—a real murderer. He's locked up on top deck. Come and see the murderer."

But the General had no desire to see a murderer, and he sat down again at his small table, looked toward the pantry door, clapped his hands, and issued a long and impatient "Pssssssssst!"

The pantry door was shut with a loud bang. The General waited and looked at the closed door.

An old sailor came into the bar carrying a tray. He walked past the General and placed the tray on the counter. He looked up and down the bar and drummed with his finger, then called, first "Steward!" and then "Batista!" The bartender appeared and the old sailor said that the captain was sending a beer up to the murderer. So he wanted three beers—one for himself, one for his buddy, and one for the murderer.

While the steward filled the glasses and wrote out a slip, the sailor said to the General, "He's a prince, the old man. He'd give you his shirt."

He left with his three beers.

The General said, "Psst . . ." once more, and the bar steward finally came over to him and served him.

The General made conversation. The steward said that he was new at the job, having just been promoted from assistant. His predecessor had quit in New York because he did not like people snapping their fingers at him and hissing. " 'Gee, those bums make me mad,' that's how he used to talk," said the steward.

"I worked with him for two trips. He used to jump every time anybody said 'Psst.' He was the tough type of barroom steward that you sometimes run across. Once, he said, somebody called 'Pssst' and snapped fingers, and this tough steward said, 'Watch me.' He got down on his hands and knees and crawled under the table where the man who had said 'Pssst' was seated. Then he barked like a dog. That man," said the steward, "never again called 'Pssst' or snapped his fingers at anybody. When he wanted something, that man, he just called 'Steward' or 'John.' "

The stevedores were untangling the cables on the loading beams, and escaping steam hissed from the winches. Later the General called, "Steward," and Batista promptly rushed to his table and brought him another drink.

Leonidas Erosa was disturbed by the unloading. He debated with himself whether he should go to the top deck and look at the murderer. By coincidence he might run into the chef and speak to him about unloading the provisions. Their port was the next one after the Canal. "No," he said, "let him come to me!"

The loading beams trembled, the winches clattered, and the

first cargoes destined for Colón came up out of the dark hold and were placed on the deck.

The old sailor came into the bar again later and asked for another beer for the murderer, donated by Madame Farah, who had photographed him. The deck below the bar was piled high with the cargo destined for unloading in Colón, and the General finally decided to go to the top deck.

The murderer was kept in a cage, which took up half of the inside of the false forward funnel of the *Céfalo*. He was a dark, half-naked man, dressed in nothing but a pair of blue linen trousers. He was leaning back on a pile of filthy mattresses, his mouth open, snoring, his head against one of the sweating, concave steel walls of the oval chamber.

Outside of the funnel were two old sailors with a toolbox. They were busy fitting a last board into the packing case that belonged to the coffin of Miss Graves. The coffin itself was between the false funnel and a ventilator, under a sheet of canvas, repaired and painted. Little Hilda danced about in her dirty yellow coat, her matted hair hanging down her face like hemp.

The General went forward to a space on the top deck occupied by the direction finder, a hooded compass, and a steering wheel. Far ahead was land. The *Céfalo* slowly overtook a freighter a few miles to starboard. He watched a sailor raise signal flags, and he walked up and down leaning into the soft warm wind that held him back as he went forward and pushed him gently on his way toward the stern. Suddenly, passing a deck-chair, he came upon the chef. Leonidas Erosa greeted him. The chef stood up and came toward him. Forgetting his dignity for the first time, he said: "Bon jour, votre Excellence."

They walked up and down as if nothing had happened—the chef relieved and scratching his beard, nodding in complete agreement with everything, while the General discussed the problem of unloading the provisions. At Guayaquil, the port in Ecuador, two river steamers, the *Reina del Pacifico* and the *Intrépido*, would come alongside the *Céfalo* in mid-river, and the cargo would have to be transferred. Then the river boats would proceed up the Guayas River to Estación Conceptión, ten miles from the Hacienda Miraflores. There would be a few hours in Guayaquil when the chef could take a trip ashore, to make himself acquainted with the stores and commission merchants there. "You make your own arrangements, Monsieur Vitasse, as usual," said the General.

The business conversation was over. They walked past the funnel where the murderer, Manuel Contreras, was kept, and the chef asked the General if he had seen him. Señor Contreras was asleep, and little Hilda sat inside the funnel, facing the iron bars, on an upturned pail. She was playing with dolls which, the chef explained, the murderer made for her. Hilda showed several of the dolls to the General. They were made out of cloth and twine, exciting little people whose noses and eyes were as wild as the face of Manuel Contreras.

The two old sailors were putting the last touches on the shipping case, smoothing the board with sandpaper. The chef, who had never been so talkative before, explained that the two sailors were in charge of the murderer. As soon as the *Céfalo* arrived in Colón, he would be transferred to another boat and sent to the Argentine.

Pointing with his thumb at the funnel, one of the sailors said, "Last trip we had a forger. We let him run around loose, but not this bozo. He's always bragging about the people he's going to murder when he gets back home.

"Down with the rich, up with the poor, Honor y Patria!" he screams. He won't even take a bath. It gets awful hot in that sweatbox, and I wanted to give him the hose, but he says he likes it hot, says he won't take a bath. He says, 'I'll take a bath when I get back to my own country.'"

The emaciated old Frenchman, who had been talking to Mrs. Bosch, clattered across the deck and joined the General and the chef.

"It took four cops to bring him on board. We got three padlocks on him," said the sailor, looking important. "He escaped once before—it took eight carabineros to catch him—and yet there is no death penalty where he comes from."

"Whom did he kill?" asked the small Frenchman.

The sailor pointed at his stomach. "The victim was a German," he said; "it was a political murder. For a week nobody had any idea who he was, Contreras fixed him up so well. He looked awful, that Heinie. He had no face left."

The assassin inside the funnel woke up and began to sing.

"That bird—he does nothing but sing and make dolls for Hilda. Anyway, nobody knew who the victim was," continued the sailor, "until they opened the stomach and found that he had eaten in a German pension before he was murdered."

"Aha! Hasenpfeffer mit Kartoffelklösse," said the Frenchman, with a sympathetic look toward the funnel.

The sailor was displeased by Monsieur Laguerrie's interruption; he silenced him with a pained look.

"Of course," he continued, "the rest was easy. First they checked on what he had eaten and it turned out to be . . ."

"Sauerkraut, of course," injected the Frenchman.

"No, beef à la mode, with potato pancakes," said the sailor with a second pained look.

"That's how they found out that he was murdered on Thursday night. Every Thursday this German pension served beef à la mode with potato pancakes, see?

"Well, when Contreras, who is employed at the German Legation and has become fond of German food also—and regularly eats at that same German pension—sees the police hanging around, he figures that the game is up. He disappears, and now the police get busy. His track leads to Venezuela, where they arrest him, and where he escapes from the eight carabineros, and from there his trail leads straight to New York. But now the police have fingerprints and pictures, and they watch every German restaurant from Fourteenth Street up to Yorkville, and, sure enough, they pick up their man a couple of weeks later, sitting there, having himself a nice . . ." He looked at the Frenchman, and ended, "Sauerbraten."

The General, Monsieur Laguerrie, and the chef straightened up. They were about to go, when the articulate sailor turned philosopher and said, "It's funny, when you come to think of it . . . in this world everythings depends on time and place. If this bozo had killed that Kraut in Africa or in a dozen other places, chances would be he'd get a medal for it. Anyway nothing would happen to him except a pat on the back. But in the Argentine they'll give him the works."

Monsieur Vitasse said, "You must look at both sides. Who knows whether the victim of this murderer was a Nazi? He might have been the very opposite. I have among my friends Germans who are remarkable people."

But the chef got no further. His compatriot, Monsieur Laguerrie, had advanced and faced him, standing on tiptoe. The emaciated old man's thin hands were up, the thumbs and fingers pressed in one line. He held them left and right of the cook's face, where they trembled like two broad knives.

"I beg of you—to say no more. I have listened to Germans explaining Germans to me, and to Italians, Englishmen and Americans. Everybody is busy explaining Germans and why they are what they are. But to hear a Frenchman explaining them—that, Monsieur, I cannot have. I have a horror of making trouble in a place that is not my home. I am a fair man, and I will defend you against anything, but not against glorifying the Germans. I am not like you—I am not a carrot to be lifted out of the ground here and then planted again somewhere else. I am a tree with long roots, with roots in the earth, and when I am pulled out, I die.

"The Germans, they killed my grandfather, they wounded my father and made him an invalid for the rest of his life, they have poisoned the best years of my own life, and now that I could have the simple existence to which I have looked forward, for which I have worked so hard, now that I could enjoy the fruits of my labor in the last few years left to me, I am chased away to a foreign land—and some people even call me fortunate. Don't say one word about them, or I shall slap your face before everybody!"

The chef, who was experiencing his third set of emotions for the day, looked pale and beaten. He said, "But cher Monsieur, I am exactly of your opinion."

"Well then, don't call them remarkable, or like any other people. Just call them swine; everything else is fantastic flattery!"

The old sailor threw a small ax and a hammer into his toolbox, ending the embarrassed silence. He said, pointing ahead,

"Well, there's Panama. It's a nice country, but if you want to have a good time, you want to go to Mexico.

"Why in Guadalajara I had a house, I and the other guy, my buddy here. It cost us with three girls eighty bucks a month—white suits included and two wines for dinner. Two kinds of wine, French, imported, both of them.

"The number one girl I kept company with when I couldn't get anybody else. Gee, she was good-hearted. I didn't want her any more, because I had someone else, see, so I called her and said to her, 'No more money, honey,' and she said, 'Oh, poor fellow—you have no money?' I felt like a heel when she gave me back all the dough I had given her. The second girl did the marketing, and the third one cleaned my shoes—as good a shine as you get in the States. . . .

"I must go and eat now, and bring the murderer his food," he said, and the two sailors left.

The group, which had understood only half of the sailor's idyllic revery, deployed. Leonidas Erosa walked toward the bow. When he reached the stairs leading down to the bridge, the chef ran after him.

"I have a duck downstairs," he mumbled. "I could cook it with oranges, or roast it plain, and I could make you a little cold Vichyssoise first, perhaps. . . ."

"No, thank you," said the General, "thank you very much. My cousin is meeting me in Colón, and we are dining ashore."

The General slowly descended to the bridge where, with his hand around Madame Farah's corseted middle, he lectured her on the Panama Canal.

Manuel Contreras stirred and looked at the little girl playing with her dolls outside his cage.

"Hilda! Little one," he said in his deep voice, "you see the nails out here on deck, the big shiny nails?" She nodded. "Bring me a few of them. Thank you, my love. And do you see that long cord hanging there, in back of you on the wall? Ah, how intelligent you are, my sweet—that's right, move the pail over, and

stand on it. Ah, ah, careful, don't fall, little one, don't hurt yourself. Thank you, lovely Hilda, my darling.

"And now go outside and see if there is anyone in sight."

The murderer put the nails and the cord under the mattress.

"You don't see anybody? Good! Now I wonder if you are strong
and clever enough to do what I ask. You see the box out there—
the tool-box—the little box next to the big one? You see it, Hilda?
Good. Inside of it you will find a little hammer and a little ax.
Now go quickly, open it quickly, take the ax quickly and bring it
to me. Oh, Mother of God, child, be careful—be very careful now.
First look and see that nobody is coming. Now the box.—Ah! give
it to me. Oh, you are so clever, little one. And now, my love, give
me your hand, your sweet little hand." He drew her hand toward
himself and sank on his knee. "Goodbye, and thank you," he said,
and kissed it.

He put his index finger to his lips. "Little Hilda, nobody knows
about my little ax—and the rope and the nails. . . ."

The little girl shook her head sadly and solemnly.

The murderer heard the old sailor's footsteps approaching.
"Goodbye, sweet—go now." She wandered away in the filthy coat.

The sailor came in. It was Thursday, and, like everyone else,
the murderer got Beef à la Mode with potato pancakes. He ate
slowly and with relish. He drank the third glass of beer, and he
asked the sailor how close to shore they were. The sailor went outside to look and told him that they were already within the break-
water. "What time is it?" said Manuel Contreras. It was dusk. The
old sailor bent down and looked at his watch.

A short while later, on the promenade deck below, appeared
Anibal Erosa, whom the General had not seen since Casablanca.
The Consul approached with outstretched arms, the curtains of
his face slowly parting. The cousins embraced each other, to the
right and then to the left, and walked ashore. The loading
machinery clattered, and the small wheels of the hand trucks rat-
tled over the steel plates again. The Indian with the Great Danes
ran up and down along the pier. Miss Graves said that she would
have a look at the town and come back on board for supper.

"I have found a restaurant here," said the Cousin, smacking his lips and turning his sad eyes to the roof of the loading shed, "a dream of a restaurant, Leonidas. We shall have a dinner, Leonidas"—he put thumb and index finger together, to signal the quality of the food—"and a bottle of wine. We shall have a wonderful evening."

They got into a waiting Lincoln touring car, an old betasseled conveyance upholstered in white linen. Affixed to the back of the driver's seat was an imitation tapestry of the Last Supper. The chauffeur was a Jamaican Negro. They drove out into the country.

"I left Portugal two months ago," the Cousin said. "I had no idea you were in New York when I passed through. I've been here a good while now, and I still can't rid myself of a feeling that I'm in Cuba instead of Panama. That's how brief the voyage was. I left Miami at seven in the morning, ate breakfast on the plane, and lunch here in Panama."

"I prefer the old-fashioned wide oceans," said the General, "even when you cross them on ships as awful as the *Céfalo*. You have no idea, dear Cousin, how I look forward to a decent meal. I am hungry as a wolf."

"Just wait," said the Cousin, and smacked him on the leg. "Just a few minutes more now."

The car crossed over a rustic bridge and drove along the shore of a small peninsula. The driver turned into a space neatly labeled "Parking Lot." A wooden hand, with "Restaurant" lettered on it, directed them to a path.

Leonidas Erosa became suspicious. The restaurant was ahead of them, in a grove of cocoanut palms. Everywhere were flowers and shrubs in bloom, and although there was ample space, the path was straight as if laid out by a surveyor. The pebbles were divided from the grass by a long line of conch shells of uniform size, their pink mouths facing the path. A second rustic sign confirmed the suspicion. "¡¡Se Prohibe!!" is all the General could read. The rest said: "to walk on the grass, to pick flowers or mutilate bushes, to bring dogs into the restaurant, Enrique Keppelmayer, Proprietor." The proprietor, Mr. Keppelmayer, stood behind a desk in front of a large clock. He was framed in antlers, old guns and ships' lanterns, photographs of Gesangvereine, stuffed owls, a mounted tarpon, pewter mugs, and fancy walking sticks that were nailed to the smoke-stained wall.

He directed the General and the Cousin through the house to the garden that faced the sea. The choice tables of the restaurant were along the beach, in booths of latticework and bougainvillaea. The chairs were gilded. Squadrons of planes with a high metallic note singing over the drone of their engines were overhead, and an electric sign on the roof of the villa read "Keppelmayer's Café Lorelei."

"The proprietor is a very agreeable man," said the Cousin. "The food is excellent."

Outside of the house was a dance floor made of red and blue tiles, brightly lit by flood lamps that hung high up in the crowns of cocoanut palms. Captain Gulbransson, wobbling with joy, with Madame Farah on his arm, crossed the dance floor and was seated in one of the green grottos.

The Cousin seemed disturbed when he arrived. "I tremble like an aspen leaf whenever I see a uniform," he said. "I am having an awful time here. The streets are full of them."

"You're not in trouble?" asked the General.

"I was in terrible trouble," said the Cousin. "I had a horrible experience."

The Cousin told the waiter to help the General first. The hors d'oeuvres were served in darkness; the arbor was lit by a small red lamp half hidden in the foliage overhead, and the General could not see what he was eating. He took a fork and stirred it around on his plate. "Herringsalat," explained the Cousin.

The cauliflower soup, with croutons, was served out of a porcelain terrine. The General was halfway through it when the emaciated Frenchman came out of the house and appeared on the dance floor with Mrs. Bosch.

"Tiens, tiens," said the General, as they were taken to a table close by.

With as much care as if he were squeezing the tiny foot of a fairy princess into a golden slipper, Monsieur Laguerrie seated his

German companion. He helped her take off her coat. He studied the menu and made suggestions. He stroked her arm.

The soup was followed by a grilled lobster; and then, over a portable oven, the specialty of the Café Lorelei was brought to the table—a whole, crisp suckling pig, with a lemon in its mouth and with a saucer of applesauce. It appeared on the menu as "Lechón Tostado con Mojo ajo." Mr. Keppelmayer himself carved and served it. A second bottle of excellent Piesporter was poured into fine glasses, and the meal wound up with small pancakes stuffed with cream cheese, cooked in sour cream. The polite General praised the dinner with difficulty. "What a restaurant," he said.

The Cousin lit the General's cigar and then his own. While they warmed the brandy glasses in the palms of their hands, the Cousin leaned over the table and said in a distressed voice: "I must talk to somebody. I suppose I shouldn't, but I must tell you what happened. They gave me a party for my birthday, on the other side in Panama—my friends. We sat around and talked at the Tivoli—and drank—and then I went home and lay down. As you know, I sometimes walk in my sleep. Well, I woke up and there I stood, out in front of my house, in my nightshirt—and smoking a cigar. I tried to get into the house but I must have closed the door as I came out, so I couldn't get back in. So what was I to do? Fortunately there is a firehouse two blocks away, and I went there and asked a fireman to bring a ladder. I walked down the street just as I was, in my nightshirt and bare feet. There was nothing else I could do. It was late, and the street was deserted.

"I found the fireman on duty sitting in a chair, sleeping, and I woke him up, and he said he would bring a ladder. I walked back and sat down at the doorstep, waiting for him. As I sat there I felt drowsy and fell asleep; a policeman came and woke me up.

"'You can't sit here like this,' he said. 'I'll have to lock you up.'

"I told him who I was, but he paid no attention. I said to him, 'Please—don't do this to me,' and I told him it was my birthday. He only told me to shut up. Just then the fireman came with the ladder and I put it up against the house, but it was too short, so I sent him back for another one.

"'Come on,' said the policeman, 'I'll take you in anyway'—and he forced me to walk with him to the police station. It was filled with people they had arrested that night. They sat all around me—men, women, and children—but to their credit, I must say, none of them gave me a second glance. The night judge came and said, brilliantly, 'Oh, somnámbulo?'

"And then the Minister and the Chargé d'Affaires, with reporters and a photographer, came and identified me. The Minister got a car and took me home in broad daylight, with a blanket wrapped around me.

"They have nothing to talk about here. You can imagine what a nice scandal it makes for them! My picture is in the paper today, and the story also, with many details invented.

"I must say, the authorities were most anxious to keep it quiet. The secretary of the President himself ran to all the papers, but it was too late. It's always funny when such a thing happens to someone else, but when you are the victim yourself there is little humor in it. Do you know what I mean, Leonidas?"

"I know," said the General.

"My friends say ignore it, but I can't laugh when I think of the Minister and the Chargé d'Affaires, and the children running after the car, and the Chief of Police in his uniform. When I hear a motorcycle I almost faint. When I see a policeman, I shake like an aspen leaf. . . . This German restaurant is the only place where I am safe. Six months ago you could not get in here, not a table free, but now it has become unfashionable, and the people I wish most to avoid—the diplomats—never come here.

"Since I am not a professional comedian, I am of little use to my government here. I shall be promoted and then I'll be quietly asked to resign. That is what my friend, the American Chargé, meant when he said that the Service mind is peculiar, that they deem it much nicer if you fail in the orthodox way than if you succeed by a violation of the rules." He looked as if he were going to cry. "By now everybody has telephoned to Caracas. Tomorrow they will read it in Caracas. . . . It will be in every newspaper in South America. Everybody will laugh."

The Cousin became nervous. He said he had heard the sound of motorcycles.

"Are you packed?" the General asked him.

At that moment a flashlight shone into Anibal's face, and a moment later blinded the General. A policeman stood beside their table. The garden was filled with policemen.

The resplendent Chief of Police of Panama stalked through the garden, accompanied by a man from the Argentine Embassy. He apologized for the disturbance and asked everyone to remain seated. As he came to the Cousin's table, he saluted. They were here, he explained, to look for a man who had escaped from the *Céfalo*. They continued their search and went away.

"He did not laugh," said the Cousin, breathing again. "That was very decent of him."

"Of course my house is yours, Anibal. Come and stay as long as you like," said the General.

"I will make myself useful," said the Cousin gratefully. "I am fond of horses. I have also studied engineering for several semesters. I will not be a burden to you."

"I have something better for you, Anibal. You need never again shake like an aspen leaf. I will make you the Commandant of the Constabulary of the Hacienda. *You* will wear the uniform, and the others will do the shaking," said Leonidas Erosa.

They watched through the smoke of their magnificent cigars. Monsieur Laguerrie kissed Mrs. Bosch on that spot in back of her ear where the soft downy golden hairs were pulled up into her turban.

"It must be the atmosphere, perhaps the magnificent Herring-salat, the Lechón Tostado con Mojo ajo, and this excellent brandy —the benevolent medicine of all these things—that makes me suddenly clairvoyant," said the General, now completely in the imperial mood. He watched the shafts of the searchlight for a while, inhaled his brandy, and said, "I have suddenly found the solution of the German Problem—the solution forever after, Anibal."

"If you have that," said the Cousin, with the curtains of his face drawn down, "then you have something."

The General looked at Monsieur Laguerrie, who was talking earnestly to Mrs. Bosch. He was sitting sideways on his chair, holding her right hand with one of his, and moving the other as if he were conducting an orchestral accompaniment to his eager words.

"You see the example before you—the problem solved." He pointed at Monsieur Laguerrie and Mrs. Bosch. "It's very simple," said the General. "But my instructions must be followed absolutely and to the letter."

"You have my strictest confidence," said the Cousin.

"First of all," began the General, "the Germans must be ordered to reduce their number to the exact number of the French. Second, every Frenchman must marry a German woman, and every German man must marry a Frenchwoman. It's as simple as that. The result: the German women will be flabbergasted by the tenderness and gallantry of their new husbands, the Frenchmen will be flabbergasted by the felicity of their sensible new wives. The perfect happiness is achieved and at last the millennium is here. . . . You will admit," said the General, "that my plan is no more idiotic than some of the formulas that have been proposed."

They got up. The General embraced the Cousin and thanked him for the magnificent dinner. The Cousin embraced the General for the invitation to the Hacienda.

"Are you packed?" the General asked again.

As the Cousin paid the waiter, some change fell out of his pocket. He stooped to pick it up. "Yes," he said under the table; and then went to get his bag.

The very black driver of the old Lincoln had eaten and found a friend, another Jamaican, who rode back to Colón beside him. They were talking together. In the dark one could have mistaken them for English actors rehearsing a drawing-room scene.

The driver said, "I'm a Panamanian."

"Not at all," said the friend.

"I've taken out the papers," said the driver.

"Don't be absurd. Your mother was a Jamaican, was she not?"

"She was."

"Your father was a Jamaican, I take it."

"Yes, he was."

"Well, mango tree and mango tree don't make papaya."

"Mango tree and mango tree sometimes make excellent papaya."

"What are you talking about?"

"If I follow your logic, His Majesty George the Sixth is still a German prince of the House of Saxe-Coburg and Gotha."

"And his mother?"

"His mother is German also, as you will have it. You will remember she was a Princess of Teck."

There was silence in the driver's seat.

"I've got another thought," said the General, "the perfect solution. After they are all married, we'll make Englishmen out of them—absorb them, with benevolence."

At the pier, when they paid the driver, he handed them a card with the name of the firm for which he drove. "BATTOO BROS.," it read. It recommended tours and quoted prices. At the bottom of the card was printed:

> *For Richer and Poorer until death do us part,*
> *For your last ride, ride in style with* BATTOO BROS.

Under this in capital letters appeared FUNERAL, and against a large M was written

M odern equipment,
odest charges,
agnificent service

"Lord," said the General, "I forgot all about Miss Graves." They found her in the bar having a lemonade.

On the ten-hour passage through the Canal, and while the ship was in Balboa, the Cousin remained in his cabin. Mrs. Bosch and her little daughter moved into first class, by the General's intercession. The old sailor, with a wad of cotton held to his head by two strips of adhesive, hosed the murderer's empty cage and recited the moments up to where he had been asked what time it was. On the Cousin's first day on deck, the General instructed him never to make "Psst" or snap his fingers at the bartender if he wanted anything to drink.

The chef prepared a magnificent farewell dinner. At the festive table, at which Frau Bosch sat next to Monsieur Laguerrie, three cases of champagne were used up, and everybody received a souvenir menu, with a picture of the General and Captain Gulbransson.

Later, in the bar, all the wounds of the voyage were healed. It was especially decorated for the Beer Evening, the last of the series of festivities with which the passengers of the *Céfalo* were entertained. Señor Guzman and Monsieur Vitasse, both in white, with newly starched chef's hats and aprons, received an ovation as they entered the bar.

They all sat at one table. The hot sausages were served, and the sauerkraut. As long as there was champagne, the beer remained unopened. Batista, the proud barroom steward, was jovial and gay, drinking and smoking and laughing with the guests. Then the captain got up and knocked on his glass. He looked around the table, made "Psst" and snapped his fingers, and told the barroom steward to fill the glasses and to fill one for himself. Mrs. Bosch suddenly blushed under her deep sunburn and looked shyly into her half-filled glass. The captain asked the company to rise and to drink to the health and happiness of the future Madame Laguerrie.

They were married on board the next day. The unhappy steward promised himself in the future to leave second class passengers where they belonged.

Monsieur Laguerrie walked about all day with the newly washed little girl's hand in his. "You know," he said to Miss Graves, "nine times out of ten, when I have seen children, I have said to myself, 'Well, it is perhaps better not to have them'— until I saw this wonderful little poppet. . . . Call me Papa." "Papa," said the little girl. He bought her shoes and dresses and a new yellow coat in Guayaquil.

Miss Graves and Plaschke also went ashore in Guayaquil, visited the places of interest, and bought themselves a Panama hat each. The Cousin went ashore by himself in a small blue launch called *Gloria*. The General had a regal day; he suffered a Municipal reception, attended a luncheon at the Union Club, made a speech, met relatives he had never seen before, was received in audience by the Bishop, and sat closeted until late with the administrator of his Hacienda.

The riverboat *Reina del Pacifico* was anchored at the right of the *Céfalo* and the cargo boat *Intrépido* at its left. The small ships sank deeper and deeper into the water as they were loaded with provisions for the Hacienda. Two companies of stevedores carried the cargo from the hold of the liner to the small steamers. When the work was finished, the chef took a launch over to Guayaquil and, list in hand, went about among the commission merchants along the waterfront, to make himself known and to make last-minute purchases.

The General, in a new Panama hat presented by the Chamber of Commerce of Ecuador, returned on a government launch. He was accompanied by a Franciscan padre, and two serious-faced young men in dark clothes who had been recommended to him by the Bishop. One of them, Señor Maldonado, was a graduate of an agrarian college engaged to help in the administration of the Hacienda; the other was a painter of sacred subjects, by name Aloysio de Alconchel. An hour after everyone else had returned, the chef came back loaded with packages, and his launch was made fast to the riverboat.

The *Reina del Pacifico* tooted three times, the shrill whistle of the *Intrépido* cut the air, and the deep horn of the *Céfalo* returned the farewell salute. Captain Gulbransson stood high up at the stern of the ship, the sinking sun sparkling on the stripes on his saluting arm. Beside him stood the radiant Monsieur Laguerrie with his new wife. He lifted the little girl whose hair was now combed, and took her hand and waved with it.

The General waved back with his new hat, the Cousin waved, even Miss Graves; and, because everyone else did, the Indian waved too.

"It's inexplicable to me that one can feel sad about saying good-bye to an awful thing like this ship. But I feel very sad," said Leonidas Erosa to his cousin, as the strip of muddy, swift water between the *Céfalo* and the *Reina del Pacifico* widened. "And I am glad that you are here, Anibal—and you, Miss Graves—and you, Anselmo."

The dogs, free again, were on the deck outside the galley, licking the cook's hands. Plaschke was setting the table for supper.

The *Reina del Pacifico* headed for Babahoya, which is halfway between Guayaquil and the Hacienda Miraflores.

10: La Reina del Pacifico

BY THE time the running lights of the *Reina del Pacifico* were set out, the slower *Intrépido* had dropped miles behind. Plaschke served dinner.

The exhausted General decided to go to bed early. He threw half of a good cigar overboard before opening the door of his cabin. He went inside, closed the door, and threw his elbows back and yawned. Then he saw that a man was standing flat against the wall.

"Shhh!" said the man, and grasped both his arms, holding him against the closed door. "Shh—don't call anyone. Be quiet and nothing will happen to you.

"You are not going to give me away," said Manuel Contreras.

"Who are you?" asked the General, sitting down on his bed.

"Don't let anyone see me in here. Don't call the valet."

"How did you get here?" asked the General.

"Purely by accident. No one thought of looking into the coffin," whispered the murderer.

"But how did you get on board? What do you want with me? Why did you come here?"

"I am sorry," said the murderer. "I had nothing to do with it. I was carried aboard inside the coffin. I will go quietly. I want nothing from you.

"I have had no food for three days. I was inside the box all day. I came out at night and sat on top of the box. I found water, but no food."

"I will send for food. I will call somebody."

Manuel Contreras looked at the General for a while. "Yes, call someone, please," he said.

Plaschke brought food to the cabin. After a while the room was blanketed with cigar smoke.

The General found the conversation of his guest so interesting and fresh that he offered him refuge. Señor Contreras thanked him. He accepted a gift of money with sincere protest, and when the brass bells of the church of Babahoya tolled for the Mass of the Roosters, he walked out on deck and waited until the boat dropped anchor.

An Indian pushed a canoe across a lagoon, and the sole passenger, with a green, tailless parrot sitting on his shoulder, paid the boatman one real and climbed aboard the *Reina del Pacifico*. Manuel Contreras departed in the same dugout.

The parrot hung upside down from a beam in the engine room and said his repertory:

"Mamasita,
Roberto,
Filomena,
Arroz a la hora de ahora,
Buenos Días."

A family of six small monkeys, whose green ropes and leafy ladders hung down from the high limbs of a venerable bread tree, sat in a row along the topmost, moss-covered branches and blinked in the dawning light. They contemplated their fingernails, looked down at a flight of pale, flamingo-colored papagayos; with small deep sounds they moved closer together and began the hunt for vermin in each other's pelts, bringing the prey to their teeth with such practice that their golden eyes were constantly roving, and their faces mobile with the grimaces of nervous, scheming, and forever wary people.

A while later, still in the pale greenery of the early morning, with the tide coming in, the *Reina del Pacifico* left the inundated houses of Babahoya. The second day out of Guayaquil, passing through a landscape of infinite desolation, the overloaded and overworked riverboat came to a turbulent passage along the River Guayas.

Like a kite on a string, she wheeled from one riverbank to the other, while her engines went full speed ahead. She was washed aside into the trembling grasses that stood in a backwater, but she waded out and tried again to find a favorable current. The river rose, and two hours after sunrise the tide came to her aid. The trembling and the labor stopped, the voices of the waters were still, the engine slowed down, and the wet deck spaces began to smoke and dry. The captain lit a black cigar and pulled the whistle cord.

At the shrill, new sound, the monkeys jumped; they all faced west and began their simian chatter, and trampling on each other with hands and feet, they fled into the greenery.

They had given the signal of alarm. Far below, at the edge of an emerald-colored warm ooze, a herd of male crabs that had stood on tiptoe holding up their enormous, brilliantly colored right claws, waving them at passing females, shifted sideways under a rotten log. In the water, which was crowded with crocodiles, an old one looked around angrily and opened his jaw so wide that the fifteenth tooth was visible. He hissed, stopped rubbing himself against a female, slid off with a complaining grunt and plumped into the water. After that only the eyes and nostrils of the herd of crocodiles were above water as the *Reina del Pacifico* passed.

Plaschke had spent the night on deck. In the middle of the night he dragged the beaten, moldy mattress out of his cabin and put it on top of the large pine box which encased the coffin of Miss Graves, and which stood against the rail on the upper deck at the stern of the boat. He got up at seven and went to wash himself, and then he took a tablecloth and some plates and went to the lower deck, where he unfolded the legs of a card table, stretched himself, and smiled at the Indian, to whom he handed a flit gun, with instructions on how to operate it.

Amidst the capricious fluttering of ordinary butterflies, of those that have scent scales at the tip of their wings, and those that look like flying orchids and sting; amidst the hummingbirds, gall-wasps, and carpenter bees that maintained themselves in the air about him, Plaschke began to set the breakfast table. As he picked a golden insect with elbowed antennae from the honey, he felt himself stung with extreme violence. While he slapped the top of his head, he was stung again on his ankle. He ran up forward and got the Indian, who was sitting at the bow with the dogs. Handing him the flit gun again, Mr. Plaschke led him back and said, "Make Fff, Fff."

The *Reina del Pacifico* sailed on, its engine throttled down to a soft purring.

The Padre stood forward on the upper deck and said his office, the sleeves of his cassock over his folded hands, the hood shading his face.

Miss Graves stood at the rail and looked at the scenery with tourist eyes; below, Herr Plaschke watched the same green backdrop and waited for the General and his cousin Anibal.

The crocodiles lay like old logs that had drifted ashore, their simple outlines dark ovals among the fat leaves of aquatic plants. Up above them on the trees perched the black gallinazos—the thieves who waited for the chance to dig up and devour the alligators' eggs—and beyond, unconcerned, standing kneedeep in a marshy field, were the first Erosa cattle.

Anibal and the General walked around the deck twice and then sat down together.

"Now that I'm coming home, I'm a little afraid," said the General. "I tremble inside a little, I have a loose feeling near my fingertips; emotions come upon me that I have not known since I was a child—a kind of hunger, something of the feeling I had when Papa called and I received a spanking."

They looked out together over the cattle. Divorced from the thick, fragrant tropical vegetation stood six majestic cocoa palms, their sad green tops swaying. A hut atop a balsa float passed, and the dog on the float barked at the Great Danes.

"I know," said the Cousin. "I'm not going home, but I feel that way when I ride up to Caracas."

"Usually, inside, I feel as if I were twenty years old," said the General. "I am always surprised when I find out that I am really much older, and here you can see why. Look—all this has remained the same. It looked just like this when I was a child—and I know it will always be here."

"But we will not," said the Cousin.

"That is sad," said the General, and dug his spoon into the cool, pale pink flesh of a papaya.

"Lemon," he said to Herr Plaschke, "please."

The river narrowed. It was barely wide enough for the ship to pass through.

The glossy ibises fled. On the two strips of soft mud were the tracks of birds' feet, the webbed imprints of the soles and toes of frogs, toads, salamanders, and crocodiles.

"And you think of your whole life as a drowning man does, and say to yourself, has it benefited me to go away? Maybe if I had stayed here all my life I would have been a happier man. Or else I should never have come back. The melancholy thought comes over me that this is the last time that I shall see it—that I shall leave it behind forever."

"I always think that when I go home, Leonidas. And I think about my mother. I thought about it all day yesterday in Guayaquil—I was there at the beginning of my career. I thought about Guayaquil and my youth a lot yesterday," said Anibal Erosa, "and about Mama. . . ."

This talk was ended by mutual, silent agreement, and both men looked happy again. The Cousin buttered his bread and explained the passing scenery to Plaschke. He pointed out lemon and orange trees, cocoa plantations, coffee bushes, sugar cane, bamboo and balsa forests, and banana trees.

Plaschke leaned out over the railing of the ship, and looked with interest at the varied plants. The botanical display made him sad. At the word "cocoa," Plaschke began smelling cocoa, although the cocoa trees along the riverbank were only in bloom.

Cocoa to Plaschke was winter. His cold childhood passed before him—he always got cocoa when it was cold—and, with the thought of winter, a song that his mother had sung in the dark kitchen of a flat in Vienna came back to wound his heart. The song was "Kennst du das Land?" His mother had sung it in German. The song of longing for the sun of Italy had nothing to do with the tropical scenery and the crocodiles, and since lemon and orange trees passed before him, he could not long for them. In the torpid heat on the River Guayas, Plaschke heard his mother sing; he smelled cocoa in a porcelain cup, and he saw a white blob of whipped cream floating on it. He suddenly felt cold—he shook—he froze—he saw small white snowflakes falling—and then he had to hold onto the rail. He was ill.

The General and the Cousin helped him up to the rear deck. There, in the shade and the breeze, he was covered up. The Padre gave him quinine. Plaschke rested on his mattress atop the box with the coffin. After a while he opened his eyes and said to the chef, who sat next to him, "I have not thought of my mother for years. Strange that you must travel half around the world, before you think of your mother and of home."

"Why did I not stay in France and take my chances? I should never have come on this trip," said the chef. He was smoking one of the General's cigars to keep the mosquitoes away, and preparing to eat lunch. He sat in front of a packing box with a spoon in his hand, which he cleaned with his napkin, then pulled the napkin through the prongs of his fork, polished the knife, and then folded his red hands and waited.

The ship's cook came up, climbed smiling over boxes and packing cases, and put a plate of rice with a piece of meat before the chef. He stood back and watched him with a hopeful face.

The Frenchman pondered the square piece of meat for a while, stuck his fork in it, and began to cut with the knife. He changed his grip on the fork, and finally held it in his fist. With a bitter laugh, he pushed the plate away.

The ship's cook advanced toward him wide eyed. He took the plate and said, "Oh, you don't like it?" Without waiting for an answer, he threw the plate with the knife and fork in a wide curve overboard into the River Guayas, and majestically walked down the stairs.

Everybody on board, except the chef, slept for three hours after lunch. Plaschke was the first to be awakened by the roar of a plane overhead. He said that he felt better, and got up. Below, the General and the Cousin awoke. Plaschke was ordered to rest, but he stood about, made cool drinks for them and said that he was all right.

"Yesterday in Guayaquil," Anibal Erosa said, "I sat with an Englishman at a marble table, over a gin and tonic, at the Club. He told me about the Hacienda. It seems that the cacao is sick."

"It suffers from the witchbroom. The tree looks sad, the leaves hang down," said the General.

"Galo Palacios told me that your administrator is a thief. He steals your horses, he also makes mistakes when counting the cattle—instead of counting the heads, he counts the hoofs. . . ."

The General became impatient with the topic. He said briefly, "The administrator is discharged; je lui ai dit, que je ne suis pas un imbécile. Fortunately it doesn't matter whether the Hacienda makes or loses money. The income is of no consequence to me. But I don't like to be made a fool of. . . ."

After a while he added, "You know why the cacao is sick, Anibal, and why the cattle die, and the horses are stolen? You know the real reason? You want to know? All because, for twenty years, there has not been a padre near the place. That is why I have persuaded the Archbishop to send the Padre along." The General pointed to the upper deck.

"Before the Padre comes I must tell you something. Something that came to my mind yesterday, when I said goodbye to Galo Palacios at the station in Duran," said the Cousin; and he began talking in Spanish, so that Plaschke would not understand.

"I was very young when I came here for the first time. I was prophesied a brilliant career, and Galo was then Chief of Protocol. He came and received me with all the ceremonial due a Minister, for which I was duly grateful.

"There was a presidential car on a siding, to which we went after dinner, elegant, in the period of the nineties—brass bedsteads, tasseled curtains, red carpets, tufted chairs, and it even had a bidet in the bathroom. We sat there for an hour, exchanging polite phrases, and then for another hour—and then after two bottles of champagne I began to move around in my chair, and I leaned toward Galo and said, 'When are we leaving?'

" 'Forgive me,' said Galo, 'a thousand pardons. I am afraid this is stupid of me—I should have told you before. We have a presidential car, but we have not a presidential locomotive, and since there is not a hotel good enough for you in this place, and since we must wait here for the regular train which goes up to the capital tomorrow at seven, I will stay here with you. There are two beds—there is more wine—and we can go to sleep when you are tired.'

"But I was not tired, and neither was he.

" 'Would you like to play cards?' he asked.

"I detest cards—and I thanked him. . . .

"He gave me a long inquisitive look, and he said, 'What would you like to do, Señor Ministro?'—he called me Ministro.

"I told him frankly—a little annoyed—what I wanted.

"His face lit up. 'Why didn't you tell me?' he said. He put his arm around my shoulder and we walked into town, like brothers. We go to a place, it is dark, you cannot see your hand, and Galo put his hands to his mouth and shouted into a dark house: 'Nelson! . . . Nelson! . . . Nelson!' After a while an immense Negro appears, bigger than I have ever seen. He talks to him, and the Negro goes and returns with a mule and a cart the size of a small table for two in an Italian restaurant—painted green—and we drive to an abandoned Presbyterian church that was built by an American who came to Guayaquil a long time ago and started to convert Catholics into Presbyterians. After thirty years he had converted forty people—ladrones—by giving them money, drink and food, and then he gave up. The natives here don't like religions where the priest lacks the power to forgive sins. . . .

"Anyway," he continued, "the giant Negro yells into the abandoned church: 'Filomena! . . . Filomena! . . . Filomena!' We waited—and a girl comes out of the door of the church. I cannot see how dark she is. I lift her up into the cart. She weighs about a hundred and thirty pounds, and I am disappointed. She has a face that is sullen, like that of a prizefighter. I want to send her away, but change my mind when we get under a street lamp. There she is all right. Her face is dark, her hair blue-black, and soft, very soft, and her face when she lifts it is friendly, affectionate. I become very ardent. She wears white cotton stockings and the strings hang out of her high shoes; she has dressed in a hurry. She bends over to tie the laces and stick the ends into the tops of her boots. I have my arm about her, and I feel that she has a very, very beautiful, solid body. . . .

"I remember the speech the Chief of Protocol made as I left. . . . He told me:

"'Be careful—it will be fatal—you will fall in love with her. She comes from the mountains, she is from the strain of Guajara, which was the greatest breeding place for slaves. She has in her the blood of the great races of the earth. She is part Indian, part African, part white. You know them immediately—those of Guajara—and the first one you will never forget. I became immune to them only recently; I am now sixty-three—et je suis saturé avec le goût tropical, même ce qu'on appelle blanche ici. I fell in love with her—as never before.'"

"Mamasita,
   Roberto,
   Filomena,
   Arroz a la hora de ahora,
   Buenos Días,"

said the parrot, climbing with the aid of his beak along the ceiling of the ship.

"Since there is no hotel to which we can go," continued the Cousin, "we drive out of the city.

"We come to the cemetery, the most beautiful cemetery in all the world, I believe. The air was heavy with heliotrope, and the tall royal palms swayed slowly in a warm wind, and I asked Nelson to stop, but she would not come out.

"'¿Por qué no?' I asked her.

"She answered, '¡Porqué no!' and crossed herself.

"And so we drive with the Negro and Filomena for half an hour until we reach a beach. The palms sway, the moon is full and made of silver, the waves in the sea are of gold, and the sand is warm. . . .

"She takes the shoes off, and the dress. We swim. And then I see that she needs no lesson. She knows all the things in the Book of Love. Afterwards, she says that she is very hungry. Nelson drives us to a small place where we knock for a long time, and a dirty man, half asleep, opens the door. Inside this restaurant is a table and three chairs. We all sit down. She eats one, two, three cans of sardines, and drinks four bottles of beer, and half of one of mine.

"By the light of the candle in that restaurant, I see that she is very beautiful, and I take her back to the presidential car with me.

"The next morning, she is still beautiful. She takes a bath in the train. I scrub her back. She talks like a bird. And Galo says, 'Take her along, send her back when you are through with her.' The train starts, and halfway up, when we come to the steep grade where the train wobbles, Filomena turns white and gets sick. The presidential car was gold and silver—beer and sardines. . . . I loved her for a long time.

"I think Filomena was one of the few women I was ever really in love with—perhaps the only one. It lasted almost two years.

"Now it would not matter; but in those days people were narrow-minded. I am told that I would have stayed in the diplomatic service and in spite of my sleepwalking would have been a Minister, instead of ending my life as a Consul, if I had not taken her to Venezuela and married her. I married her over all the protests of the family, one year after I met her, and for me it was the right thing to do."

A shot from a large-calibre revolver punctuated the end of the story.

The arrival of a canoe, a mailboat, or a river launch was always a great event at the Hacienda Miraflores, and was usually celebrated with the ringing of a bell which hung in the slender spire of the branch chapel of the church of Nuestro Señor de las Aguas Santas.

The overseer of the Hacienda had declared a holiday in honor of the arrival of the General. He had shot his revolver into the air the moment the *Reina del Pacifico* came in sight. The chapel bell began to yammer in high, hair-thin peals, old guns placed along the road to the Hacienda shot salvos into the sky, and the leader of a band raised himself on his toes, lifted his eyebrows, and, wetting his lips, blew into a trumpet and began to intone the first bars of a barbaric potpourri of triumphal music.

The monkeys fled to the uppermost branches of the trees, and the vultures flapped their wings and rose into the sky.

The General, in one of his best imperial moods, stood at the prow, the black lock hanging down his forehead. He waved. He smiled benevolently at his people. He looked up at the festooned and beflagged watertank on which, in green and yellow letters was written:

"Viva El Benefactor. Viva Leonidas Erosa."

The fear of Papa's spanking came back to the General, and for a moment he suffered the pain near the fingertips. Coming home, he felt homeless and lost. On a spot where his mother had stood and waved farewell to him, a young girl stood now, in a dress that seemed made out of a curtain. She was barefoot and held a bouquet of flowers, and she smiled at Leonidas Erosa. Then she quickly and silently moved her lips—she was rehearsing a poem.

"Mamasita,
  Roberto,
  Filomena,
  Arroz a la hora de ahora,
  Buenos Días,"

said the parrot, all the way up on the mast of the *Reina del Pacifico*.

11. *Man in Tears*

AT ONE time the Estación Conceptión, the river port of the Hacienda Miraflores, presented the desolate aspects of an industrial suburb. It was a place of cranes, machinery, tanks, a repair shop, and an abattoir, grouped around the branch chapel of Nuestro Señor de las Aguas Santas, and ringed by abominable small houses and sheds. Now it looked like a gaudily camouflaged bombing target. Only the chapel and the abattoir had survived.

Geranium trees, studded with their vulgar brick-and-flesh-colored blossoms, commanded the entrances of most of the roofless houses. A row of them ran along the center of the torn-up trackage of the freight yard. The pit of a turntable, like a giant jardiniere, was crowded with fern trees.

A small Maffei shunting locomotive lay on its side in the volatile arms of a cotton tree, its wheels wrapped in green bandages, the boiler shaded by the thousand and one umbrellas of plants whose green hunger drew the locomotive slowly back into the jungle. In the green fire-box lay a boa and her brood, and the porous chimney blew away in wafer-thin, rusty flakes.

About a dozen of the people of the Hacienda Miraflores, who had come to celebrate the arrival of the General, had climbed to the top of a barrack-like wreck of a building. They were the first to see the *Reina del Pacifico*. They waved their arms and jumped with excitement, and scrambed down in a cloud of golden dust to run to the dock.

On the planking of a boat that was half in the water and half out of it—an ambitious undertaking that someone long ago had begun and then got tired of—they sat down again to wait for the *Reina del Pacifico*. She plowed through the last two miles of river.

Out of the white, loose Sunday blouses of the women shone throats and shoulders in all the shades of cigars and of the earth. Here and there a man stood out because of broad shoulders and height. One, leaning against the mast of the unfinished boat, had a red beard; several had livid complexions and eyes that were dulled with malaria.

A dark mother hung her feet in the water and splashed her children with them. The two little girls, who were naked, had African features and skin as white as porcelain. Standing next to them and teasing a tame ocelot was a boy who seemed to be of English parentage. His features were so clean-cut British that you looked for the line where his make-up ended; but he was indigo to the soles of his feet.

The three hundred barefoot, simple souls of the Hacienda Miraflores had one common attribute. They all possessed long, intelligent toes, a result of walking during several years of their sunny childhood up and down in a street in which cocoa beans were spread to dry on large tarpaulins. Using their feet like plows, sliding along in the beans, they turned them over and picked the bad ones out with their agile toes, never having to stoop. They could perform with their feet all the tricks of armless people.

The texts of their songs and their conversation were for the most part unburdened with the luxury of past and future tenses, and they had no need to count anything above the number of their toes or fingers.

The wonderful man who could count higher owed this accomplishment—and the added distinction of being able to read, to write, and to speak French—to the Bonnes Sœurs de la Sagesse of Quença, at the doorsteps of whose asylum he had been left at the age of two months. Don Modesto, the major-domo of the Hacienda Miraflores, referred to his people conveniently as "Indians." He himself was a halfbreed, with a small, black mustache, thick blue-black hair, and green and yellow patches on his sallow face, his hair, his fingers, and even his fingernails. The spots were the result of a labor of love. He himself, lying on his stomach, had slowly painted an inverted exclamation mark, and then the first letter of "¡Viva El Benefactor!" The letters were green with a yellow outline. The sign was nailed on the water tower.

Don Modesto stood on the wide marble portico of the chapel. He was the proud possessor of a silver watch and chain, and of a colossal revolver which dangled in its holster on his left hip, the handle forward for a quick draw. He supervised the last arrangements.

A worm-eaten confessional with its doors removed had been carried out of the chapel, and stood waiting in the center of a carpet of flowers. Several of the Indians draped the mutilated statues of saints which stood five feet apart, like lamp posts, between sections of marble banisters. A woman fastened the wooden shutters of the chapel, which flopped and ached in their joints whenever a wind blew. And when all this was done, Don Modesto looked at his watch and ran down to the wobbly dock. He threw his right leg in the air, and then his hat; he shouted a vibrant "¡Viva El Benefactor!" and encouraged the crowd to full-throated roars of welcome, which lasted as long as it took the *Reina del Pacifico* to come up against the dock, setting all the planks at an angle. A child handed the hat back to the major-domo. He put it on, jumped on deck, and took it off again as he sank to one knee and kissed the General's hand.

Then he got up, twisting the rim of the hat and looking as if someone had given him an impossible riddle to solve, and a moment later as if he had found the brilliant solution to it. Accompanied with operatic gestures, the overseer launched his speech. He spoke of the illustrious General and the long voyage home, of God, love, and his own worth. He vowed fealty to the returning master, and wished him eternal life. He ended with several profound observations about the state of the world and the blessed peace of the Hacienda. At the end of the address, and after three cheers had been given, he took Don Leonidas Erosa by the arm, led him over the planks and through the cacao street, and marched with him under a triumphal arch to the confessional at the portico of the chapel.

With the booming of the guns, the shouting of "Viva" and the ringing of the chapel bells, the Indians followed them from the ship up the street, and spread themselves over the wide stairs and portico of the chapel.

Herr Plaschke really smelled winter and breakfast now, and he thought the fever had returned. But this time it was real cocoa, stored in the ruined chapel.

The General drew the largest crowd; but those who grew tired of standing on their toes to get a glimpse of him moved over and formed several groups around the others. The Padre and Miss Graves were surrounded first. Plaschke had a few admirers, around the chef and the Cousin a small group gathered, and only a few stragglers watched the two serious men in black.

The small bell stopped clanging overhead. The young girl with the curtain dress, whom the General had seen standing at the dock, detached herself from the crowd and carried the bouquet of flowers to him. She knelt down and kissed his hand, as the major-domo had done, and then stammered a poem, at the end of which she ran back to the protection of the crowd. There she turned and smiled at him with snow-white, perfect teeth. She was a half-finished, pretty girl, of soft soles and small breasts.

The General walked a step forward from his throne, to see her better. He looked at her while he made his speech, during which the Indians slowly approached. At the end they were standing so close to him that he could have kissed all those in the inner circle without even leaning forward. A small soft hand touched him on the cheek, and then he felt himself caressed by several hands. Somebody reached up at his last words, took his hat from his head, and threw it up into the air. It was a Monte Cristi of finest weave, the one he had acquired in Guayaquil. It sailed back into the crowd, and a second later it went up into the air once more, as high as the spire of the chapel. At the third throw, the major-domo pulled his revolver out of the holster and shot a hole through the hat. The shot threw the hat off its course; it side-slipped onto the roof of the chapel, and there it stayed.

The Indians looked from the hat on the roof down into the General's face. For a few moments they feared his anger. But he did not look at his hat. The girl was leaning on his arm; she stemmed her narrow haunches against him. He asked her name, and she turned her lovely head with slow grace. The large blossoms in her hair brushed against his cheek. She looked up at him as if they were all alone, and she told him that her name was Chimène.

"What a pretty name," said the General. He asked her in French how old she was.

The girl shook her head and giggled.

He asked her, in Spanish, who her father was.

And she laughed and shrugged her shoulders.

"Anyway," said the General, "we know two things about him. . . . He was a Frenchman, and he must be an admirer of Corneille."

"And I know nothing of what you talk," said the dark girl. She thought for a while and added: "I am called Chimène because I was made along the road."

"Yes, yes, that's true."

The General laughed.

The scene, the General's face, and the laughter and the girl's grimaces, were all unconsciously mimicked by the Indians. They smiled with complete satisfaction. They had forgotten the hat up on the roof, but they suddenly remembered what day it was and began shouting "¡Viva El Benefactor!" and "¡Viva Don Leonidas!" They shook his hands, danced, picked the flowers off the floor, and showered them at the General.

The band played the "Golondrina" for the fifth time, now without self-consciousness, in sad, slow, weeping tones.

The major-domo threw his own hat into the air and shot at it twice. It fell on the marble floor and he danced around it, stomping with his thick legs. By way of invitation to dance, he pulled a colored kerchief from the shoulders of a woman, and led her through the intricate figures of the "San Juan." At the end of it he looked at the General as one in a trance, ran up to him, embraced and kissed him; then he rushed to the chapel, where he leaned against the wall, buried his face in his folded arms, and began to cry loud and bitterly, like a small child.

From the breath of the girl and from her soft lips, which were red as if she had eaten jam, the General discovered that she was drunk. The Padre came and told him that the entire population was; and the General said that he knew nothing that could be done about it, to which the Padre agreed.

Large tears ran down the cheeks of the major-domo; they slid down a wet path into his mustache. He detached himself from the chapel after his crying spell was over, shot his gun into the air, and announced that now the festivities would begin. He ordered the band for the sixth time to play the "Golondrina." The major-domo spread his arms wide and embraced Leonidas Erosa, with a face that seemed racked with the pain of all the martyrs. Holding his neck in a tight grip with one arm, Don Modesto pointed at the sign which he had painted, at the crowd, at the chapel, into the sky, and lastly at a large vessel which two Indians were bringing. Suspended from a bamboo pole, like a captured tiger, it swayed wildly as the Indians climbed the stairs with it. The great bowl was filled with chicha.

The band followed after the chicha, and automatically a procession formed. The General and his party marched behind the band, then came the major-domo and the girl, and after them the Indians. They circled the chapel twice and then marched inside, where cornbread, roast pork, homemade sausages and kettles of soup stood on ovens, benches, tables, and on boards that were placed over sacks of cocoa.

The General was offered the first dipperful of chicha and swallowed it, making believe that it was a delightful drink. The Padre bravely drank the next dipperful.

Plaschke left quietly. He ran down to the boat to attend to the baggage.

The Padre advised Miss Graves to drink, so as not to offend the Indians, and she did it with gracious discipline—she was royalty at a garden party for the natives. The chef stood in a corner, looking doubtful; but the General called to him, "Allez donc, venez ici. Courage." The major-domo in his best French repeated the phrase; and Jacques Vitasse, intimidated by the shooting, afraid of the dark faces around him and the wild leers with which he was encouraged, took one hesitant step out of his corner, and was pushed the rest of the way to the brass vat. He took the sticky cup in his red hands, looked into the revolting and still bubbling brew. It was the color of honey and smelled like stale beer. Closing his eyes, he gulped the bitter medicine and then shook as if he were freezing.

A toast was drunk to the General every few minutes. The Indians crowded around him, telling him of their circumstances, imparting freely their most painful secrets. They stuck their fingers into his stomach to get his attention; they were suddenly his closest friends. The girl claimed his right shoulder; she had folded her hands and clamped them so that her chin rested over them and she could sing innocent songs directly into his ear. The General was Godfather returned, his pockets suspected of being filled with most wonderful gifts.

The major-domo was a punctual man. He looked at his silver watch, drew his gun again, and was about to give the signal for the races to begin, when he saw the chef standing alone again in the corner of the chapel. The gregarious overseer, who could not bear anyone to be lonesome and unhappy, went over to cheer up Jacques Vitasse, his big revolver in hand. He found the Frenchman an ardent admirer of Ecuador, and of the United States, glad that he had come, a lover of all things he himself liked. The major-domo stood with his free arm around him. They drank five ladles of chicha while the cement of their new friendship dried, and they called each other "vieux copains."

At last Don Modesto looked at his silver watch again. It was high time to shoot the shot that announced the races. He pulled the trigger and found that the gun was empty. He ran outside into the light and, seated in the confessional, with the salty streaks of his tears on his cheeks, he reloaded his revolver with uncertain, wobbly fingers. He shot into the air three times to announce the cock racing. After all the celebrants were out on the terrace, a beautiful black rooster, its feet tied, was handed to the General. A man in a black silk costume, on a black horse, with silver stirrups, rode up the stairs of the portico. The General gave him the fowl, which the man held high in his gloved right hand. He trotted down into the square and waited. A fanfare of trumpets sent him galloping—he was away, followed by six other riders who tried to take the rooster from him. He wheeled his horse again and again so that the pursuers overshot him; he dodged, jumped ditches, and used his excellent horsemanship to take advantage of the terrain. He kept his rooster a long time, but eventually he was cornered, lost it, and the game began over again. After the third sorry bird had changed hands, and both riders and horses were exhausted, the major-domo came to the General, saluted extravagantly, declared the celebration ended, and announced that now he was ready to ride with him to the Hacienda Miraflores.

The General looked for Anselmo, whom nobody had seen. Someone went running to fetch him.

"No, not you," said the General to the disappointed overseer. "It is he who is coming with me—" and he pointed to Anselmo.

The Indian had been found on the stern of the *Reina del Pacifico,* sitting with the three dogs. The General told him to mount one of the two black stallions that stood waiting at the chapel. The Indian swung himself into the saddle, took the reins, and the two galloped off, down into a *quebrada,* out and up across a sugar field, over yellow, baked, camel-back ground, past marble quarries, and on toward the dense gray-green curtains of the jungle. They rode through a torrential stream that came up to their knees. The horses lifted their heads and neighed; they fell into a dancing trot as they came into the shady road; they trotted along under orchid-laden trees, under immortelles whose blossoms covered the road so that it looked as if it had been dusted with paprika. Beyond this straight, vivid red, narrowing line, set behind a row of the tall silver columns of royal palms, the old, ochre-colored Amelita came into view. They rode into the grounds between the bronze gates, over paths as orderly as they were in Biarritz, past bushes and plants green and fresh like Brussels sprouts packed into grocers' baskets. In one of the tall windows of the lonely villa stood a servant in a white coat, who bowed politely.

"The horse is yours, Anselmo," said the General. "Go home." The Indian wheeled, to ride back and around the grounds, but the General stopped him. "No, go this way, take the short way. Ride down the stairs and over the bridge."

He watched the nervous animal dance sideways and then carefully descend, skipping and sliding, the flight of six wide architectural stairs that led down from the terrace to the river where it wound below the villa. At the bottom were two bridges, long, low, easy, like the curve of a hunter's bow. It was as if the Pont Alexandre in Paris had been sawed in half, and one-half placed at the right of the villa, the other at the left. The horse approached the left bridge, then backed away, and finally got across the other. The Indian rode up the opposite side and was swallowed by the first hills.

Leonidas Erosa was alone now. He looked from the terrace at the water below, at the hills, and over the fields to the mountains. He was home; he remembered everything with clarity. He was back in the first dark tunnel of unhappiness, when the eyes had come out of his teddy bear, when life extracted its first toll from him. He recalled the detail of his mother's dress, how she had come out and consoled him on the terrace where he stood. He saw her on another day, standing in the sun, and showing him how, by tilting his head and with a little imagination, he could find a bishop's mitre, the outline of a cannon, and the face of a dead man in the silhouette of the mountains. He tilted his head now, searching for the mitre; but the mountains blurred as the wave of lonesomeness broke over him anew. He passed his hand over his eyes and walked into the house.

As soon as they were off the bridge, the Indian dug his heels into the horse's side and raced into the landscape, up the road that had remained faithful in all details to the homesick dream-picture which he had carried with him on the long voyage. It unwound itself in front of him exactly as it had lain in his mind's eye all the years he was gone. The low, smoky huts came into view, the fields undisturbed, soft and warm like the fur of a sleeping animal, and behind them the copper mountains in the fading sunlight. From the hills came the beat of drums, and the wail of the flutes of Indian shepherds.

He rode through the village, past a row of windowless, smoke-stained hovels, out to a depression in the landscape, where another such earthen house stood beside a pond. A door opened, and a man carried an old Indian woman piggy-back out into the road. Her face was bestial; she was filthy as an animal that has wallowed in dirt. She stuck out a withered arm and clutched Anselmo's sleeve.

"You," she said, "do you hear . . .?"

"Who?"

"You."

"I?"

"You go down?"

"Where?"

"To the boat."

"I, to the boat?"

"Yes, you. Is he back?"

"Who?"

"Anselmo?"

"Yes, he is back. . . ."

She made a sound like the hooting of an owl; then she said, "I am coming back," which is the Indian's goodbye, and she was carried back into the hut.

Anselmo rode on for a long time. He got off his horse at the side of a mountain, and lay down and waited until the moon rose. He found himself in the land of goodness, whose sky was of the purest blue—blue now even in the night. He heard the flutes, he heard the songs of angels, but it was all much farther away than it had ever been. Where was his young mother, where was his Indian father, where was the love of his youth, the little girl in the white dress? Only the road was there, and the mountains; everything else had fallen into the waters, together with his life. He had been away too long.

The cheated, wet, and trembling Indian lay and stared at the moon. He wept as bitterly as the drunken major-domo, and when he got up, he returned to the other dream, the one about killing Leonidas Erosa. He rode back to the old Amelita. The dogs met him at the gate, they sat with him on the terrace, and they slept alongside of him, their heavy faithful heads at the edge of the blanket on which he lay down outside the General's door.

12: The Laughter of the Indians

WITHOUT SONG or shooting, the freight boat *Intrépido* arrived two hours after the *Reina del Pacifico,* and was made fast alongside of her.

A few Indians who had heard the ship's shrill whistle came down from the Estación Conceptión and sat along the shore to watch the unloading, which was done by stevedores who had been brought along from Guayaquil.

They carried the heavy crates and boxes across the pier to a loading platform, where a wagon with two small horses waited to take baggage to the Hacienda Miraflores. Plaschke had put the General's luggage in order. He came out of the cabin and was walking down the gangplank from the *Reina* to the dock, carrying one of the General's Vuitton suitcases, when Señor Maldonado, who had been leaning against the rail of the *Intrépido,* ran after him as if Plaschke had stolen the bag. He told him that he could not carry anything off the boat, and when Plaschke asked him in his slow, correct, newly learned Spanish: "¿Por qué no?"—Señor Maldonado answered excitedly: "¡Porqué no!"

"Because not! Because it is not done, Señor! Because that is what these animals are here for, Don Alberto!" He called two of the stevedores from the *Intrépido* and assigned them to the other ship, where Plaschke directed them to the rear deck. He gave them the radios first, and then asked them to take the coffin of Miss Graves out of its box and carry it ashore. It was taken to the loading platform, where it stood alone, more important than anything else.

The Indians moved a few inches forward. They sat with their rumps suspended in air, leaning out over their knees and balancing

184

themselves like modern chairs. In this position, they looked at the coffin, carefully, studying the silver handles, the claw and ball feet, the nameplate, and admiring its satin blackness. After they had seen enough of it, they sank back and rested with their hands folded over their knees, and leaned toward each other exchanging whispered comments.

As if he were preparing for customs inspection, Plaschke had the baggage of the passengers assembled in separate, neat stacks from left to right—the General's, Don Anibal's Miss Graves's, and the small bag of the Padre. He looked at the idle Indians, walked over to them, and asked them to be so kind as to help him to place the luggage on the wagon. The Indians looked to each other with blank faces, consulted in whispers, and one of them stood up, removed his hat and bowed politely. He looked with much compassion directly at Plaschke, and slowly said to him: "Thank you, Master, but we rather not."

Plaschke quoted to himself a proverb, "Other lands, other customs," and walked back to the ship, where he disappeared into the cabins of the passengers to look for articles left behind.

After he was gone, the Indian who had spoken to him went down on his knees, putting out one hand to support himself as he leaned forward. He stretched and reached up with his right hand to the lid of the coffin, and slowly lifted it.

All the others leaned forward again and watched. When they saw that the coffin contained an umbrella and a hat instead of the usual tenant, they were surprised for a moment; and then they smiled silently, their mood changed, they got up and with dispatch loaded everything into the wagon, including the coffin, stacking it neatly with room to spare.

Mr. Plaschke appeared with the two stevedores who carried his two imitation leather bags. The Indians sat as before, but the wagon was loaded. For a moment Plaschke felt uneasy. He thought he saw snow falling again; he shivered, but it passed. He climbed up beside the driver. He looked at the Indians, who smiled at him, and when he smiled back, they all jumped on the wagon and rode along up to the chapel. "Oh, these children of nature," said Mr. Plaschke.

The return to the Hacienda Miraflores had been loosely organized by the major-domo. The first to leave after the General and the Indian was Don Anibal Erosa, who rode away at the head of the twelve horsemen. They were followed by the band, and then by the Indians, who went on foot.

In front of the chapel stood a painted, festive wagon, as long as a railroad carriage, drawn by four horses, decorated with ribbons, its wheels plaited with camellias. In this wagon, on benches, seated according to a strictly observed precedence, the upper middle class of the Hacienda returned home.

Up ahead on the first bench, next to a box with knives, forks, and glasses, sat the tall, bearded painter of holy pictures, Señor Aloysio de Alconchel.

On the next bench was the wife of the major-domo, the native electrician, and the *escribiente*. Behind them a stucco worker and a stonemason from Guayaquil, and the girl in the curtain dress with the tame ocelot, which she tried to protect from the curiosity of the three Great Danes. The dogs sat at the end of the coach. As soon as Señor Maldonado came and was seated, next to Aloysio de Alconchel, the vehicle started off.

Miss Graves was sitting in the cool church, in the confessional, which the Padre had dragged inside. The worried, kind, and honest man of God wandered about among the debris that was piled in every corner of the edifice. He lifted boards and pushed stacks of rubble away. For an hour his robe picked up dirt and cobwebs in every corner of the chapel, where he searched in vain for some forgotten symbol of belief. He heard a rooster crow above him, and climbed two notched trees that served as a stairway to the choir. He heard birds pecking, and their querulous, gurgling talk.

As he came up through a hatch, he saw a statue of the Lord seated on a throne covered with a coat of yellowish dust. It was surrounded with fighting cocks. Most of them inhabited bamboo cages; some were attached with cords to heavy stones and to the four handles of the wooden litter on which the statue was seated. The birds' breasts and thighs were plucked. As the Padre appeared, they stopped drumming on the floor and straightened up. Their blood-red wattles, earlobes, and combs were small upraised flags of defiance. They looked at him obliquely with furious glassy stares, jerked their heads, and stood away as he walked to the Image and knelt down.

Taking a handkerchief from his breast pocket, carefully, as if he were washing the face of a badly wounded man, the Padre began to remove the dirt. The statue was so worm-eaten that it looked as if someone had sprayed it with buckshot. The Lord sat on a throne of gold, and had silver sandals on his feet. He was four feet tall. The statue was old and neglected. It was not the work of the most talented of sculptors. But it was there and it was whole; and that, thought the Padre, was a good omen.

The Padre cleaned the pedestal and found written on it, "Nuestro Señor de la Portaria." The birds went on pecking yellow corn from the floor. The Padre, with furious determination, went down the notched trees and dusted himself off.

Outside the door of the chapel waited the next vehicle for the cavalcade—a landaulette. The unsteady, red-eyed major-domo, with much effort at gallantry, escorted Miss Graves down the stairs, and almost fell into the carriage as he tried to make her comfortable. He opened her umbrella for her and swung his hat down in the dust. The Padre took the seat next to her and the major-domo climbed on the box, cracked his whip and started off, followed by the wagon with the baggage, Plaschke, and the smiling Indians, who swallowed dust until the landaulette was out of sight on the road to the old Villa Amelita.

"Have patience, and it happens," said an Indian who, impeded by his wife's embrace, was straggling along the same road. They were walking in back of a swaying mare, a creature whose body seemed made of barrels, with honey-colored mane and tail. The beast of burden clop-clopped along through the scenery, flattered with shiny headstall, bit and reins, and a broad-beamed saddle in which sat Jacques Vitasse, the besotted chef, his face a ghastly purple.

Jacques Vitasse had refused to ride in the wagon with the second-class citizens. He announced that he would rather walk than ride with halfbreeds, dogs, and the like. He finally persuaded the major-domo to think of him as a person of greatest importance and a horseman. The mare was saddled for him and he started off sitting straight, one red hand on his hip and clucking his tongue. He rode in this majestic position, very satisfied with himself, for about two kilometers, and then he became very sleepy. He began to nod in the rhythm of the horse's hoof-beats, and the reins fell from his hand. From time to time the mare stopped to rub its nose on the knee of its right or left foreleg, or halted at the edge of the road to rip a mouthful of leaves from a bush. At each of these interruptions, the chef awoke, reached for the animal's neck, lost his balance, and slid down over its head. The benevolent old horse stood still until the two Indians came and helped him back into the saddle.

Since they had left the Estación Conceptión, the chef had fallen three times. . . .

"Have patience, it will happen again," said the Indian to his wife as the landaulette passed. The wise mare got out of the way of the major-domo, and the chef fell off at the side and rolled into the bushes. The Indians laughed and lifted him up, steadied him and pushed him back on the horse once more.

Almost at the main portal of the grounds, within view of the villa itself, stood a bridge that was called old when Leonidas Erosa was a child. The decaying piers of the bridge were covered with mantles of flowers. The river was indolent for half the year, and for the other half turned into an unreasonable, tumultuous demon. Its water was always icy, sweet, and rich in fish. A mile below the bridge the waters became a sluice, and beyond a semicircular silvery edge they fell three hundred feet, with a roar that vibrated in the timber of the bridge and every stone and tree that stood within hearing. Except for the waterfall, the bridge was the center of a sentimental, peaceful landscape, made for the brush of a pastoral painter.

Weary of long years of being a picturesque landmark, the hesitant complaints from its moss-covered beams inaudible in the noises of the falls, it chose the day of the return of Leonidas Erosa to fall into the water.

The bridge became unreliable under the pounding of the hoofs of the constabulary, and it gave up its efforts completely when the flower-wagon with the second-class passengers, pulled by four horses, was on its back. Mutely and with the leniency with which all inanimate things in the jungle pass away, the bridge began slewing and yawing. It ended its flight over the waters, slowly sagged, and settled. The horses broke loose and galloped away. The wagon itself rolled on its side and spilled the occupants into the river. Their shrieks were silenced by a few mouthfuls of water; but no one was hurt. Only the box with the knives, forks, and glasses was lost.

The band and the Indians, who had followed on foot, arrived at the scene as the girl in the curtain dress, with the pet ocelot clutched in her arms like a doll, was fished out of the river. The wheels of the overturned wagon stuck out in the air and slowly spun in the current. The Great Danes lay on their backs in the grass, twisting their bodies, drying themselves, and barking.

The Indians looked at the collapsed bridge and at the river. The women picked up their skirts and held them high as they waded into the water; the men took the little children and carried them on their shoulders; the musicians held their instruments over their heads, and they all passed over to the other side, where they sat in the sun to dry themselves.

The landaulette with the Padre, Miss Graves, and the major-domo arrived on the near side where the casualties stood, wringing out their clothes.

"Bi not sad," said the Padre to Miss Graves, when he saw the wreck of the bridge, "we will get across."

The landaulette was driven into the shade of a bamboo thicket. Miss Graves, with umbrella in hand, sat under a balsa tree.

The three Great Danes shook themselves and sprayed water over everyone; they barked, rubbed their noses between their paws, and ran back into the river for another bath.

The girl in the curtain dress leaned backward and shook her hair in the sun, and the wet dogs ran into the jungle. One of them came back limping and ran to the Padre, who took his right front paw and pulled the spine of a cubaya plant out of it. The dog licked the paw and the Padre's hand, and the Padre said to Miss Graves, "Dee dog is dee frend an companen ov man, no?"

"Excellent," said Miss Graves, and spent the next few minutes trying to teach him to say "the." Small monkeys in the crown of the balsa tree overhead amused themselves by throwing dead branches down on her umbrella.

The overseer supervised the making of a portable chair for Miss Graves. The stonemason cut down two young balsas with a machete, while others chopped bamboo poles and split them. During the construction of this litter, the wagon with the baggage arrived, and the sleeping chef came into view seated on the swaying mare, followed by the straggling Indian couple, still embracing.

"Be patient, it will happen," said the Indian again to his wife, as the mare came to the river with the nodding chef. Slowly, clumsily, with forelegs lifted, the horse walked in until the water was up to its knees; closing its nostrils, it sucked long, loud draughts of water and waded downstream with careful fumblings. The chef woke up when the water reached his knees. He screamed like a woman in a bad dream, sat up straight, and took his bearings. The situation slowly communicated itself to him. He wanted no advice and turned his back on the people whose hands pointed the way for him. He made his own calculations; he saw the portal on the other shore and beyond it the Villa, the wagon in the water and the broken bridge. He headed the horse into the stream and guided it to the other side where, fully awake and majestically, again with his red hand on his hip, he passed through the disappointed Indians.

The chair was finished—a seat woven out of bamboo strips and attached to two balsa logs, the ends of which fitted in yoke-like fashion over the shoulders of two men, about ten feet apart. The litter was tested by the heavy stonemason, who was lifted up and even bounced in it, to show Miss Graves how solid it was.

It was decided that Aloysio de Alconchel and Señor Maldonado were the only two people who were sober and also strong enough to carry Miss Graves through the river. They were also still wet from falling off the bridge. They bowed with extreme formality, and Señor Maldonado offered his hand to Miss Graves as she took her seat.

The chair was lifted by four people. Señor Maldonado stepped in front and placed the yoke on his shoulders; Aloysio de Alconchel supported the rear; then, one starting duly with the left foot and the other with the right, like the four legs of a horse, they walked down the bank and into the river, Miss Graves holding her umbrella high in one hand, and raffing up her skirts with the other.

They were halfway through when Miss Graves let out a scream, like the chef. Señor Maldonado, ahead of her, had sunk away in the river. The water was up to his chin. She dropped her umbrella into the water and held on to the sides of the chair with both hands.

She screamed again, long and loud, as the conveyance began to tilt sideways. The river tugged at her skirts. It seemed inevitable that Miss Graves would be dropped into the water at the most inopportune time, exactly at the spot where the current was strongest. At the last moment Señor Maldonado, holding the balsas high above his head, recovered himself and came up. He opened his mouth and stood straight and still. He took a deep breath and, turning his head, he tilted the chair again in an effort to look past Miss Graves at his colleague.

"¡Vamos!—let's go!" shouted the artist, but Señor Maldonado only stood still, with terror in his eyes. The man in back shouted again impatiently.

Señor Maldonado observed another period of silence and then said, "I am thinking."

"But why don't you move?" said the other.

"Because I can't," answered the front man.

"¿Por qué no?" screamed Aloysio de Alconchel, who was getting cold.

There was a period of silence again, after which a rapid discussion in Spanish took place.

Finally one of the horses was unhitched from the landaulette, and the resourceful Padre rode to the three people who were marooned in the middle of the river. Miss Graves still gripped the sides of the chair with icy fingers, her face mobile with nervous, uncontrolled grimaces.

The Padre said to her: "In spait ov dat, Señora, Ýu uill go di rest, bi not sad!"

Señor Maldonado begged the Padre to come closer, and as the Padre bent down to him, the unhappy man confessed why it was impossible for him to go on. His trousers had come off in the water.

"It is you who will understand, better than anyone, why I cannot go on," he yammered. He could not think of walking out of the river as he was, exposed to the eyes of Miss Graves.

The Padre found the simple solution. He placed the front ends of the litter across his horse and held them there while Señor Maldonado ducked down into the water, between the poles, and moved with chattering teeth to the rear to change places with Aloysio de Alconchel. Miss Graves watched the perilous maneuver with lips silently moving, as if she were praying. When it was completed, the chair proceeded to the other side of the river.

The Indians watched the litter and its occupant emerge from the water. They saw that the man who had been in front was now in back, and they wanted to know why. They waited until Señor Maldonado passed, and then they discovered the reason. They began to laugh. Señor Maldonado tried for a moment to impress them with his physique. He looked stern and unconcerned. He marched with measured steps, every muscle taut. His efforts brought nothing but laughter. He turned his head and cursed them—and they laughed more. He could not let go of the poles without dropping Miss Graves; he had to follow the man in front.

"Are you going all the way to the Villa?" he screamed at Aloysio de Alconchel. "You are nothing more than an idiot!" He finally succeeded in persuading his partner to walk to the nearest bush, where the chair was swung around so that when it was lowered Señor Maldonado could retreat into the foliage. He sat there like a pelican in his nest, shaking his fist and making fearful threats at anyone who laughed at him.

The Indians leaned against the palm trees, lay down in the grass, and crept about doubled up with laughter.

Miss Graves asked the Padre what the Indians were laughing about, and he said, "Ai canod ekspres mai sell in Inglich well, becos ai am not in di chabit ov spicking it." But he succeeded in telling her, with the Indian's economy of words, what had happened.

"Di trouser sink," he said.

"I have never heard you laugh before, Miss Graves," said the astounded General, as he welcomed her on the portico of the old Amelita. It was the second good omen on that day.

The third omen was reported late, by the worried Plaschke. The radio had just begun to work; the electrician was on the terrace hooking up a loudspeaker. The General was watching him when Plaschke came up and took him to some statuary, behind which was hidden the cover of Miss Graves's coffin. The coffin itself, said Plaschke, was unfortunately gone—his fault and the fault of the Indians. They had promised to take it through the river for him. . . .

"They took it down to the river carefully, and there they opened it, and told me they would carry the top across first and then the bottom. They carried the top across, and they came back from the other shore with an old woman. While I was busy unloading the baggage, they sat her in the coffin, put the hat on her head and the umbrella in her hand. They had prepared everything carefully. The music played on the other side, and two of them carried the coffin through the water. In the middle of the river they began to laugh, and they bounced the old woman up and down in the coffin. She screamed, like Miss Graves, and threw the umbrella into the water, and then she fell in. They went after her, and when they had her safely ashore, they remembered the coffin. They waded after it, but it was too late—the current was too swift, the coffin turned slowly, and then it went down over the falls. They think you are angry with them. They are standing out there in the bushes. They are afraid you will punish them."

"You know what the Indians call the moon, Albert?" the General asked Plaschke. "They call it the Dead Mother." He pointed up through the baroque archivolts. "Look at her," he said, "how soft her light is. And there, Plaschke, on the bluest sky in the world, with the last golden pencils of daylight the mountains are drawn. With a little imagination and by tilting your head, Albert, you can see a bishop's mitre, and next to it the outline of a cannon, and at the end the profile of a sleeping man. Can you see it, Plaschke? Tell them to take the cover of the coffin and throw it in the river—and give them each a cigar."

The Indians' cigars shone like glowworms under the black cedars. Silently they moved up from the river.

"The old bridge waited for me, Albert. I have brought Anselmo back to his people, Miss Graves has laughed, and the Dead Mother with the stars dancing around her sends her soft light down to me. . . . The world is full of wonders," said the General.

As they stood on the terrace, he turned a dial on the radio. Virginia Vanderbilt, all the way from the Kiss Royale, was singing "Cockles and Mussels." As she came to the words, "Through streets wide and narrow," the Indians passed in front of the General, knelt to kiss his hand, and trotted down the stairs and across the left span of the Alexander Bridge to their hovels beyond the hills.

"OH, IT'S YOU," said the chef to Plaschke, removing a blanket and sitting up. "I don't know who covered me up last night.

"I had a nightmare; I woke up and thought I was in hell or the house was on fire. And then I ran out here where it was cool, and lay down and had beautiful dreams." He added in French: "Someone was kissing me. I was afraid to open my eyes; but I know it was not a dream."

He sat under the left span of the Alexander Bridge and held his head. A man was fishing sheets of paper out of the placid waters out of the river, and Plaschke put them in the sun to dry. "It was I that covered you up," he said.

"What are you doing with my recipes?" asked the chef.

"You threw the recipe book into the water last night. We're fishing out the missing pages."

"Oh," the chef yawned. He rubbed his aching legs.

Plaschke folded the blanket and discovered that the ground was covered with money. Together they counted one thousand seven hundred and fifty dollars in United States currency.

"It's all there," said the chef, and explained that it must have fallen out of his money belt during the night.

Plaschke helped him to his feet. He stepped out of the shadow of the bridge and stood in front of the glorious façade of the Villa. He was dressed in an armless flannel gilet, around his neck was a foulard muffler, and he wore a womanish camel's hair kimono, a rubber stocking over his left knee, and gray, formless carpet slippers. As he fished around behind his back to find the cord of the kimono, the gown fell open in front and disclosed an intricate, wide abdominal belt of dirty pink rubber, on which was stamped

195

the trade name "Rassurel" and under it "Manufacture d'Armes et Cycles, Saint-Etienne, Loire." Jacques Vitasse tied the cord and walked up onto the bridge. He put both hands on his hips and surveyed the building in front of him. He looked at the water, at the bridges, at the moss and fungi covering the lower platform and the stairs.

"I will die of rheumatism here, with all that water," he observed. He studied the oxidized green Churriguerra obelisks, piers, and spiral columns that festooned the lower floors of the old Amelita. "I grant you," he said, "the house in Biarritz was a barracks compared to this."

The Villa was an altar of indulgence to every architectural caprice and whim. Not content with the play of light and shadows, the architect had filled any vacant spaces with coats of arms made of gold. Flamboyant amber-colored glass statuary was set in front of panels of red lava, and up on the cornices white figures stood in niches paneled with sky-blue glazed tile. The building was flanked left and right by the festoonery of gala stairways, burdened with marble benches and neoclassic statuary. The sun, made into a chandelier hanging from a cloud, would have turned the scene into a ballroom.

The monotony of frozen stone was eased with the play of water, which followed the baroque stairways from the sky down to the river. The display began with two plastic fantasies up above, at the sides of the Villa, where the water sprang from the nostrils of six prancing horses—borrowed, like the bridges below, from Paris, from the fountain in the Luxembourg. Under the first downward and outward sweep of the wide stairs the water disappeared in two liquid, shimmering bands—an effect obtained by sending it rippling and babbling down over twenty onyx shells. With a sound of cymbals it splashed into two small pools. It was smooth by the flat mouths of stylized dolphins that spewed it in silent silver bands into two lagoons, in which the Villa and the bridges were mirrored, and beneath the pools it rose again in arm-thick columns, up to the full height of the Villa. In its last appearance, the two descending streams poured into a pool which was set in a double row of Tuscan columns. From this round, cold bathing place the water flowed without ceremony, through an underground duct to the river.

"One must have courage," said the chef, "to build anything like this."

The sun came up over the Villa. The water turned greener and the statuary shone. The General descended the stairs, slowly and with pride. He waved his hand in greeting. He was surrounded by the dogs, and the Indian walked six feet in back of him.

The General came up to the chef and greeted him, and the dogs licked his hands and jumped up on him.

"Monsieur Vitasse, you may throw away the girdle," the General said, "and the thing on your knee, as well. One bath, and you will be jumping around like a deer. I have seen people carried here on stretchers who could not move a small finger and screamed at a draft, and a week later they played tennis and ran up and down these stairs."

"I hope so," said the chef. "It is moist here, and in a valley, and the sun comes late. Water, water, water—I feel as if gills were starting to grow in back of my ears. I swallow like a fish already," he gulped.

"Everyone would die of rheumatism here," said the General. "That is why we have the hot baths inside." He preceded the chef and Plaschke through the two rows of Etruscan columns, halfway around the cold pool, to the entrance to the baths. The doors, which were carved in elaborate, deep relief, were opened by the Indian, and the General explained, as they walked into the pool, how carefully the house had been planned.

"The doors," he said, "are all of hardwood, of lignum vitae, which grows in our own forests. The sculptor found it harder to work with than granite. The safest place, in an earthquake, is always to stand in the frame of a door," said the General. "Stand under this door and nothing can happen to you.

"Before we go into the baths, I want to show you where I played as a child." The General opened a door at one side and admitted the two to an empty room. One wall was covered with a nursery landscape—Don Leonidas pointed at it—in which a painter had rendered all the animals occupied with human pursuits. The black cat was a chimney sweep, the secretary bird a doctor, the wolf was a policeman; and a poodle chef, with the white cap on his woolly head, was stirring in a casserole.

"The poodle you see there, the one who is the cook," said the General innocently, "belonged to me. He was a dumb animal, but very kind." The chef was furious; the purple veins disappeared as his face flooded with anger. The General walked ahead.

In the vaulted room stood four silver lions, which sent streams of warm water into an oval pool of black marble. They stood on pedestals which were drowned with ornament. "This was Papa's favorite room; it has everything you need," said Leonidas Erosa. He showed the two men the steam room, massage tables, showers, and three doors over which was written respectively "Messieurs," "Mesdames," and "Pour les autres."

The General said, " 'For the others' means the *escribiente*, the overseer, Aloysio de Alconchel, and such vegetables. They can come here when no one is here and use those dressing rooms. You, of course," he said to the chef, whose eyes had become hysterical, "and Albert can come from your rooms as you are now, in robe and slippers, and bathe here." The chef remained silent at the gracious offer. He stared up at the ceiling, where Queen Omphale of Lydia sat in shining mosaic, with Hercules dressed in the maiden's costume in which the Queen made him spin for three years.

The General added, "Any time you two wish to."

The crisis passed out of the chef's eyes when the General opened another door—heavy, yellow, and again deeply carved. Beyond it was a second door, such as one finds on the refrigerators in butcher shops. It opened with a sucking moan after two heavy brass levers were thrown back. Inside was a cave which, the General explained, went back into the mountain for half a mile.

"This is the cold cave," explained Erosa. He spoke like a guide in a castle. "Here is the pipe that brings the miraculous water. You can run cold water from it into the pool. This is the valve where you shut it off. The hot water comes from the other side, in a five-mile subterranean pipe, all the way from the Chapel of Nuestro Señor de las Aguas Santas. The steel beams you see above the door support the floors of the Villa. My papa was always afraid of earthquakes, and just before he died, he got an American architect to reinforce the Villa. The floors are all of steel and concrete." The door closed with a liquid swish and a deep "oomph."

"This is a good icebox," said the chef.

Sulphur fumes filled the hot chamber on the opposite side of the pool. The floor was covered with a maroon-colored brine, and planks laid over stones led to an apparatus where the miraculous cold water was mixed with the boiling hot Aguas Santas of Tingo and sent to the mouths of the four silver lions.

The General took the chef and Plaschke out into the fresh air. The sun was bright, the fountains sang and gurgled. He showed them the outflow of the pool, still steaming in the cold air that hung over the river. It splashed from black stone below the Villa out of the side of the slope and into the river. The General turned, put his arm on the shoulder of Jacques Vitasse, and said, looking toward the Villa: "Here is where all my treasures lie. . . ."

Then he left the chef and Plaschke and walked toward the terrace alone.

"That cave would make a nice icebox," said Jacques Vitasse to Plaschke. They passed the General as they went back to the Villa. "That would make a nice icebox," the chef said, his red hand pointing in the direction of the cold cave.

The General's mood had changed. "When you get dressed, Monsieur Vitasse, and find time to look into your kitchen, I think you will find adequate facilities."

The chef was purple again. Mr. Plaschke collected the dried pages of the recipe book and followed him through a door at the side of the building.

The General wandered once more, alone, up and down the stairs and through the rooms. He rode in the elevator and stood in front of the fountains. The Villa was no more bizarre than any of the dreams in stone and stucco which people of the General's means and temperament had inherited and called home. Examples of such adoration for things curved, grandiose, and carefree stand all over the world, and water splashes among most of them. The largest indulgence is at Versailles, but it has also been used in praise of God, as in the Church of Santa Maria della Salute in Venice. The Trevi fountain in Rome is cluttered with its statuary, and the architect Pöppelman has assembled a catalogue of all its possibilities on the façade of the Zwinger Palace in Dresden—a classic example of the style after which the old Amelita was first sketched. She would have had a good pedigree, even with the glazed tile and the alabaster, had not the General's father become attached to an art current in Europe at the time of his last visit to Paris. The forms of this movement are uncertain and undisciplined, and, fortunately, they survive only inside a few old theaters, on the ornamental gates of a few palaces, and on the entrances to the Paris subway. "Art Nouveau" was mostly green and gold. It consisted of uncertain ornaments such as floating waterplants and lilies, designs like columns of smoke frozen in the air, and women dressed in veils who smiled like salesladies in a department store.

The General's father imported the Art Nouveau at the time he decided to reinforce the floors of the Villa and install an elevator. It was a green art, artistic in jungle growths, and the plants and flowers recommended it to its new surroundings. In Paris it was the height of fashion; it became the rage in the capitals of South America; and its manifestations at the Villa in Miraflores were an envied wonder, constantly pointed at and admired.

Throughout the Amelita, inside and out, sometimes coyly hidden and coming upon the visitor with the sudden surprise of their commercial smiles, the full-bosomed women danced in their sheer veils. Sculptured in onyx, they hid along the walks and played tag on fountains. In bronze, inside the Villa, they held up lighting fixtures; and they smiled from the wire mesh of the elevator shafts at the passengers who entered the golden cage. In wood, two of them bent down and lit the fire on the mantelpiece in the salon. Out of love for his father, the General left them. He gave away or hid only the movable objects which they adorned, and to which the Art Nouveau should have been confined, such as book ends, ash trays, and umbrella stands.

Later in the morning, the General took Miss Graves on a tour of the Villa, through the ballroom, the music salon, the library, the grand salon, the petit salon. In the dark unused apartments of his parents, he showed her the bed in which he was born. His mother's rosary still hung over one of the posts. The Villa, like its humble sister in Biarritz, was an auctioneer's paradise, only here the objects were harder to move. Everything was built to outlast time. Adjoining the bedroom was a private chapel dedicated to the Virgin, who smiled down out of a pale pink sky, surrounded by pastry angels flying above faint pastel landscapes which pictured his mother's birthplace.

The altar resembled a Russian Easter egg. It was tufted, lacy, bespangled and alight with ribbed Gothic spires that were stuck on it like candles, and covered with small golden doors inlaid with miniatures.

The Padre brought the statue of the Madonna which the General had taken to Biarritz, and put it back in its old niche. The trinkets and other holy articles were also restored to their places. The General knelt on the priedieu and prayed silently. He took holy water from the silver turtleshell.

The Padre informed him that he had good and bad news. The new administrator, Señor Maldonado, unable to bear the memory of the Indians' laughter, had given him a letter of resignation to deliver to the General, with his regrets, and left on the *Reina del Pacifico*. The good news was that Aloysio de Alconchel was already at work restoring the statue of Nuestro Señor de la Portaria.

The General was explaining to Miss Graves a mural on the ceiling of his dressing-room—one of six paintings of the Education of Achilles—when Plaschke came and told him that the chef wanted to know where the iceboxes were.

"I suppose," said the General without looking down from the ceiling, "I shall have to send for a detective to show him where the oven is. Tell the old maniac to open the door on which is written 'Refrigerator' and he will see the icebox."

Jacques Vitasse was rosy and sweating with kitchen warmth. He was sharpening knives and screaming happily at his assistant and at several women, when Plaschke came in and told him where the icebox was.

"Oh," said the chef, "he calls that the icebox. Oh, pardon me—that is the icebox. That makes me laugh, alors." He laughed bitterly. "I wish he would come down here and look at it." He waved the knife. "I would like to show him . . .

"Follow me, come with me!" he screamed at two Indians. "Here, pick up these two boxes first—and come with me. I wish he would come down here, so he could see what I am doing. Come with me! And you too, Monsieur Plaschke—come with us." He knotted the serviette around his neck and adjusted his chef's cap.

He was purple again; with the carving knife in hand, he walked out and down the festive stairway, followed by the Indians and Plaschke. In his dirty kitchen shoes, misshapen from use and one of them mutilated with a razor blade to accommodate a bunion, in his black-and-white-checked cooking trousers, he walked through the marble bath, opened the outer and the inner door to the cold cave with sudden, determined jerks, and, pointing at the Indians with the knife, he said to Plaschke, "Tell them that I want everything that is in the kitchen, in the boxes, brought down here pronto!"

"Yes, but the General said . . . the pool . . ." began Plaschke.

The chef's wrath colored him—he was purple in half a second. "The pool, Plaschke, I spit in. Tell him that. Tell him I want everything down here, in this icebox. I want iron hooks on the wall there, a lock on the door, storage closets, shelves for the wine, a fan to turn the air!" He showed the Indians where he wanted the boxes. "And if he cannot bear the sight of 'the others' going through his miraculous bath, then let him get the madman who built this house and let him break a hole through the ceiling of this cave up to my kitchen and put a ladder there!" He said this long piece in one breath. He took enough air to continue his tirade in a changed and pathetic tone:

"I am a simple man, Monsieur Plaschke. I don't even ask for a stairway, I dispense with fountains and statuary." Then he ended by screaming suddenly: "Tell him that the poodle who is dressed up as a chef would like to have a wooden ladder so he can get into his icebox without disturbing His Holiness! Oh, good God!" he said like an actor, in a fourth variation of his many voices.

"Why didn't Jacques Vitasse stay in France, and take his chances!"

The Indian who cleaned the pool had barely erased the traces of the chef's shoes and of the bare feet of the Indians, when the General entered with Miss Graves.

"In the mosaic on the ceiling, Miss Graves, you see the Rouet d'Omphale illustrated. This was Papa's favorite room. Papa was always scared of earthquakes," recited the General, "and just before he died . . ." At that moment the two Indians returned, each one carrying two cases containing fifty cans each of Captain Cook's famous herrings in tomato sauce. They walked silently through the room. The first one put his load down and opened the outer door, and then the inner, and both of them disappeared into the cave.

"You cannot teach Indians ever to close doors," said the General to Miss Graves. He walked to the cold cave, shut the door, and pulled the two levers that locked it. "The hot and cold water," continued the General, "are mixed here in this room"—he opened the door to the hot chamber. While they were in there, Plaschke came and announced luncheon.

The strained relations between the General and his chef were reflected in the mildewed, lukewarm Vichyssoise, in soapy strips of larding bacon sloppily left tied to the breast of birds, and in the soufflé that stuck to the spoon with which Plaschke served it. The General made faces but he said nothing.

After luncheon he sat with Miss Graves in a small green summerhouse and smoked. The Padre declined the cigar and brandy. When the General went to take his nap, the Padre excused himself. He rode away, back through the stream, to the Estación Concepción. The statue of Nuestro Señor de la Portaria was emerging from the dirt, with flakes of gold shining on its wooden mantle.

Around three, Plaschke drew the curtains. The General sat up and said, "Albert, go down to the pool. Inside the cave, if they are not dead, you will find two shivering Indians. Let them out, and tell Jacques with the red hands, for once and for all, to keep out of my pool."

The good-hearted Plaschke ran down the stairs as fast as he could, to let the Indians out of the cave. But the Indians were already set free. The outer door was open, and from the inner, which was part open, came a shaft of light. The startled Plaschke advanced, and high above him, unreal, in the triangular space at the top of the half-open door, he saw part of the chef's face: half of the nose, the chin, and the malicious mouth under the black mustache. The chef was enjoying himself. The cave was brightly lighted with a string of electric bulbs; it was immense like the inside of a circus tent. The chef, with his foulard muffler around his throat and a tape measure in his hand, was standing on the cold water valve, directing the activities of a dozen people. The electrician stood looking up at him and translated his plans to a carpenter. The Indians stacked cases against the wall containing boxes of sardines and anchovies.

The chef greeted Plaschke with a great show of pride in his icebox. "Look," he said, "the vegetables here, the hors d'œuvres there—I have one thousand cans of petits pois alone. He thinks," said the chef, "that I brought along the material for a dinner for eight people in the country. I would like to hear him yell when something he asks for six months from now is missing, or gone bad. He will accuse me of stealing again. He keeps track of every cent I spend—and that is why I want a steel closet here with a strong lock for the caviar and the pâté foie gras. You understand . . . hooks over there for the hams," he said to the electrician. "And another lock on the outside door." The electrician nodded.

Plaschke said that everything was admirably arranged. He praised the chef's courage and intelligence. The chef crowed; he asked the electrician for the time, and said that it was enough for one day. "Clean up," he yelled at the Indians; "tomorrow we will continue, tomorrow we will also start with the wine cellar, which is here." He pointed to a huge recess in the cave.

Plaschke ran upstairs again, pasted his hair down on his flat head, and delayed the General as much as he could.

"Did you speak to him?" asked the General. Plaschke nodded.

The General and his cousin later descended like two Romans in white togas. They hung in the buoyant brine like two frogs with all four limbs stretched, and floated about. The lions spewed warm water on them. Later, after they had been rubbed and rested, the General told his cousin about his victory over the chef.

The sun, as it sank along the side of the bishop's mitre, cast the shadow of the agonized Laocoön across the terrace. The General leaned against the balustrade; he was in the highest of his imperial moods. Still in his robe, he put the binoculars to his eyes and surveyed his land. The old Amelita was the perfect retreat for a sovereign. Every wish was fulfilled here—above all, his wish for the happiness of his people.

Leonidas Erosa invented a new and lovely world. He called Plaschke and gave him the glasses and explained it to him. "Look over there, beyond that depression in the landscape. On windless days you see columns of smoke rising from their houses. There, Albert, live the Indians, in a democracy unattained elsewhere in this world, without fear of tomorrow, with the assurance that things will never change for them."

Plaschke hesitantly adjusted the glasses to his eyes. He looked beyond the white peacocks and the promiscuous birds of paradise, beyond a high fence of ancient yews that had been acclimated with patience and trimmed by a landscape architect in self-indulgent, grandiose lines that were sympathetic to the baroque façade of the Villa and the silhouette of the mountains. Plaschke saw a woman, her neck behung with two strands of golden beads, leading a cow through a field and down to the river. The General continued his idyll.

The men earned twenty reals a day, and they were happy because they had many children. No mother ever said "My poor boy" here. Each day was a vivid picture in greens, with the sun, a cow, or a little rooster painted into it. They never repaired their houses, because it was much easier to build new ones out of the earth on which they stood. The streams were filled with fish, the forests with game, chicken was their monotonous everyday diet. And on Sunday they cooked a simple red soup, their specialty, made of the things that grow around them, and ate it out of wooden bowls, with silver spoons, sitting inside their houses in the same position as they had sat when the coffin of Miss Graves appeared. They drank Agua Gloriada, a mixture of rum and water.

They spoke in melodious low voices; no one was impolite; and for three hours at noon there was not a sound in the village. For love they rolled in the grass, and after submitting to its brief sweet agony they slept under trees in each other's arms until the drumming of the rain on the grandiose foliage woke them. They laughed easily and were never engrossed in troublesome thought.

Everything was done by hand, as slowly as possible and with the delightful, spine-tingling idea of doing as little as possible of the little work assigned to them. Because they took promises for polite conversation, they were all the more delighted when anyone kept a promise given them. And now, since the Padre had come, they could look forward even to dying. He would tell them of the joys of the Heavenly Kingdom, and Aloysio de Alconchel would paint it for them so they could see that it exists.

"Sometimes," said the General, "I wish that I were an Indian, Albert. I have never seen one of them worried—they have nothing to worry about. They lack the talent for it; they are free as the birds. They never cry, not even when they are babies. What have we got for dinner, Albert?"

Plaschke pulled a pad from his pocket and read the menu:

CRÊPE AUX OEUFS DE STERLET

CONSOMMÉ SANTA MARIA

SOUFFLÉ D'ÉCREVISSES

AGNEAU À L'ÉCOSSAISE

SALADE LORETTE

LE BISQUIT GLACÉ AUX PERLES DES ALPES

FRIANDISES

"He's formidable, that chef," said Leonidas Erosa. "Here one day, wastes half his day annoying me, and serves a dinner like that at the end. It was lucky I brought him along. Can you imagine what it would be without him? Albert, can you imagine? You know how it would be—it would be awful. Hungry, Albert? Start serving dinner. . . ."

"The dinner was superb. I had my doubts about the lamb, but my respects to the chef. Take a glass of wine down to the old maniac," said the General, "and tell him I am grateful."

The dinner was served on the terrace to music from New York —from the Waldorf's Starlight Roof—at a table with four Hepple-white chairs, in the light of a dozen candles in a silver tree chandelier which rose from the center of the table. The English schoolboy with the indigo skin helped for the first time. He showed great promise. He bowed in snow-white linen, and walked on his toes in unaccustomed shoes. He lit the Padre's cigarette, and opened the door for Miss Graves.

The boy whispered good night. The Padre put his elegant white hand on the boy's head, and, as he left, the boy watched Herr Plaschke put a bottle of that most drinkable of all champagnes, Dom Perignan, into an ice-filled silver cooler. With this vintage wine, especially bottled for the Vatican, sealed with black wax, and labeled with restraint, "Le Lait du Pape," Leonidas Erosa was well supplied. The Pope's Milk was his rarest possession. Mr. Plaschke slowly turned the bottle in its container, and then cut the strings which served instead of the usual wire to hold the cork in place. The boy quickly put his hand over his mouth to still his cry of surprise as the insufficiently cooled wine, which was furthermore disturbed by traveling, popped the cork loudly out of the bottle and past Plaschke's face. And he was bewildered when he heard the invisible Virginia Vanderbilt singing "Cockles and Mussels." The General and the Cousin got up, said good night, looked for a while at the play of the waters below, and went to their rooms.

The General, after Plaschke had undressed him and left, picked up the telephone and called the number of the Palace Hotel in New York. It was one o'clock in Miraflores, and two o'clock in New York. The Beauty was not at home, and he left a message. For a while he speculated whether it was good or bad that she was not here. Then he stared at his beautiful ceiling, folded his hands and prayed.

Outside the Villa, the fountains had been turned off. There was a great silence, as if the door to a noisy room had been closed. In the new stillness, clear as a silver flute, a bird in the limbs of an acacia tree began a simple tune and repeated it after measured pauses.

Red frogs jumped and fell to the moist stones with a smack, and then spoke of their love in bloated voices; blue ones talked with a doleful primeval wail, and others sent an unconvincing signal from their throats that was like the measured blow of a hammer on a small anvil. Fireflies with three lights on their heads and two on their bellies, which they switched on and off at will, hovered in the trees. Like the sails of an incoming fleet, sheets of vapor rode over the river from the jungle, drifted past the Villa, and sank away at the waterfall.

The little bird sang all night, and kept the General awake. Leonidas Erosa sat up; he turned in his bed and lifted the net. Over the sorrowing palm trees sailed the moon, and the fungi and mosses on the stairs of the villa glowed in its light. In this silver landscape, out on the terrace, stood Anibal in his nightshirt, smoking a cigar.

The General got up and went to his afflicted cousin.

"When I think of her, I always dream of looking down the inside of a factory chimney," said the Cousin in his sleep. "I see glowing embers at the bottom. Don't let her get away—she goes with the estate. . . . Mamasita, Roberto, Filomena. She is a link between us all, half Indian, half Negro, half you and me. She danced here for me, before you came, like a leaf that falls out of the symmetry of a tree. She danced in her poor little shirt while the nightingale sang for her.

"I reached for her eyes, but there was a band of blood from her mouth to her ears when I wanted to kiss her, and then she fell. . . . It would be like father and daughter sleeping in the same room. A bird has built its nest at the top of the factory chimney—a bird whose cry is like a carnival trumpet. Her ardor is for you. But I warn you—she is from Guajara. Her nostrils, her hair are above beauty; it sings all over her. She is the goddess although she is poor—and I am alone. I only came up the stairs to say that I'm alone, so alone, so altogether alone. I will always be alone, because I understand too many things."

Anibal Erosa carefully shook the ashes off his cigar, and the General took him by the arm. In the tree the bird still played his monotonous piccolo music.

Halfway to the door to Leonidas's room, the Cousin began to drag his feet. He became heavy; he resisted and turned. His face large and flat, and filled with unspeakable sorrow, he stood and looked up at the moon. . . . Then he walked all alone to his room and got into his bed.

The General returned to his own room and lay down. He was staring at the ceiling when the frogs stopped their noises once more. He looked through the mosquito tent and recognized the chef, who was in his dirty kimono. An ocelot growled and nipped at his heels.

The cook came into the room without ceremony. He opened and closed his mouth several times. Eventually he spoke. His words escaped between spasms of heavy breathing, like the sound of a broken concertina, and he had massacre in his eyes. He said: "I find bestial and inconvenient everything about this ménage. Not at all is anything the way it was described to me. In the kitchen are four women who are supposed to help me. They smell worse than your dogs. The dishes are not washed here—with all the water inside and outside the house, they are cleaned in a box —with sawdust!" He stared at the General and held his head in his hands. "Last night, I slept under the bridge. I have in my room an admirable antique bedstead, but on it, instead of a mattress, is a stinking pad. The sanitary conveniences are inaccessible. Two bridge tables, a dresser and a rocking chair are piled into the bathroom, and the tub is for a child. If I were to sit in it, my knees would be up under my chin. I repeat it—everything about this establishment is abominable. You have carried the joke too far this time. . . ."

The chef paused, then spoke about the icebox, and what he needed for the cave.

The General had folded his hands behind his head and was looking up to the ceiling. "Oh, you bloody cook," he said secretly, "to bring your awful kitchen smell in here. How I hate you and your red hands! I will send you back tomorrow on a plane—a ship is too slow."

But aloud he professed great concern. He sat up in bed and nodded. "Yes, yes, of course; and why not, Monsieur Vitasse?" He understood, he saw, he would take care of everything in the morning. When the chef finally threatened to leave at once if he was not given another room, the General climbed out of bed and walked him to his mother's apartment. He showed him the beautiful bathroom and the chapel. He tried the mattress. There was no linen, but the General himself found a sheet for him. He told him that the next night he would have a lovely room of his own and everything would be in order; and then he wished him good night.

"I have never seen bugs like this before," said the chef, holding up an insect between his fingers. But the General was already gone.

Leonidas Erosa sat down on the stairs outside. He was weary, and after a while he was cold. He looked into the Cousin's room; Anibal was sleeping soundly. And then he walked up to the terrace and to his room. The light had been turned out. In the center of the room, like one of the statues, shining in the white splendor of her newly washed curtain dress, stood the girl with the tame ocelot.

The toads plopped on the terrace again, the bird sang in the acacia tree, the bed creaked and the vibrating "dongggg" of a loose bedspring accompanied a small cry. The bleating of the red toads and the hammering sound of the black ones were resumed until the pleadings of the fortunate ones were heard, and they reached out with their cold wet hands to embrace their mates.

14: *Do Good to the Poor*

FIVE MONTHS after the arrival of the General at the Hacienda Miraflores, the routine of Biarritz was installed in every detail. The General progressed again smoothly from one pair of hands to another. When the fear of attack came, the Indian gardener came to the house, slept outside his door, and followed him with the dogs on his promenades. Besides Anselmo, Plaschke was constantly in attendance, even during the crisis. When Leonidas Erosa fell, when the garroting began with the animal cry and the hopeless man sank into unconsciousness, the good Plaschke wrung his hands and began to tremble. In order not to watch the disgraceful performance, he fastened his eyes to the Indian's face and formidable shoulders. He saw how he knelt down and silently took over. . . . And what Plaschke observed there, during the attacks, made him give a silent promise to the unconscious man—never to leave him alone with the gardener.

A masseur, a second cook, a valet, half a dozen other servants, an *escribiente,* and a housekeeper gradually arrived on the *Reina del Pacifico;* also several kinds of meats, and fish from the ocean sewn in sacks and packed in ice and sawdust.

Extraordinary provisions, medicines, art materials for Aloysio de Alconchel, magazines and newspapers, were flown in twice a week by a small yellow plane that circled over the square in Estación Concepción, dropped is cargo there, and flew back.

The Cousin supervised the reconstruction of the bridge, and occupied himself with horses. He arrived in time for all the meals, which he honored with great appetite.

Miss Graves read aloud to the General in a small temple that overlooked the waters and the Villa. On its cool stone floor the chef rested his feet, after dragging himself up the marble steps, when he came to discuss the menu. Then he went down through a private passage built to his own specifications, leading from his kitchen to the cave. The cave was completely installed with the hooks, shelves, and closets he had asked for, as well as an ice cream freezer.

Aloysio de Alconchel, the sacred dauber, had seen the General's art collection and discovered his weakness. He painted him badly but as the brooding Napoleon, the sardonic Napoleon. He planned Napoleon on a horse, Napoleon at the side of the Tuscan columns, and Napoleon with the three Great Danes standing around him. He painted the General mornings at the Temple of Diana, unashamed and with fury.

At the one sitting, some time after the arrival, he posed the General in profile, the left side of his face toward the painter. Stuck to his right cheek that day were two pieces of adhesive tape, and his right hand was bandaged.

When the General became restive, a small wagon with steaming casseroles, a basket of fragrant bread, and a cooler with a bottle of wine on ice was trundled across the terrace to the pavilion. He got up, inspected what the artist had done, and said, "Very nice." Seeing that the painter eyed the casseroles, Leonidas Erosa lifted his arm and said, "I salute you." He added in French, "Until tomorrow, dear friend," and turned his back on him.

While the footman set the table, Aloysio de Alconchel threw his palette down, dipped his brushes into a bottle of turpentine, and left in a rage. He ran to the kitchen, where he usually ate at a small table.

"It is not important," he said to the chef, "but tell me, were the artists who painted him before treated as abominably as he treats me?"

"He treats everybody abominably," said the chef.

"After all," groused the painter, "one has feelings. He could at least have asked me to stay for a glass of wine. Monsieur Vitasse, I am asked to the best houses in Guayaquil and Quito. I am a man of culture . . ."

"One can plainly see that," said the chef.

The painter picked up his knife and fork and threw them down with a loud clatter.

The girl in the curtain dress came into the kitchen; she was barefoot. She came every day and feasted on a herring in tomato sauce, eating it slowly, pensively, the way children let ice cream melt in their mouths. She loved coffee. The chef gave her a large cup of it and the girl put a piece of butter into it and stirred it.

While the assistant cooked a pork chop for the painter, the chef said, "Ask her why he has a plaster on his cheek and a bandage on his hand. What happened?"

"Oh," she said, "we were playing. He was running after me in the park, and he fell into a thorny bush."

The chef sat down with the painter and gave him a glass of wine. Aloysio de Alconchel wore a smile from ear to ear.

"What are you thinking about?" asked Jacques Vitasse.

"Oh, nothing—Naples, San Francisco, a thorny bush, a plaster on the face, a girl and a miracle."

The painter left and went over to paint in the Chapel of Aguas Santas. On the way he met the Padre going to the Villa. The Padre lived in a shed near the chapel, of which he was supervising the restoration. He said Mass at an open altar for the Indians in Tingo, and rode from there to the Estación Concepción, to attend to the needs of his small congregation there. He traveled on a meek horse, seated between saddlebags in which he carried small gifts.

He arrived at the Villa in time for dinner, placed his cheap Panama hat on the piano in the grand salon, rubbed his hands, and threw one leg over the other. After a while he said to Miss Graves: "I uill nod offend yu, to pratis dee piano?"

He sat down, rubbed his hands again, and played, while the General, the Cousin, and Miss Graves listened to him. He thanked them, embarrassed at the applause, and nervously drew his breath as he bent forward to take a glass of sherry from the silver tray which Plaschke offered him.

He drank a glass of wine with dinner, and discussed with the General the plans for the Feast of the Holy Waters—a glorious event at which the restored chapel was to be consecrated anew, and to which the General contributed a good deal of his imperial thinking. He worried about the procession while floating in the brine, thought about the decoration while being massaged, and while walking he planned the pageantry, the shooting of mortars, and the police problems. He concerned himself with every detail, from the little girls marching under the banner of the Virgin to the constabulary who were to be taken off their horses and given the honor of carrying the statue of Nuestro Señor. At the end of the dinner, with the coffee, the Padre begged every evening for his barefoot congregation.

It was always the same need:

"He has many children," the Padre said; "he needs a calf, or a sheep."

"Give him a cow," said the generous Leonidas Erosa.

"He needs a tercio of barley, or corn, to grind for his raw meal for mashca. The woman needs a piece of cloth. They will be married and the children baptized, and he also wants a wax candle for the most holy sacrament, and cloth for the woman."

The General granted everything.

The Padre looked at the General with great kindness after such grants, and said to Miss Graves, "Du guud tu dee puur, av compachôn on dee unfortunet, and God uill tek ker ov dee rest!"

He also consulted the General about all the difficulties that arose.

"They are most happy, Don Leonidas, and are looking forward to the Fiesta of the Holy Waters. They all want to carry the statue. But they have costumes," said the Padre in Spanish, "that I can't altogether approve of. They have shown me a devil's mask with long blue horns, and monkey masks. Two men intend to appear disguised as Negresses; they want to wear black masks with wigs made of flax, and they want to beat their drums and dance all the way. In addition, they are going to drag the cauldron of chicha with them, and we have seen what that means. And the overseer, Don Modesto, with his cannon strapped to his leg, insists on making all the arrangements."

"Send Modesto to me," said the General. "I have already made all the arrangements."

The Padre took one of the General's cigars from the silver casket every evening, and carefully put it away in the breastpocket of his robe. He left soon after dinner. In the uncomfortable cloth of the Franciscan Brotherhood, the honorable man walked down the stairs and crossed the left bridge. He rested beside the river, removed the Panama hat, and dried his tonsure. He wore flat, heavy-soled leather sandals and black socks. The banisters of the bridge and the hedge still trembled in waves of warm air. When he left the Villa, he walked over to the Indians and talked to them about the statue of the Lord. He described its red robe and explained how it was protected by a small blue heaven on which golden stars were painted. It sat on a wonderful gilded throne. Its feet were in silver slippers. Soon they would be allowed to see it, and some of them would be allowed to carry it to the Chapel of the Holy Waters in Tingo.

The Indians ran the five miles to the new chapel several times a week, to see if it was finished. The Church was their theatre. They learned the first simple acts of devotion; they were serious and came to pray an hour before he told them to. They sat around him listening to his stories with open hearts, and when he called on them for help, they gave him much more than he asked for.

When they leaned forward and began to look like people who are trying to listen through a thick wall, he knew he had over-taxed them. He ended his visit with a prayer and said his blessing over their bowed heads.

The only difficulty he had with them was in the confessional. They knelt at his side, but they found that they had nothing to confess. The indigo boy was his first problem child. He spoke to him of the Lord: "You are approaching Him now. You will neither see Him nor will you hear Him. But you are kneeling at the feet of His priest and He hears you. Come now, my son," he said to the worried youth, "and tell me. He is very kind and He has told His priest, who is in His place, that he must be kind also, so the Padre will not scold you, no matter what you say, and the Padre will not tell anyone else. There is nothing to fear. The Padre himself must go to confession; he knows how difficult it is. He will not be surprised at anything you say. Many others have told him the same sins that you have to tell. . . .

"Well, my son? . . .

"Have you examined your conscience?"

"Yes, Padre."

"Let us say a prayer together and ask God to help us make a good confession."

"Yes, Padre."

"Well, my son? . . ."

Again there was silence.

The Padre discovered eventually that he had to assume the role of prosecutor and accuse them. The first time he did so, they joyfully confessed, almost shouting their delinquencies. "Yes, of course I do that," they said.

"How often?"

"Oh, continually—oh yes, very often." They burdened themselves with lies while they were confessing—their hearts were black with all the sins except murder—and they prayed their penance with an insistence as strong as hunger. Their favorite penance was a string of Ave Marias which they said on their knees, singing the words with an ecstasy that was written in every line of their faces and strong bodies, from the uplifted hands to the toes. After they prayed, they ran back to the confessional, and pushing the penitent there aside, they looked through the grille and asked like children, "I do my penance well, Padre?"

"Are you really sorry? Do you repent?" asked the Padre.

"Oh yes, oh yes!" they sang, and when he smiled and nodded, they ran out, sorry that it was over, and eager to fill up the blank pages again, so that they could confess once more.

As important to the village as the Padre and the new pleasure of confession, were the visits of six fortunate youths—the indigo schoolboy, the intelligent youth who helped Plaschke, the new second valet who loved to hang up the General's chamois gloves, and three others who had been taken over and were allowed respectively to run the golden elevator, keep order in the cold cave, and assist in polishing silver. From time to time they came back over the hill to bring gifts to their families.

On such visits a pair of the General's gloves and a cigar were likely to disappear. The boys also wore shoes and hats. They did not go into the Indians' smoky hovels, but waited under a tree beside a well; when the villagers came and had seated themselves on the ground, the boys performed one-act comedies of manners.

At the beginning of the play, one of the brilliant youths—the silver polisher—stepped before the audience and described the scene and the actors. He pointed at the tree and explained that it was a door, the fountain a piano; a small stone was a chair, a second stone another chair, two stones a couch.

The one with the yellow gloves and cigar was the General, the indigo-colored one the Padre; the third played Miss Graves, and a fourth, who was the director, author and moving spirit, spoke to the audience and pushed the actors on and off the stage.

The play began with the entrance of the Padre, who rubbed his hands, threw one leg over the other, and sat down on one of the small stones. Then the General entered with the cigar lit, blowing smoke; slowly pulling off his gloves and squinting, he sat down on the other small stone. Miss Graves entered with the umbrella. The director himself came on the stage, in a white shirt, and impersonated the Cousin.

After a pause and some prompting, the General got up and said, "Good evening, Miss Graves, good evening, Padre, good evening, Anibal. Please put your hat on the piano, Padre—Anibal." The General, Miss Graves, and the Padre all put their hats on the piano.

After another pause, the General said, "Oh, how do you do, Miss Graves."

"Oh, I am very well," said Miss Graves, "and how are you?"

"I am very well," said the General, "thank you very much."

Again a pause, and then Miss Graves said, "Please, Padre, play the music." The Padre got up, bowed and rubbed his hands, and squatted next to the fountain, waving his hands over the stones. The Cousin hid behind the tree in his shirt and moaned the melody of "Cockels and Mussels" into a hollow shell formed by his hands. He reproduced the effect of the orchestra first, and then aped Vanderbilt's singing with uncanny skill.

"Well, I must go to the people, dear friends," said the Padre, getting up. He bowed. "Good night, Padre—good night, Miss

Graves." Everybody said good night, and they filed out past the tree.

The director of the theatre came back and addressed the audience.

"I," he said, "am Anibal. I speak not much during the day. I walk at night and talk to the Dead Mother. You have seen the 'good evening' at the Villa," he said. "We will show you more about the morning soon. Morning is until the General eats; it is also 'good day.' All morning you greet the Padre and the General and all friends and acquaintances by saying 'good day.' We eat in the middle of the day, at a table, just as the General does, in a dining room especially for us where we sit on chairs and are attended by a woman; and after that it is 'good afternoon,' and you say 'good afternoon' to everyone. The evening begins in the bath. When the General comes out of the bath it is 'good evening'; when you meet your family you say 'good evening.' 'Good night' starts before you go to bed; when it is dark, when you are tired, you say 'good night.'

"I say 'good night' now to you, dear friends; we must go back to our rooms, where we sleep in beds. I also say that we will see you again. We thank you for watching us."

In this manner the elegance of life at the Amelita—the absolute authority of the chef in his kitchen, the benevolence of the General, the stately manner of Miss Graves, and the musical talents of the Padre—were made known to the Indians who sat in awe under the tree, the mothers envious of the mothers of the clever boys, and all women envious of the girl with the curtain dress.

The General named her "Baby"—he discarded Chimène. Chimène sounds like a carillon, and not like a name for a girl one loves. In the imperial mood he called her Zulaya, which means Daughter of the Moon, and sounded a little like a Nubian slave girl—which is the way he liked to think of her. But Baby was what she became for everyday purposes.

Leonidas Erosa had looked through his small belongings, after the first night, for a gift for the Daughter of the Moon. He could not send her orchids; they grew wild everywhere. He emptied his desk and searched through the drawers of his dresser. He found several India silk prints, bandannas, but he was too fond of them to give them away. He sat at his desk unpacking, and she stood beside him with the ocelot in her arm. He found the menu of the farewell dinner aboard the *Céfalo,* a pamphlet made of shiny metal paper, on the cover of which appeared a life preserver framing a colored view of the steamer. The *Céfalo* seemed bigger than the *Queen Mary.* Inside the paper cover was a snapshot of the captain and Don Leonidas standing together on the bridge. On the opposite page was the menu. A satin ribbon held the souvenir together, and Baby reached over his shoulder to take it. She also chose her second gift. She came up behind him one day when he was standing in a room that was used as a shoe closet, holding a pair of boots which had been made for him complete with trees, by Peel in London. He looked at the date—the shoes were twenty-one years old. The original soles were still on them, and while he held them, he became a little homesick for Paris, London, and Biarritz, thinking of the streets, the squares, good restaurants and rooms he had stepped into with the small, beautifully aged boots on his feet.

He owned over forty pairs of boots, and he had the same pleasure in handling them that jewels give. He passed his hand over the smooth forms and held them close to his eyes to look at the dates and the names of the makers. He had done this several times when Baby, hanging on his left shoulder, her chin on her folded arms, announced a wish. She pointed at a pair of shoes, the only pair that the General didn't like, a pair that Plaschke, who couldn't throw anything away, had bought in New York to be used on the boat. They were rubber-soled sneakers. The General had refused to wear them. He gave them to her, and she put them on and ran immediately to the village, leaving the provocative imprint of their waffle pattern all over the dusty road, next to the bare footprints of the Indians.

On the morning of the day the celestial dauber had finished the decoration and pictures for the Chapel de Nuestro Señor de las Aguas Santas in Tingo, Plaschke and the indigo schoolboy hung up sixteen pairs of the General's chamois gloves. Then Plaschke went into the General's dressing room. He found the drawer of the dresser open, and inside of a ring of stiff, high collars, a nest. The bird who occupied it looked about with proprietary airs and made small singsong. While Plaschke called for the schoolboy, to get him to remove the bird, the bedroom door opened and Leonidas Erosa, in nightshirt, dressing gown and slippers, led by the Daughter of the Moon in one of the General's bathrobes, was pulled into the room and up to the dresser. The bird, she said, was a gift from her to the General. The General thanked her and led her back to his room.

Plaschke clapped his hands in despair about what to do. The bird rose, flew around him, and settled back on her nest. Tilting her head, she looked at Plaschke out of one eye and then the other, and Plaschke said again, "Oh, these children of nature!"

The General rang for his clothes and an immediate breakfast. He wanted to go to Tingo and to look at the new paintings in the chapel on the way.

Leonidas Erosa and the girl were singing. She carried the small rug on which he prayed, and led her ocelot. Halfway to the village of Tingo they came out of a tunnel of greenery and flowers. Plaschke, who walked in back of them, sank into the moss-covered ground at every step, as if he were walking on carpets. In the fulvous amphitheatre of a quarry at the top of the cliff, its only tenant a century-old tree with roots that reached as far out as its branches, the General stopped. A long stone formed a seat, and in the shade of the tree Leonidas Erosa sat down and took off his coat. He asked Plaschke whether he had brought along anything to eat or drink. Plaschke unhappily shook his head.

"O Lord," said the General, with his arms outstretched, "how beautiful is your world!" The General anchored his thumbs along his suspenders and looked around. He said to Plaschke that in all the world there was not another spot so grandiose and beautiful as this. He tugged at his walking stick, which he had stuck into the hard ground, and pointed at the scenery with it. Above them were the tops of volcanoes—beneath them the River Mona, a calm, wide band, green like polished onyx, which curved to the falls just across from where they sat, and fell with a thunderous roar of perpetual catastrophe to the boulders of the lava-lined gorge below.

The General pointed at the waterfall; Plaschke leaned over the precipice to see it better, and his straw hat blew off his head. It wavered upward and touched the wing of a bird, traveled out over the falls, and in pendulous descent from one edge of the abyss to the other, rode down and danced in the foam among the boulders for a while, and was drowned in the smooth-flowing waters where the river turned green again. . . . After it was gone, Plaschke listened while the General explained the village of Tingo and the chapel, two miles farther along. The wind blew in Plaschke's face again; his hair danced around his head like small lassoes, stuck to his ears, fell down to his chin, stood out sideways and then up straight. Plaschke took a handkerchief from his pocket and tied four knots in the corners. He turned, facing the wind, caught the sixteen loose strands of hair and held them down while he slipped the improvised cap on.

The General pointed ahead along the cliff. So high that it seemed to come out of the clouds, a thin, icy band of water fell down across the dark green walls. The silver band divided the village of Tingo from the newly calcimined Chapel of the Holy Waters. A beam of sunlight came through the clouds; a solid compact shaft of liquid gold lit up the cross on the spire. Its walls shone through veils that rose from the cataract and vapors from the miraculous hot springs beside which it had been built.

"Oh, Lord, to be allowed to see this once more!" said the General to Plaschke.

The General was lost in beauty. He was sad again with the thought of the passage of time. It had been exactly like this when he stood here with his mother, only he and the tree had grown old.

When Leonidas Erosa was ready to go, he looked around for the young girl, and found her squatting in a position from which she could look up and smile at him. The roll of carpet was under her arm, she had a flower in her white teeth, and she smiled. There were rocks and bushes in back of which she could have disappeared, but she attended to her needs where she was. Plaschke, with the four knots around his head, looked away. He said again, "Oh, these children of nature!" The General smiled back at the girl and said to Plaschke, "Beauty and realism, Albert." He waited until she stood up, and they walked toward the waters of Tingo, arm in arm and singing.

The ideal valet is always a man with feet, head and size of collar the same as his master's. Plaschke, who wore the General's socks and a pair of his trousers, now also received a hat—a much better one than the jipijapa straw that had blown away. The General, who was tired of carrying it, put it on Plaschke's head. He sang— the girl sang—and Plaschke hummed. The three happy people stopped at the edge of a pond choked with bushes, whose flowers were forget-me-not blue. The pond lay like a bouquet in front of the Chapel of the Holy Waters of Tingo.

The chef who had arrived with his assistants hours before, stood beside a buffet under a tree in the chapel garden. The General picked up a piece of chicken and gave it to the girl. He offered the dish to the Padre and to Plaschke and then ate some himself. The bones were thrown to the pet ocelot, who gnawed them like a dog. The General licked his fingers, and held his glass toward a bottle in Plaschke's hands. He leaned to the Padre and proclaimed again how lucky it was that he had brought the old maniac along.

Aloysio de Alconchel had up to now sat behind his tarpaulins and scaffold, and had come out only long enough to say that he had to be left alone to do his best. He had done a Madonna, a Nuestro Señor, and several angels; and over an altar in a side chapel he had expended his best efforts on a picture of Saint Francis—a copy of a canvas that hangs in the Church of the Franciscan Fathers in Quito. His masterpiece was called "The Temptation of San Francisco." He had lettered an explanatory text under the picture. "In the Convent of Gaeta, in Naples," it read, "the sainted Father, San Francisco, was sorely tempted once upon a time by the alluring arts of a licentious woman. To preserve his chastity, the Saint threw himself naked into a thorny bush. The spines bathed by his holy blood were at once transformed into beautiful and fragrant roses."

It was unmistakable that the painter had taken Don Leonidas and the girl as his model. She was whiter and more voluptuous than in life. The General's Napoleonic lock had been removed, and was replaced by the tonsure of the Franciscan monk.

Again Leonidas was the privileged man—he was the only one who did not see the resemblance to the girl and to himself. He congratulated the painter and promised to reward him. Then he inspected the Sacristy and visited the confessional.

The confessional was also newly painted and equipped with curtains that assured adequate privacy, a board for the penitent to kneel on, and a silver grille. As the Padre entered, the General knelt down on the rug placed over the wooden board for him, and the curtain was drawn. He was an unusually long time with the Padre.

When he came out, he walked up and down on the red stone terrace outside the church, praying and in deep thought. He looked like a child who has been scolded; he was wholly devoid of the joy that the Indians felt when their sins were left behind them.

On the way back, he watched the girl with curious eyes, embraced her, and looked at her longingly and close when they were alone. He kissed her on the forehead and stroked her hair. She was full-bosomed and voluptuous as the temptress in the painting of Saint Francis, because she was with child.

In his room at the Villa, the General sent for Anselmo. He sat on the edge of his bed while the valet took off his shoes and massaged the balls of his feet. When the Indian entered the room, the General asked him to come close. He motioned the girl to his side.

"You will marry her," he said to the Indian. "Right away! Go see the Padre."

And since that was the way it was always done, there was no dismay. Without tears or rebellion, with the gift of a piece of land and cattle and an obsolete battery-operated radio, with the blessing of the Church, with singing, dancing, and the shouts of "Viva El Benefactor," the wedding took place the next week. The cauldron of chicha swayed from its bamboo pole to the village over the hill.

15: The Feast of the Holy Waters

In the candle-lit chapel of Nuestro Señor de las Aguas Santas, the Indians of Tingo, who for three days had been decorating it with palms and flowers, were assembled for the early Mass. One of the intelligent boys, who served as sacristan, with a bell rope in each hand and one foot through the loop of a third, waited until the Padre turned to the congregation and pronounced the Ite missa est. Then he set the bells in motion, pulling the mouth of the largest, the sermon bell, first, to let the clapper strike. He waited for the humming sound which follows the first note, a moment after the bell is struck, and then he rang the passing bell, and last the tenor bell, repeating the changes for half an hour.

The first salvo of the mortars rolled through the valley. The dogs' barking cut through the white stillness around the Villa. The falls of the Mona and the jungle lay bedded in mist; above them into the starlit heaven rose the mountaintops draped in Bordeaux-colored cloaks.

In the river, near the Indian village, stood the barelegged mothers of devout little girls, whose sticky hair suffered under the pull of unaccustomed combs. After they were washed and combed, each one of them slipped into a white dress. A sky-blue sash was twisted around the waist, and on each small chest gleamed a blessed medallion of the Madonna on a silver chain. Finally each one was handed a white lily to carry in the procession. The little girls assembled under the banner of the Virgin, as the Padre had shown them, in two straight lines, and stood waiting for the morning. It was so beautiful and godly that none of them dared to speak except in whispers and of holy things.

The indigo schoolboy was the standard bearer. He waited for

the ringing of the bell of the branch chapel in Conceptión. When the high note sounded from that direction, he lifted the flag, started off with the right foot, and began the litany:

"Holy Mary . . ."

"Pray for us," answered all the little girls in chorus, with whistling voices and with their bare right feet outstretched.

"Holy Mother . . ."

"Pray for us."

It was half-past six when the musicians assembled at the Estación Conceptión. The wagon for the second-class citizens of the Hacienda Miraflores, swaying with palms, its wheels braided with lianas and heliotrope, passed over the new bridge. The constabulary with polished boots and spurs, their helmets in their arms, sat on the steps of the branch chapel, waiting to shoulder the beautiful statue of Nuestro Señor de la Portaria. The wild dancers with the flaxen wigs and the devils' masks were inside the church admiring the work of Señor Alconchel, who had gilded the statue and restored the face.

With his colossal revolver strapped to his leg, his hands in gauntlets adorned with embroidery, the major-domo galloped from one place to another, in sober and serious mien. Since the General had himself assumed the role of Supreme Grand Marshal of the Procession and Fiesta, made all the plans, and decided on every detail, Don Modesto put as much importance into his role of Adjutant as he could. He inspected the constabulary, rode back to the bridge, exchanged extravagant salutes with the electrician who was the chief of the small fire department, and rode on the pump-wagon. The major-domo looked at his watch and saluted again, then rode to inspect the little girls, who had passed the Villa now and were halfway to Conceptión, their prayer rising in the soft air:

"Thou Tower of David . . ."
  "Pray for us."
"Thou Ivory Tower . . ."
  "Pray for us."
"Thou Golden House . . ."
  "Pray for us."

The major-domo dismounted from his horse and knelt as the flag went by. Then he rode to the stables to get the horses for the Cousin and the General.

He swung out of his saddle at seventy-thirty, just as Miss Graves left the Villa for her morning walk. She was dressed in white; she carried her cream-colored sunshade and as always her large handbag. The major-domo almost threw his hat away in saluting her. He pulled the gauntlets over his wrists, adjusted his tunic, turned the three horses over to a groom, and marched into the Villa, where he had a conference with the *escribiente*. They stood at a window on the top floor, and the major-domo pointed across the landscape, with his shiny, embroidered glove, along the course the procession would take toward Tingo.

The new butler had set the table with gaudy Dutch porcelain for the holiday breakfast. Plaschke had gone downstairs to the pool, where the General and the Cousin were bathing. The chef was buttering a roll for himself in the kitchen.

It happened without any warning, much quicker than it can be told; it took place in just two seconds.

The sun at that moment was halfway up the side of the bishop's mitre; it shone like a petroleum lamp through heavy smoke. Suddenly the earth trembled in darkness, the ugly faces of bats fluttered through the air, there was a sound as if heavy furniture were moved overhead, and everywhere were the cries of animals and people.

In a sickening lurch, in a clockwise turn, the ground about the Villa moved. The valley closed, and where the Villa and the fountains, the bridges and the stairs had been, was a new scene, resembling Botticelli's "Adoration of the Magi." Three split stone arches remained standing, and from them wildly swung an electric wire. One of the stone horses of the fountain pawed the dust. So brief was the disaster that, at the side of the ruin, the major-domo was walled up in stone, his gloved hand still pointing at the chapel in Tingo.

At the beginning of the earthquake Miss Graves was on a path along the River Mona. She first thought that someone had jumped on her back and thrown her to the ground, but there was no one near. As if a pan half-filled with water were tilted violently, the River Mona rolled back, disclosing its bed. In three great shocks, the bed split and the agitated river came back in a wall ten feet high. The ancient tree across the valley, under which the General had sat, danced through the disaster; it tore its roots out of the stone, reached skyward with them, and plunged head first over the cliff.

The dark quarry behind it at the same moment became fissured split, and opened like a gigantic theatre curtain. Distant places that had been hidden by the fulvous rock were suddenly visible. It was over as suddenly as it began, and the sun shone as if it had risen to celebrate the most peaceful day.

Miss Graves was on her knees. She stood up and ran, with umbrella and bag, in the direction from which she supposed she had come. In her tear-filled eyes the new landscape and the road became even more uncertain than the catastrophe had made them. A black horse, dragging its saddle, raced past. She tripped over the roots of fallen trees and cut herself on stones and on the spines of plants.

After a while she stood still to orient herself. She looked at her watch. She heard voices in a small window of the forest. Beyond a corridor of leaves and air roots, she saw a cross of gold passing and a banner with the picture of the Virgin; she wanted to call but she had no voice. Miss Graves walked toward where the cross had been, she came to the road as the constabulary trotted past carrying the statue of the Lord, followed by the Indians in the flaxen wigs and the masks. A few yards ahead was the ruined gate of the Villa. The little girls arrived at the ruin with their banner and the lilies still held in their cramped hands.

The hand of Don Modesto was discovered by the Indians, and his body was dug out. But then all possible rescue was halted by the flames that rose as if torches had been thrown into every part of the ruin. The second-class citizens of the Hacienda cried and lit their candles, and in front of the statue of Nuestro Señor de la Portaria, the Padre said the prayers for the dead. After three hours the inadequate fire apparatus of the Hacienda arrived and played a thin stream of water on the flames. In the late afternoon a plane passed overhead, and at night it began to rain. It rained for two days without letup.

The trembling horses were rounded up by the constabulary, the Indians began to build new houses for themselves, and Miss Graves, who was installed in a hut, looked out of a window and waited for the Indian woman to bring back her dress, which she had taken to wash in the river.

She put it on, unpressed, and also the torn shoes, and walked over to the branch chapel. She was at the confessional when she saw the Indian sitting in it.

He got up and came close to her.

"I salute you," he said in Spanish. He raised his arm as the General had done when he dismissed someone. He knelt down and repeated, "I salute you, Patronsita."

Miss Graves stood still, and he got up.

"You are displeased with me, Mother?" he said.

"Go away, you smell, you are drunk," said Miss Graves to him.

"Oh, you are displeased with me, Patronsita." He looked at her a long while, and his lower lip began to tremble like that of a child about to cry. His eyes slowly filled with tears. He moved the jacket of his white linen suit aside and disclosed the major-domo's revolver strapped to his hip. The dream of killing Leonidas Erosa had ended—Anselmo was red-eyed with weeping for his lost master.

"The Padre said to me, Patronsita, 'Anselmo, you are the new major-domo.' What good is it, to be major-domo now, Patronsita—what good is anything now?"

At this thought he broke into violent weeping and accused himself of having been a bad servant to Leonidas Erosa.

"You are right to be displeased with me, Patronsita."

He took the gun out of the holster and raised it to his temple. He pointed it in several directions, and even at Miss Graves, before he found the proper place. He held it, digging the muzzle in his black hair as if he were going to make a dent before firing it off. Miss Graves looked at him. He removed the gun and wiped away his tears with the back of his hand. He recited his worthless life, and then he raised the gun once more and this time slowly squeezed the trigger so that the hammer gradually moved back. "I will kill myself," he threatened. "You are displeased with me. I will go and kill myself on the grave of my master." He pulled the major-domo's watch out of his pocket, and held its face toward Miss Graves. "This is when Anselmo dies," he said, and resumed his suicidal pose.

She took his arm and pushed the gun away.

"You are not displeased with me, Mother?" he asked.

Speaking more to herself than to him, she said, "No, no, Anselmo—I am not displeased with you."

He looked at her and asked, "And the General?"

"He was not displeased with you, either," said Miss Graves. She kept the gun, and the Indian wandered away.

The *Reina del Pacifico* appeared on the third day. Aboard her was Don Lorenzo Erosa, representing the bulk of the inheritors, very distinguished, very brief and formal. Also on board was a man with red hair, so plentiful, electric, and intensely carrot-colored that it looked as if he were wearing a tight cap. As he disembarked, walking with hands in pocket, he presented the picture of healthy, athletic youth of no particular nationality, with green-blue eyes, wide mouth, and the total absence of an expression either troubled or gay.

He stood a little away from both Don Lorenzo and the Padre. When they spoke to him, he answered and shrugged his shoulders. After a promenade over the wrecked building , they had a conference in the branch chapel at Conceptión. As the whistle of the *Reina del Pacifico* let out its first shrieking signal of departure, the young man started toward the riverboat.

Miss Graves, with the handbags her only baggage, and with her umbrella, was on the way to the ship. The Padre and Don Lorenzo talked to her. "Olues lov God and yu chal bee hapi boz in diss laif and in dee next," said the Padre. They waited to wave to her as the ship drew away, but Miss Graves remained inside the cabin. It was the one the General had occupied on the way from Guayaquil.

While the thin whistle's echo sounded through the silent afternoon, and the engine began its long sucking noises, and the feeling of motion invaded the room, she sat on the bed and said goodbye as the little girls said their litany. "Goodbye, Leonidas; goodbye, my love; goodbye." She said it over and over until it was dark, until the smell of cocoa was gone and the boat was in the swifter currents of the Guayas.

Next morning Miss Graves came out of her cabin and went up on deck. In the early morning sun she began her traditional shipboard promenade. On her dress near the right shoulder gleamed the green salamander with the ruby eyes.

The young man with carrot hair was on the top deck. As she passed, he pulled his immense feet out of the way and sat back in his chair against the cabins. He drew his knees up to his chin; the socks hanging down disclosed part of a freckled leg. He disarranged himself again, the second time Miss Graves passed, by sitting up straight and saying, "Good day," to which Miss Graves answered briefly, "How do you do?"

After she had done two more turns of the deck, he stood up and followed her.

"I don't think you remember me," he said, "but we have met before."

"I'm afraid I don't," said Miss Graves.

"We crossed on the same boat, on the *Xenaide Ybirricos,* from Casablanca to New York."

"Oh," said Miss Graves.

"I regret to see you looking so pale," said the young man. "There isn't much one can say, but I would like to offer you my deepest sympathy, and if there is anything I can do . . ."

"Mamasita,
    Roberto,
    Filomena,
    Arroz a la hora de ahora,
    Buenos Días,"

said the parrot of the *Reina del Pacifico.*

"Thank you," said Miss Graves, "don't bother—I know your business. I know very well why you are here."

"That is more than I know," said the young man, smiling sadly.

"I have six coffins downstairs, all of them empty. My papa will be very unhappy . . ."

"There is nothing I can do for you," said Miss Graves, and she hurried on. He followed her.

"Dear lady," he said at the stern of the ship, "believe me, no one is more delighted than I am; and in fact Papa, when he gets over his first disappointment and stops jumping, will be happy also."

"You're not very professional," said Miss Graves.

"After all," said the young man, "my papa is entitled to a few moments of rancor over the posthumous client who has cheated him."

"I suppose so," said Miss Graves at the bow, and stopped to look at the banks of the river.

"My good papa," continued the young man, "whom I honor and love, Miss Graves, has dreamed of this funeral for months. He saw the General when he arrived in Guayaquil and attended a luncheon at the Chamber of Commerce at which the General was also present. From then on, he watched him like an apple ripening on a tree. 'Rich,' said Papa, 'immensely rich. Had a good life, loves pomp, and has obviously come home to die; the perfect client.'

"Of course he never dreamed about a disaster. But in this land, where man and nature are violent, such things happen, and Papa was prepared for it.

"On top of our first-class hearse sit four angels, one of whom has had a broken nose for the last two years. It was immediately dispatched for repair. The uniforms of the master of ceremonies, the twelve coachmen, and the six deaf mutes whom Papa employs as pallbearers were sent to be pressed and cleaned. Mama and my little brothers were busy beating the purple velvet pillows on which ceremonial swords, decorations and trophies are carried in the funeral procession. Even the horses' hoofs were lacquered.

"Here in my pocket, Miss Graves, is the estimate for the funeral. It was all ready, like an obituary in a newspaper office. Papa walked to his desk, took it from the top drawer, and handed it to me—as simple as that. He pushed me out of the house, and on the way to the boat he calculated the additional cost, the difference between the Erosa Gala Funeral and the catastrophe. You will not be angry at me, Miss Graves, when I tell you that you were included in this sad estimate. What a disaster—two Erosas, at least four more people of consequence, entitled to a first-class funeral, and untold others.

"The boat was held up until the six first-class coffins arrived, and here I am. I have always wanted to see the River Guayas— I am on my vacation. Miss Graves, I have been traveling like a lord, for my pleasure. Would you like to see the coffins?"

"No, thank you," said Miss Graves.

The man in the dirty shirt who was the deckhand and steward of the *Reina del Pacifico* announced that luncheon was served. Miss Graves and the young man sat down.

"My name," he said, "is Reinaldo Moraru."

The soup was served and eaten. Two small pieces of square dry meat, with white, hard rice and a hot sauce, were served next.

"We are refugees," he said; "Rumanians."

Miss Graves looked at him and swallowed a piece of the tough meat. Reinaldo Moraru thought that the expression on her face was an answer to his words.

"People say that a Rumanian will sell his country. When that is said to my papa, he answers, 'True, true, we sell our country, but we never deliver it.'"

"The sauce," coughed Miss Graves, "is very sharp." She drank a glass of water.

"I have never been in Rumania, Mademoiselle. I was born in Nice, at a time when Mama was entranced with the songs of Reinaldo Hahn—hence my name. Mama loves music—when she whimpers Reinaldo Hahn songs, Papa, by way of revenge, plays very loud and very bad Wagner. He almost breaks the piano with *Siegfried*; and *Lohengrin*, he says, is not music but an aphrodisiac."

"I am very fond of the music of Wagner and of Reinaldo Hahn," said Miss Graves.

The young man looked at the River Guayas. "Forgive me for what I have said, Miss Graves; it seems heartless, but it has never happened to me before, and I must laugh now. I cannot arrive in Guayaquil laughing in my poor papa's face."

"Will you tell me, Mr. Moraru, what is so amusing?" said Miss Graves.

"It's like in school when you have to laugh; even if they will punish you, you have to laugh. Imagine, Miss Graves, all these sad people. The coachman with his black tricorn washing the hearse and carefully polishing it. And all the people who have ordered flowers, and bought black hats and gloves, and now because it is the rainy season, black umbrellas, and everything of much better quality than if they had an idea that there would be no gala funeral. All the top hats that are being polished, all the false faces—they all hated him—and we come empty-handed.

"No one has died! . . .

"You are not angry with me, Miss Graves?"

"I like you very much."

"Thank you, Miss Graves. For that I will tell you a secret. Death, dear Miss Graves, is a completely misunderstood phenomenon. It exists only for the manufacturers of black cloth, and for the florists, the padres, and our poor dear mutes who find it so easy to look sad. . . .

"It exists only for the others, for the bereaved, for the readers of newspapers and the scavengers. You and I, we ourselves, never never experience it. Each of us can only experience life. . . . I have celebrated it, among the paraphernalia of death, ever since I could walk.

"I will not bore you, to talk of my life?"

They walked to the upper deck. The young man, who neither smoked nor drank coffee, sat on the deck in the bow of the ship, and Miss Graves sat on a chair next to him and listened to his talk.

"The City of Nice, Madame, had two Pompes Funèbres who had sworn to inter each other at the first opportunity. The struggles which they carried on to accomplish this end were fertile with amusing incidents. Actually, over a period of years, the burials were accomplished under conditions of siege—and sometimes after hard blows had been exchanged. The war was declared when the wife of the director of the Terranova Funerals slapped one of the canvassers of our firm on the street. At another time, just as our men came out of a church, six pallbearers employed by the rival firm set upon them. Our men got into a pitched battle over a coffin which the others said they had a right to take away. Fortunately, my grandfather, who had had the idea already of employing deaf mutes, could make it clear to the court that our men had not started the argument, and so the other men were arrested and persecuted for violation of the sepulcher. It was not pleasant.

"This ghastly rivalry was finally terminated by a marriage of convenience. The moment for ringing the bells for this happy event came when Papa married Piedad, the daughter of Señor Terranova, owner of the rival establishment. That gave us a monopoly. The only thing the bereaved were allowed to furnish was the corpse, and just as everything was going good, and I was born, my grandpapa died.

"And Papa, who is a Gypsy, and hated palm trees, decided to go to Vienna.

"The twins, Oldemar and Waldemar, were born there—and from then on we had plenty of travel. First we moved to Rome, where Mogador was born. My fourth brother, Abdullah, was born in Casablanca; and the baby, Bolivar, was born six months ago here in Ecuador.

"Our house teems with life—with children, rabbits, birds, and a turtle five hundred years old. My papa's soul is always gay, like Offenbach music, like a red manège in a circus with horses trotting in a circle, little bells at their throats. When we came into the harbor of New York, when the ship approached that most exciting city in the whole world, Papa almost fell into the water. We stood, all of us, all the way up near the bow of the ship. Papa looked at the houses; I looked at the bridges, particularly at the first bridge over the East River. I saw people walking over it. A distant thunder came down to us from above; small lamps shone in the blue evening. And suddenly I saw that the Brooklyn Bridge was the illustration of life. It was a very important discovery, because I had made it all alone, after thinking about it endlessly.

"The wheel of fortune is spun by a hand as careless as a gambler's. It is arbitrarily decided whether you will be black or white, sympathetic of countenance, repulsive, or just dull. Your wit, your mood, the color of your eyes, and your impediments are thrown into the moist, ancient sac of flesh in which you crouch.

"We come out of oblivion like blind-born animals. We cry, but we see nothing, and if we were to die then, Miss Graves, nothing would die. On our walk across the bridge, we placed little mirrors along the way. In the first mirrors, in that first day of my life when I begin to see something, I see the face of my mother, and then I see a palm tree, and I think that all the world is a tropical country.

"I am still helpless, but the wheel is spun again and I find myself in soft pillows and clean linen, and I think that all the world is clean and rich. And if I die then, nothing much dies. The world impresses itself on us, not we on the world.

"In the next mirrors, I see my papa and later I discover that he is an undertaker, and I think that everybody's father is an undertaker; and then I find out that other children will not play with me because of that, and then I find out that my father is unhappy because he is an undertaker.

"And on this account, I, his oldest son, must become a doctor. . . .

"And you know why my papa is unhappy? Curiously enough, it's because he has nothing to do with dead. . . .

"When they come to Papa, it's all over. He can kick them, throw them off a mountain, or drive a nail into their heads. 'It doesn't matter, they have pulled their golden ships ashore and gone away—and all I can do is clean up the rubbish.' That is what he says.

"And at the end of the bridge, Miss Graves, we again become blind, voiceless, and immune to trouble or good fortune. The last mirrors are like the first—we return to anonymity, with all the trouble, the power and the glory swept into the coffin; and since we come as strangers, and go as strangers, all we can do in this life that is of any consequence is to sweep the bridge over which we pass, to keep it in good repair, to make its approaches inviting, its end a pleasant and secure promenade.

"You and I will not remember this the next time we come, but it is evident that we come back again. I am an interne; I work in Quito. I hear them crying every day, and searching for their mirrors, and they are all of them alike as worms."

The *Reina del Pacifico* was in Guayaquil. She swung on the incoming tide and headed for shore. The reception was as the young man had promised. . . .

Torches burned in the dusk; the pier was draped in black and gold. Throngs of people, in top hats and fashionable mourning garb, stood in a reserved enclosure. The six deaf mutes waited in their tricorns and professionally sad faces, their black-gloved hands folded in front of them. After the *Reina* docked, Miss Graves walked through them in her white dress and hat and with the cream umbrella and the handbag. The young man's father ran from one group to the other. On the waterfront stood the refurbished hearse, and the bells began to ring.

Reinaldo Moraru spoke earnestly to his father.

"But you could have telegraphed from Babahoya!" screamed the father.

"But, Papa, all the wires are down."

". . . Or done something. . . . What do I send you to school for?"

"But, Papa, there was no way!"

"But, Idiot—you make me look like a fool."

"I am sorry, Papa—"

"At least you could have detained the boat."

"But, Papa, Miss Graves has to catch a plane."

Walking to one of the numerous Erosas, wringing his hands, the elder Moraru told the dreadful news. It began to pour. The mourners protected the ladies' black mantillas and satin robes with the new umbrellas, and took them to the waiting funeral coaches, in which they discussed the bad end of Leonidas Erosa.

Miss Graves left a few hours later on a plane for New York. She stayed at one of the hotels in the Fifties that bear the names of forgotten presidents of the United States. She ignored the financial arrangements the General had made for her. She wanted to do everything, as she had always said, "on her own." She made arrangements for passage to England, and while she waited for a berth on a freighter, she followed the General's track through the park. As she came to the golden statue at Fifty-Ninth Street and Fifth Avenue, she stopped as the General had done, and she was intensely glad that she had never identified it, but allowed him to continue believing that it was a monument to Bolivar.

"Also, the Old One is back," said Dr. von Despard to his wife. "She sits downstairs in the Palm Garden and listens to the music." The Beauty saw her on the Avenue once and fled into Bergdorf Goodman's. And, on the day before she sailed, Miss Graves ate at the General's table at the Ermitage. The smile of the proprietor, the respectful service, were like the altar candles of the Padre; and when she finally walked across the gangplank, old and alone, up to the gray hulk of the steamer *Newcastle,* it was hard to imagine that someone once had loved her very much.

16: Now I Lay Me Down to Sleep

LEONIDAS EROSA looked around for his valet, from force of habit; and because he had never taken his robe off himself, he left it on.

"I'm not an opera man," he said. "Tell me, Albert, who wrote *William Tell?*"

"Schiller," said Plaschke.

"I mean the music, Albert."

"The music, Your Excellency, was written by Rossini."

"That's what it sounded like, Albert," said the General. "Not the storm part; the beginning, when it goes 'baaaaa papapapa papapa paaaaah pah!'"

"I thought it was some more of the shooting outside—the beginning of the Fiesta is what I thought," said Plaschke.

"I should have listened to my papa. He said to me, 'Always expect the unexpected,'" said the General.

The valet was shaving the General by the light of a candle.

"How often I have cursed that black-hearted cook, Plaschke. At least once a day I think I cursed him. God rest his soul, how I hated the old maniac, with his iceboxes and his red hands. And here, Plaschke, his icebox has saved our lives. What are we having for lunch?"

The General sat on one of the silver lions and the Cousin was in the pool.

"It was more like Berlioz," said the Cousin. "I thought, like Plaschke, that it was the shooting at first—it was definitely like Berlioz. Once I attended a performance of his *Requiem* in the courtyard of the Invalides in Paris. They had sixteen kettledrums, and cannon outside the city. 'Un Concèrt à mitrailleuse' they called it. That is what it was like."

238

"What are we having for luncheon, Plaschke?"

"Turtle soup, Your Excellency."

"Again? We had it only two days ago."

"That is what we have the most of," said Plaschke.

On a folding card table, next to the lion, he served the meals. Turtle soup, petit beurre biscuits, plum pudding, chocolate wafers, or rusks, prevailed on the menu.

"I would give a lot for some boiled beef and a glass of beer, or a plain steak, or even a rizotto—if we could only have a rizotto with some lamb, or a mushroom soup! I would be grateful even for a dinner at the Café Lorelei, or a plate of Herringsalat and the food on the *Céfalo*—a bœuf à la mode, for example."

On a tray, as neatly as it is done in a good restaurant, Plaschke served the soup for the General and the Cousin, and then ate his own in the cave.

Although he had never discussed it with either the Cousin or Plaschke, Leonidas Erosa had thought, when the earthquake shook the building, that he was coming out of one of his spells. There was the roaring of a train, the thunder rolling away into deep distances and then returning; pressure on the eardrums, and the violins playing madly. But the steel and concrete had held. It had moved, and he had fallen on the floor; but then he had touched his legs and his hands, he had heard the voices of the others, and suddenly he had felt as if someone had thrown a pail of cold water in his face. The pool was in motion—the waves rolled up the walls and splashed the ceiling—but not one stone fell out of the mosaic. In the darkness he did not move. The water in the pool spilled over the side and then subsided.

There was utter darkness, which changed to a reddish glow as he rubbed his eyes. It had seemed like a place strung with invisible threads for bats to fly through. The Cousin announced that the pool was caved in at one end; but that was only for a day and a half and then it slowly filled again. The water was kneedeep at the upper end, and occasionally a thin stream of fine dust was heard raining into the water. A patch of light as a sign of daylight outside—a faint, far-away emerald light—shone up out of the water; it was lukewarm. At the lower end of the pool, to measure it, they tied strips of cloth together in a string about thirty feet long, weighted it, and let it down; but it never touched bottom.

They talked about the door to the cold cave for two days before deciding to open it. The Cousin said that the cave might be flooded and they would be drowned. The General argued that beyond the door might be daylight and freedom, and that if the door remained closed they would starve to death or drown in the rising water of the pool. It would be better, said Erosa, to have it over with quickly, instead of sitting there slowly starving to death, suffering the tortures of Tantalus, knowing that beyond the door was a cave filled with food and wine. He named a few of the things that were in the cave, and when the green glow disappeared they sat silent for a while and became very hungry—and Plaschke agreed that it was best to open the door. The Cousin thought it might be blocked. At any rate, he said, it would be hard to open. They tied several sheets together and twisted them into a stout rope. The Cousin said that if the cave were flooded, they might have a chance to close the outer door quickly and save themselves.

The levers were thrown back, they pulled, and the door opened so easily that the three almost fell into the pool. The cave was dry. Everything was exactly as it had been. They found candles. They ate. Plaschke opened a bottle of the Pope's Milk while the Cousin occupied himself with the building of sanitary conveniences

In the light of the candles they looked at each other for the first time since the accident. They felt like homecoming brothers. Temporarily all the disturbing and pitiful mementos were gone in the flames of their hope. They drank each other's health and made impertinent speculations; they emptied a whole bottle of brandy and kissed and embraced one another. The General and the Cousin lay down on two massage tables.

There were great stories of rescue under catastrophic conditions, said the Cousin, in the dark. People had survived on rafts in the ocean, or in the sun and the desert; without food and water for days; explorers had been rescued from the jungle; miners had been dug out after weeks of being locked in subterranean shafts.

The General folded his hands in prayer for the victims of the disaster, among whom he included the chef and the Indian. He prayed for Miss Graves and for his own rescue, and then he went to sleep.

"Also, I have heard that they have taken people weeks later out of buildings that were bombed," said the General at breakfast the day after they opened the door to the cave, and the Cousin agreed that the chances for rescue were extraordinarily good. The Cousin proposed that when the digging started they should go to some safe place—a stone or beam might be loosened. To protect themselves, they built four solid towers of cases of wine, and whenever they heard a sound which they thought was the work of picks and shovels, or whenever the thin streams of sand rained down into the pool, they retired and sat in this shelter. The third week began.

Whenever the General sensed that Plaschke was downcast, he said to him, "Don't worry, Albert, they have gone back to get machinery. They have sent for a steamshovel and a crane, and that takes a long time to get up the River Guayas. I am sure there is an engineer outside. I know I heard them knock again during the night; the stones moved and some earth shifted. You will be all right, Albert; we will all get out, maybe tomorrow."

From time to time they heard rumbling as of furniture being moved, and for a few days they were certain again that someone would find them. They retired and sat in their shelter, to the right of one of the silver lions. The fourth week they began to hammer on the metal massage tables. They soaked the labels off the turtle cans, wrote messages on them, dropped them into the water, and watched them drift around for a while, curl into cones, and sink down toward the light; and they hoped that they floated out. And then they shouted again. But no one heard them.

"Yes, yes, Your Excellency, they have gone back for machinery," said Herr Plaschke when he saw the General staring into the pool. "I heard them knocking again today." They heard a stone move; but it was only the Indians poking through the debris.

It occurred to the General, at the beginning of the fifth week, that they were lost. He became most convinced of it whenever the Cousin banged with the meat cleaver on one of the metal massage tables and then listened for an answering signal. The

General had an impulse to tell him to stop the noise and say a prayer.

Leonidas Erosa bathed in the shallow end of the pool, Plaschke kept order, and the Cousin went exploring in the cave. He had already gone into it for a mile and a half. When he reached the second mile, he returned with a reward and reason for hope. He brought with him a handful of roots. He had found them at the roof of the cave, hanging from soft earth. It only remained to dig through some four or five feet of earth, and they would be out.

They sacrificed a can of goose liver paste and drank another bottle of the Pope's Milk. They sang and embraced each other again, and after dinner the Cousin and Plaschke, equipped with a kitchen knife, the cleaver, and a ladder, went into the cave.

Four tall, flickering wax candles stood at the edges of the marble pool. The Rouet d'Omphale was mirrored in the green water. Leonidas Erosa felt the myoclonic twitching, the first signal of the attack.

"Don't be afraid," Plaschke had said to him. "I will be there to help you; I will know when you need me."

"Plaschke!" screamed the General. "Plaschke!"

He looked at the water. In the dancing surfaces swam the reflection of Hercules in the maiden's white dress. The background of pale gold mosaic flashed in the water, and the reflected face of Leonidas Erosa looked as if it were made of the moving wings of yellow butterflies.

"Anibal!" he screamed. "Anibal!"

There was no answer.

The face of Hercules was made of red and amber pieces cut in triangles, lunettes, and squares. In the reflection the General could count them plainly, and the arrangement of the shapes was so clear that he could have drawn it forever after. The eye was made of one hundred and ten small pieces of brilliant enamel, the lips of eighty-five purple lunettes, the hair of six rows each of one hundred and ten square black chips. Erosa crawled to the silver lion and embraced him.

"Oh, there is disaster everywhere now, and people who have never known how to die—the simple people with the foolish faces, the obedient faces with eyeglasses and ill-chosen names—know how and all at once are heroes. You will be well behaved, Leonidas; you will not tremble."

He leaned out over the reflection of Hercules, who had become the Cousin in his mind.

"Anibal—I am an extremely moral man, Anibal. All my appetites and all my play, dear Anibal, were only to decorate the lonesome house in which I lived. And now it is all over. Still I pray to her soft eyes, to her young mouth, to the pulses in her wrists. Anibal, you never pray, and here my voice is praying again over the water. Again I die for her in loneliness—again she comes to me in the water. Oh, I am thirsty like an ox, Plaschke. Life is not vertical at all—it's horizontal; life is nothing you can collect or stack up. This is one day like any other day—like the day on which I was nineteen or thirty-five. It's Thursday, Plaschke, and as long as any other. The rest of life is filled with such small moments that I can tell you all of them in three seconds. When you have lost your first love, you have lost all the women in the world, Anibal. Why is it that the more women you have, the more lonesome you are? And why is it, Anibal, that coffee is never better than in the kitchen of a whorehouse—and that nothing is as awful as the need for it?"

These were the last spoken words of Leonidas Erosa.

There was no grip on arms or legs, no twisting, no kicking, and no cry. He was leaning over the water; then, voiceless, he rolled on his back. The small pieces of porcelain and gold up in the mosaic became audible like furious exercise on the high piano keys. The forty-six dark brown pieces in the ear of Hercules moved.

A fair slim golden angel, the most honest and kind messenger, came silently into the room. He stood beside the silver lion, knelt down at Erosa's side, and took his hands.

A regiment paraded somewhere through the General's memory. The musicians, in the blue and silver glory of a marvelously uniformed band, raised their shining instruments and began to play. Miss Graves, now young and in an emerald-green gown, with jewels in her red-gold hair, sat next to him in the old Panhard, and they drove across the Place de la Concorde with all the fountains playing. They came to the Restaurant Robinson. The chef, the old maniac, was the proprietor and stretched his red hands in welcome. At the tables up in the stout branches of the tree were friends. The Cousin waved, and Monsieur Laguerrie; the wobbly head of the captain of the *Céfalo;* Mlle. Borotra, and the dirty little girl.

"There is disaster everywhere," said Plaschke, stretching out his hand to help the General walk up the tree. "Be careful."

"Give me your hand—your honest hand, Plaschke," said the General. "We are not afraid—we do not tremble. I am thirsty like an ox, Plaschke. I would like to stand under a waterfall."

Plaschke said, "Be careful."

"Oh, I don't particularly worry about being careful any more, Plaschke. I'll stay exactly where I am."

The General leaned out over the branches. The hotel's façade was crowded for a moment with beautiful golden letters that spelled "Compagnie des Wagons-Lits et des Express Européens." And through the windows of the hotel shimmered the silver coast of Biarritz, the rock in front of the Hôtel du Palais; in one of the rooms was sand and a shorn poodle, and in another was Miss Graves and the sea.

"She's waiting for me there in the water, Plaschke. I will go out to her." He pushed himself away from the silver lion.

The cool fingertips of the merciful angel reached to his temples. He thought that he had safely carried him across; but Leonidas Erosa balked.

"Good God, as you wish it. Now and here if I must, and without tears. . . . O God—I will be good, I will be good—let me come back once more to your beautiful earth. If you would let me live once more, for ever so small a time and in no matter what shape, I would be good—I would be kind and generous. Once more, dear Father in Heaven . . ."

The powerful god who attends to the smallest details of life with the same care he gives to his stars, who provided the vintages at the Table of the Immortals—the arbitrary god of the Kiss Royale and of sweet-faced little girls on crutches—the god who in his inscrutable judgment placed the Germans next to the French—stirred himself and sent a sign of his awareness to the old beggar in the pool of the Amelita. . . .

On the silver lion's head appeared a small green salamander, in his elegant jeweled pose of constant alertness.

Then the soft black bandage was put over the General's eyes. "Tiens," said the General, "listen to who is applauding me." And all was over.

The jungle wove its fierce emerald blankets over the ruins of the Amelita. The eyes of animals watched from split marble; toads and salamanders, snakes and birds, found desirable locations in the ruin; and all nature said, "Forget, forget. . . ."

In a scene that was like the Nativity, close to the moist muzzles of the cattle that had been a wedding gift, with shepherds guarding their flocks on the horizon, the wish of Leonidas Erosa was fulfilled.

Not long after he left this life, he started across the bridge again, unburdened with any ills of the flesh; his new impediment was poverty.

He was the pride of the village. He reached out of his reed basket and cried from full lungs. He was given the name of Francisco. He was well born.

He sat up straighter than any other baby. He was imperial. With a bamboo stick for a sceptre and chickens in a ring around him, he sat in the sun and laughed at his new fate.

Anselmo brought him playmates from the jungle, small monkeys and birds. The Indian gardener had become a man of greatest importance. He wore shoes now, and while his wife and all the visitors sat on the floor, he occupied a chair and frequently looked at his silver watch. He drew roosters in the sand, and at times he took a piece of paper and some chalk and gave the impression of writing. And he was determined to teach all this to his son.

END